FOURTEENTH COLONY

FOURTEENTH COLONY

JEFF ALTABEF

TATE PUBLISHING
AND ENTERPRISES, LLC

Published by Tate Publishing & Enterprises, LLC
127 E. Trade Center Terrace | Mustang, Oklahoma 73064 USA
1.888.361.9473 | www.tatepublishing.com

Tate Publishing is committed to excellence in the publishing industry. The company reflects the philosophy established by the founders, based on Psalm 68:11,
"The Lord gave the word and great was the company of those who published it."

Book design copyright © 2013 by Tate Publishing, LLC. All rights reserved.
Cover design by Allen Jomoc
Interior design by Caypeeline Casas

Published in the United States of America

ISBN: 978-1-62510-452-6
1. Fiction / Thrillers / General
2. Fiction / Thrillers / Political
13.03.04

DEDICATION

This book is dedicated to my family and friends, especially my wife and two girls who continue to be the light of my life. A special thanks to all of my "readers." Without their encouragement and wisdom, this book would never have been possible.

1

April 14, 2041[1]

Warren Scott quickly approached room number 9 with a deep scowl etched on his face. He did not enjoy surprises, and the message from Michael had been abstruse at best. He took long confident strides down the empty hallway. The old-fashioned door was stained black and made of solid, heavy maple wood, the number 9 engraved in shiny brass toward the top. Warren breathed deeply, took hold of the brass doorknob, turned it, and quickly pushed his way inside. Confident that no one saw him enter the small guestroom, he quietly shut the door behind him.

Inside the room, Michael sat alone and agitated on the edge of the bed with a tablet computer tossed to his side. Upon seeing Warren, Michael abruptly stood, relief clearly evident on his face.

---

[1]   The characters portrayed in this book are real and the events factual. Some of the characters have become famous over the past two hundred years while others have drowned in the ocean of time. The dialogue and internal thoughts of the characters are fictitious, however, where possible, I have tried to use actual speech patterns gleaned from personal papers, videos, and public interviews. With the benefit of the past two hundred years, I believe that the events described in this book represent a tipping point in American history and deserve to be told.

"Thank God you were able to meet me so quickly. I didn't even know that there were rooms up here."

Warren studied Michael closely, noting the sweat running down the sides of his face and stress lines creasing his forehead and the corners of his eyes. Even in the cool air-conditioned room, his golf shirt was heavy with moisture, sticking tightly to his body. Michael was of average height, slightly overweight with weak facial features that were only made weaker by his thinning light brown hair. He was young, only midtwenties. Warren's employer had paid for Michael's college education and still owned the rights to his income stream for the foreseeable future. Michael worked in the technology department. He didn't work directly for Warren, actually no one worked directly for Warren, but he did special projects for Warren from time to time—all in all, he was a talented individual that Warren had known for just under five years, but not indispensable.

Warren smiled in an effort to put Michael at ease. "Yes, there are ten guest rooms up here for out-of-town guests. They rarely ever get used but can come in handy for a hasty meeting like this one." Warren lightly crossed his arms over his chest. "Now, tell me what you discovered, Michael. It can't be half as bad as you look." Warren liked to use first names, believing that it gave him power over the person he spoke to.

Michael began pacing back and forth with quick, short strides, looking toward his feet as he spoke. He felt more comfortable talking as he moved. "I started hacking into Mr. X's computer just like you said. It took me some days before I got past the security, but once I did, I stumbled upon something truly shocking." Michael reached for his tablet, opened it, and brought up the keyboard.

Warren sat stiffly on the bed and waited, his internal clock ticking loudly. Warren sighed; he had an important meeting to attend. He glanced at his handmade Swiss wristwatch. It was paper thin, had a large white, rectangular face with blue digitally projected hands, and a narrow platinum band. It was the thinnest watch ever made, outrageously expensive, held a charge for three years, and kept terrible time. He didn't have much time to handle this situation. Michael slowly handed the tablet to Warren. Michael's hand shook slightly, the sweat from his fingers lingered on the edges of the computer.

An open memo appeared on the screen as well as a number of supporting documents that were tabs behind it. As Warren started scanning the documents, his eyes grew wide in surprise. This was more than he had imagined.

After a few minutes, Warren placed the tablet on the bed and stared into Michael's eyes with a piercing gaze; shock and maybe fear were reflected in those eyes, but Warren thought he detected something else, something dangerous.

Michael stammered, "You see, it is both great news and terrible news. I can't believe it, but all the backup documents look authentic. I'm stunned."

Pushing the tablet away from him, Warren calmly asked, "Is there any way to trace this information to you? Did you leave a trail of some sort?"

Michael hesitated as he contemplated the question. "I left no trail. If he figures out that the information was hacked, he will reach a server in Singapore and never be able to follow the trail from there." He was good at what he did, and he spoke confidently.

"Have you told anyone else about this?"

Michael rocked back and forth on his heels with his arms crossed against his chest. "No one else, Mr. Scott. I knew that you would know what to do with this information. You would know how to make this public." Michael unconsciously glanced beyond Warren toward the head of the bed, but Warren didn't notice as he was deep in thought, contemplating what he should do next.

Warren smiled. The situation wasn't as bad as it could have been. "You did absolutely the right thing, Michael. Sit down while I think about the best next steps. As you said, this is such good news wrapped in an awful secret. We must be careful."

Michael sat on the edge of the bed as Warren walked over to the only window in the room. From here, Warren could see the long road leading toward the clubhouse. A few cars were already arriving. Soon, the road would be full for tonight's benefit. With his back turned to Michael, Warren twisted the large stone on his college valedictorian ring, revealing a small needle on the other side. Glancing out of the window, he said, "This discovery might change everything."

Drained, Michael sat stiffly with his head held in his hands. He stared somberly at the floor. "I still can't believe it."

Warren turned and slowly approached the young man with a wide smile on his face. "You've done really well. You have performed beyond my expectations." He smiled again and slapped Michael firmly on the back, his hand hitting him at the base of his neck.

Michael felt the sting immediately as the small needle punctured his neck, injecting a fast-operating poison into Michael's bloodstream. Michael became instantly paralyzed. The only part of his body that was moving was his heart, which raced in panic. *Thump, thump, thump.* Warren gently grabbed Michael's shoulders, letting him fall to the bed. "I am sorry it has come to this. You really did achieve so much more than I thought was possible. I will have to deal with Mr. X later."

The oxygen left Michael's lungs. *Thump...thump...thump.* His heart stopped beating, his face turning a bluish-white color. Warren watched closely as the life faded from his eyes. He regretted killing Michael, but he had enjoyed watching as he died.

Warren carefully twisted the ring back into its original position. Michael wasn't the first person that he had killed, but Warren didn't take much joy in this one. He did the best he could to enjoy the moment, but without the careful planning and anticipation, it felt oddly hollow. There was little Warren could do about it.

Michael had left him no choice. He proved that he was valuable, but Warren wasn't willing to share this information and was certainly not going to let it go public.

Warren pressed a button on his small cell phone and started talking. "Steven, I need a cleanup crew here at the club. Come to room 9. It is one body. There is not a lot of time. The place is going to be crawling with people soon. I need you to pick it up immediately, and we never want it found."

Warren abruptly shut the phone not waiting for a response. Michael was one thing, but how was he going to handle Mr. X and this information? Warren hastily looked around the room, making sure that nothing was left in sight. Grabbing the tablet, Warren folded the device and put it in his pocket. He didn't have time to examine it closely right now. Later tonight he would study it, and perhaps he would give it to some trusted tech guys in the morning. Now he needed to leave without being seen and distance himself from Michael and room number 9. He glanced at his watch and frowned. He was late for a meeting he needed to attend, but he left with a bounce to his step. He felt surprisingly good as he closed the heavy maple door behind him.

The breeze felt good running through Jack's curly brown hair. It was only the beginning of April, but the weather was already hot. *Easily eighty degrees*, thought Jack. Each year, summer came a few weeks earlier.[2] Spring was mostly reduced to a concept that happened when old people were young. At most, spring lasted one week in early March, if you were lucky.

Jack expertly weaved his motorcycle through the rush of lower Westchester traffic. He turned eighteen two months ago, and his mother had somehow saved enough money to buy him the used, bright-red Indian Chief motorcycle. Jack's tall, lean frame felt comfortable on the leather seat. It was a few years old but remained in pretty good shape and rumbled powerfully beneath his legs. Jack had plans to fix it up. He used his savings to buy a white racing stripe for the body, but that just hid some of the

---

2   Despite the overwhelming scientific evidence to the contrary, at this time, the government's official position was that manmade factors had nothing to do with global warming. Oddly, many people were convinced that proponents of global warming were intent on perpetrating an elaborate hoax on the world in a bizarre attempt to redistribute wealth from rich countries to poor ones. Large energy consortiums had funded "research" that supported these claims. Luckily, Project Refresh was already underway. Within the decade the scientists behind Project Refresh developed the technology to remove greenhouse gases from the atmosphere, saving the planet from a near cataclysmic event.

scratches and dents. The bike really could use a new paint job, but he needed to make enough money first, which was not an easy task.

The fuel gauge hovered near empty. *No time to stop for gas at this point,* Jack thought as he looked at the long line at the public gas station[3] and shook his head. He was already late for work, and at twenty dollars per gallon, Jack was forced to find other ways to improvise his fuel acquisitions. It was either that or take a lot of buses, and Jack hated buses. He would rather hitch a ride.

Jack twisted the accelerator, passing one of the private gas clubs—no lines and no published prices. Jack heard one of the members at the club complain about having to pay thirteen dollars per gallon. Jack shook his head. *Thirteen dollars and someone pumps the gas for you!* Gas hadn't been that low in years at the publics. The private gas clubs had a process to accept new members, requiring a financial commitment and vetting. They didn't let just anyone in, which meant that Jack would never get in. Well, there were other ways to get fuel. He pushed the Chief onward, hoping that he had enough gas to make it to the club.

The sun had already set as Jack glided the motorcycle through the large metal gates at the Ronald National Country Club[4] in

---

[3]   In 2041, motor vehicles were still powered by fossil fuels, most notably gasoline and liquid natural gas. It was an expensive, inefficient, and environmentally detrimental way to power vehicles. Ten years later, Finnish zander fisherman Nars Larrson publicly announced his discovery of a biofuel based upon algae, an inexpensive, safe, and renewable form of energy—a discovery he freely shared with the world. Within a month of the announcement, the top three energy companies independently sued Larson for stealing trade secrets, claiming that they developed the same technique as far back as 2007.

[4]   The Ronald National Country Club still exists as of the writing of this book. The original club changed its name upon the death of its famous founder who was a controversial real estate and media mogul. Within five years of his death, his family invested all of their net worth in a highly leveraged venture to purchase and develop

Chappaqua, New York. Jack waved at the guard at the gate, Bob, the head of security for the club. Bob was in his middle forties, six feet tall, built wide like a refrigerator, and specialized in solving discrete problems for some of the club's privileged clientele. If any of the members had a problem with one of the lower classes, they spoke to Bob. He was discrete, effective, and fast. He wore all black and slung his assault rifle over his left shoulder. Bob rarely spoke about the private jobs he did for members. Only when he was high did he ever talk about his "other" job and then only in the most general terms. Most people were afraid of Bob, but Jack liked him. He had a surprisingly dry sense of humor when you got him to open up. It took time and effort, but Jack thought Bob was well worth it.

Jack swung the motorcycle around the back of the main clubhouse toward the member lot where the valets parked the members' cars. A new gold BMW convertible screeched to a stop inches from him. Jack was in luck. Julian, one of his closest friends, bounced out of the car with a wide grin on his face. He was in his early thirties, rail thin, and always had a deep tan. His left leg was slightly longer than his right, which caused him to have a small but noticeable limp. He yelled at Jack as he got out of the BMW, "Hey, you can't park that piece of junk bike over here."

---

an island off the North Carolina shoreline aptly called Atlantis. The island was intended to be the latest adult Disneyland, offering enhanced gaming and entertainment options for wealthy clientele. One week before the official opening of the complex, a one thousand–year hurricane leveled the entire island. Due to a clerical error, the venture was uninsured, bankrupting the real estate family. To avoid liquidation, the club was purchased by its members in 2032; however, a life-sized bust of its namesake can still be found in the men's restroom in the member's male locker room. Golfers rub the head for good luck.

"You almost hit me!" Jack groused back. He jumped from the bike, approached Julian with hands at his side, palms open, and a sly smile on his face. "How about you do me a favor? I am a little low on gas. I'm late as it is. I didn't have time to wait on one of those lines."

Julian frowned as he darted his small black eyes from left to right. As usual, the member parking lot was empty. "You get me fired from this job, and I'll kill you." He reached out his right hand, palm up and wiggled his fingers. His lips were turned downward into a frown, but his eyes told a different story. Julian was always pressed for cash. He had a gambling habit, and he wasn't that good of a gambler, which was a horrible combination.

Jack pressed a twenty into Julian's outstretched palm—the usual amount for his cooperation. "No one will know," said Jack. At least Jack hoped that no one would find out. He cringed at what he imagined Bob would do to them if he ever did.

Julian pointed to two dark sedans in the back of the lot. "Use those two. Don't take too much from either car. Mr. Cullen owns the black one. He has to be ninety years old and can barely see. Mrs. Torio owns the blue one. I doubt she even knows what day it is. Both driver side doors are unlocked. Be quick."

Jack groaned. "I can't take the gas from Mrs. Torio. She reminds me of my aunt. How about the white Mercedes?" Jack pointed to the car next to Mr. Cullen's.

Julian smirked. "That one belongs to Judge Smelts. Don't take too much from him. He'll probably blame it on communists and start an investigation." No one liked the judge. His *investigations* were notorious. Good people were often locked away as communists or terrorists with only the slightest shred of evidence against them.

"You're the best. I'll only be a minute."

"When you're done, park that bike in the employee lot, or I'm bulldozing it."

Jack grinned. "Don't worry about the bike. It doesn't take up much space. No one will notice it. I'm late, and I have to deal with Wendy." Jack started up the Chief and swung it toward the two cars in the back. He leaped off the bike, grabbed a clear plastic hose and a plastic funnel from his luggage compartment, and in a few minutes, he siphoned off a full tank of gas equally from the two luxury cars and parked the motorcycle in the back of the member lot. In a hurry, he raced his way toward the kitchen entrance in the back of the clubhouse.

CHAPTER

3

Jack skidded to a stop outside the employee entrance to the kitchen, kicking up loose gravel against the door. He carried a duffel bag, which contained miscellaneous belongings, including his all-black waiter's uniform. Waiters were required to blend into the dark edges of the room unless a member or guest needed something, and then it was up to the waiter to anticipate the need or desire before the member or guest had to ask for it. "Members should never wait for anything" was the first and last rule every waiter at the club had to learn.

Jack checked his reflection in the windowpane next to the door. He was six-foot-five, thin, tanned, with well-defined muscled arms. His curly light brown hair was cut short, his brown eyes had a bright shine to them, and he left the slightest trace of stubble on his chin. Jack did his best to tame his curly hair and strode purposefully into the kitchen. The kitchen was already buzzing with activity: burners were lit, fans sucked smoke away from stoves, and kitchen workers scurried from one place to another. The vast room was replete with the continuous sounds of an endless war waged between stainless-steel cookware and utensils, each side clanking bravely as they briefly clashed with each other. Jack recognized the steady beat of knives meeting wooden cutting boards as one table busily sliced vegetables for the salads.

The club's three chefs stood out from the jumbled mass of kitchen workers; they were the officers of this particular army and were dressed in all white with large chef hats proudly placed on their heads. Each one knew his responsibility for tonight's event. The head chef, Antonio, carefully watched his team as they began preparing tonight's entrées. His face was bright red as he angrily pointed at one of the assistant chefs who was pounding chicken cutlets in a manner not to his liking. He noticed Jack's tardy entrance and disapprovingly pointed to the clock on the wall. Very little happened in his kitchen that Antonio didn't notice. With a guilty shrug of his shoulders, Jack hustled toward the exit, the smell of garlic and onion filling his senses. He was careful not to interrupt the kitchen's rhythm.

Jack burst into the short hallway that led to the dining room. He took a quick left toward the employee bathroom, and as he was about to reach the bathroom door, he heard a shrill voice call out his name. Jack didn't need to turn around to realize that the head food coordinator, Wendy, had spotted him. He froze as a feeling of dread swept through him. He spun slowly around as his sneakers squeaked on the tile floor. He had hoped that he could have somehow blended in with the rest of the waiters without running into her.

This part of the club was off-limits for members. The hallway was dimly lit, the paint was peeling in spots, and instead of plush carpets, gray industrial-looking plain tiles covered the floor. Wendy looked irritated, with her eyes narrowed and her lips pursed together tightly. She was in her late forties. Her straw-colored, shoulder-length straight hair framed her oval-shaped head full of sharp features. She probably didn't go outside much as she always had a pasty complexion and wore a severe look on her face like a mask. Jack couldn't remember seeing her smile, unless it was one of the forced grins she felt obliged to flash to members. She wore a dark blue suit with a nametag identifying her as Wendy—Head Food Coordinator. Lucky for Jack, Wendy wasn't his normal boss but only supervised him when he worked events. Jack regularly worked for John, the head tennis pro, as an assistant tennis instructor. He only worked events to earn some additional money.

Jack turned on the charm. "You look lovely tonight, Mrs. Mitchell. I'm sorry I am a little late, but there was this terrible accident on Route 100, and I had to pull two kids from a burning car. Luckily they're both okay." Jack smiled innocently and shrugged his shoulders, giving his best impression of a humble heroic figure.

Wendy looked at her wristwatch, with her lips turned down in a disapproving scowl. "You are twenty minutes late. That will cost you one hour's worth of pay. I don't care what John says. Next time you're late, it will be the last time you work for me. Get changed and report to section 2. And if you can, limit the fraternizing to a minimum. This event is important to Mr. Hoffman[5],

---

[5]   Dr. Robert Hoffman owned a nationwide chain of state-of-the-art private hospitals. At this time in American history, about one-third of Americans were insured for private hospitals and private doctors. Another third had insurance that covered clinics (where typical waiting times were one to two months), and the remaining third had no coverage at all. Within three months of this benefit, it became publicly known that Hoffman was conspiring with the three large insurance companies by inflating costs and fees. The larger the costs and fees, the greater the premiums charged by these companies and the higher the net profit to the insurance companies and the hospitals. The arrangement was not illegal because any governmental organization that might have prevented price fixing was disbanded in the name of free-market capitalism. Still, the wealthy clients of the insurance companies and Hoffman Hospitals were not happy with Mr. Hoffman. His membership from the club was terminated, and he suffered a mental breakdown. Hoffman disappeared. It is believed that he reemerged months later as bearded Toby Nate Tyler (aka "TNT"), living out his dream of being a country music singer and songwriter. TNT enjoyed some popularity among the ghettos for a short time. His most popular song was *Better Pack Your Bags, My Wife's Got a Tazer*. Unfortunately, Hoffman received an infection from a cut on his lip during a bizarre beer shot-gunning inci-

and I want everything to go smoothly." Wendy shot Jack one last disapproving scowl that made his stomach turn, before spinning in a tight 180-degree turn and crisply walking back to the dinning room. *So much for the charm,* Jack thought. Maybe the heroic stuff was a little much, but he had no chance, he had to go big. Nothing would have worked anyway; Wendy was an iceberg. He had never met Mr. Mitchell. Much of the staff refused to believe that there was a Mr. Mitchell, but if he did exist, Jack felt sorry for him.

All the members of the club were supposed to be treated like royalty, but it did not take long to realize that some members were more important than others. Mr. Hoffman was close to the top of the list. Today's fundraiser benefitted the Founding Fathers' Brain Cancer Research Corporation, a charity that Mr. Hoffman supported since its founding.

An extremely aggressive version of brain cancer was first diagnosed ten years earlier, and since then, it had continued to show up with increasing frequency. It typically attacked men and women in their early sixties, moving through the body with extreme swiftness with no known cure. Once detected, it was too late to do much of anything. The clinics didn't even offer chemotherapy as a treatment. At most, chemo bought people a few additional months and was deemed cost prohibitive. Jack had already lost a number of relatives and friends to the disease. The government stated that one in seven was expected to come down with the cancer, but in Jack's neighborhood, the number was closer to one in four.

---

dent. The infection grew out of control, with Hoffman returning to one of the private hospitals that bore his name. Unable to prove who he was, the hospital refused to treat him. He later died in the parking lot, clutching his guitar under a sign that bore his likeness. It was not until the Human Rights Wave of the 2050s that the universal single payer health insurance was adopted by the United States under the name HumanCare.

Jack dived into the employee bathroom and quickly changed into his uniform in the cramped dingy confines of the poorly lit employee bathroom. Alone, he stuffed his street clothes into the duffel and squeezed it under the sink for safekeeping. There was not enough time to get to his locker, and there was nothing of real value in the duffel anyway. Despite the nastiness with Wendy, Jack felt good. He was close to obtaining some information that he really needed, information that might prove valuable and could change everything.

4

As Jack swung open the double doors leading to the ballroom, he was greeted with the soft sounds of jazz. Jazz was very popular among the rich and powerful. No expensive benefit was complete without a live jazz band. He could tell how important the benefit was by counting the number of musicians in the band. From the look of the crowded stage, this benefit was top-notch. Jack preferred the driving beat of the latest new rock, but he had to admit that well-performed jazz involved a certain artistry that appealed to him, a certain freedom of interpretation that made every song unique.

The large ballroom was polished to a high shine. The immense crystal chandelier sparkled brightly. It took a team of four people three hours each to get it in that condition. On one end of the ballroom stood a raised platform where the band performed. A new lead female singer, who Jack hadn't seen before, stood at the front of the stage, a microphone grasped gracefully in her hand. Her long, wavy, striking red hair fell well below her shoulders. She was tall, thin, and young looking. Her voice sounded highly polished, powerful, and expressive as she sung the lyrics to a popular love song. Ten other musicians joined her on stage; most looked familiar from other performances at the club. They played everything from electric guitar to the saxophone, but Jack struggled to take his eyes off the singer. Only when the trumpet took over for the vocalist did he break free from his trance and glide toward his section.

An all-glass–enclosed greenhouse room was connected to the main ballroom, and stood opposite the stage. The dividing wall that sometimes separated the two was gone, making the three glass walls and the vaulted glass ceiling part of the main room. A long table filled with a variety of appetizers on large white china serving plates stood at one end of the greenhouse room while a long wooden bar manned by a team of bartenders was set up at the opposite end. Most of the guests had not yet arrived, but the bar buzzed with activity. The men wore suits, and the women wore cocktail dresses. Apparently, black was in fashion for the upcoming summer season. Most of the men looked as if they were in their forties or older while the women in the room appeared at least a decade younger on average. Enough diamonds sparkled in the room to fill Jack's duffel bag.

Jack noticed a few intense conversations among small groups of two or three. Mr. Johnson and Mr. Bennett were engaged in a charged discussion with a third man who Jack did not recognize. They both leaned in close and spoke adamantly to their companion who stood silently with his arms crossed. Jack's keen eyes moved from group to group imagining what type of business deals they might be discussing. The business world and high finance was, however, far beyond his reach. Jack loved tennis from a young age and had won a few tournaments in his early teens but had never finished above the semis in the county tournaments. The competition from teens who enjoyed private lessons and unlimited court time was too much for him. While Jack had never attracted the attention of a corporate sponsor to go pro, he had more than enough talent to teach, and scored high grades in the one year he spent in tennis instruction vocational school. After a few years apprenticing under John, Jack might be eligible to be a head instructor himself. *A lot of good that would do me,* he thought with a smirk. There were only a few jobs for tennis instructors, and he was unlikely to find a more prestigious place to work than at the club. Besides, he liked John.

When Jack was sixteen, he had a fleeting hope to go into business, but he was just not smart enough. He took the preliminary college assessment tests and scored better than most, but not good enough for a corporate sponsor. Without a corporate sponsor, advanced schooling was not an option for Jack, so he threw himself into tennis instruction. Tom, Jack's younger brother, was, on the other hand, quite brilliant. He dominated his preliminaries last year and scored a contract with ICS (International Commodity Sellers). Tom may have sold his soul to the devil, but there was a chance he would make his way out. Jack smiled. His brother had a chance. Few people scored high enough to earn a corporate scholarship, and ICS was one of the most prestigious places to work in the country. As unlikely as it may be, he hoped that one day Tom would be having an intense discussion at a benefit just like this one. *Maybe I'll take his order*, he thought with a chuckle.

Jack started filling water glasses while the smell of the appetizers made his stomach jump. He hadn't eaten anything since breakfast except a dried beef stick. One of the perks of working a large benefit was the leftovers. At least a third of the food prepared for tonight would go uneaten, which was more than enough for the staff to split amongst themselves.

Once the guests were seated, Jack planned on sneaking into the kitchen for a quick go at whatever was available. Antonio liked Jack, usually taking pity on him.

The lights flickered on and off, alerting the guests to the end of the cocktail hour and the beginning of the formal dinner. Jack glanced over at the band and thought he caught the eye of the female singer. She was well out of his league. Maybe it was just his imagination, but she seemed to be staring at him. She looked vaguely familiar, but he was sure that he would have remembered her if he had met her before. *Probably just my mind playing tricks on me*, he thought as most of the guests filled the main room.

Jack spun into action, pulling out chairs, dispensing compliments freely, and flirting where appropriate.

Once the initial activity calmed down and everyone's orders had been taken, Mr. Hoffman took to the stage to address the crowd. He was in his early fifties with a bulging stomach, balding light brown hair, large round face with a ruddy complexion, and a nervous smile. He cleared his throat awkwardly and started speaking about brain cancer research and the need to find a cure. At least that was what Jack assumed he was talking about. Jack paid little attention to him as his voice droned on, preferring to glance at the crowd instead, checking out the latest styles, and getting a feel for the mood in the room. People let their guard down when they thought no one was watching, and Jack could tell a lot from body language. Jack had just noticed Mrs. Bennett playing footsie with someone who was not Mr. Bennett when he sensed that someone had silently slunk up next to him.

The unmistakable scent of Heather's perfume, musky with a hint of honey, lingered in the air like a light cloud. Without turning around, Jack spoke softly, "Can I help you Mrs. Benson?" Heather was in her late twenties, had a thin muscular body toned from many hours at the gym, long blond hair that didn't resemble her natural color, and crystal blue eyes that exuded sensuality upon command. She often wielded them like daggers. Heather was Mr. Benson's third wife. He was a media mogul in his late fifties, and certainly a member of the inner circle, which made Heather dangerous.

Rumor had it that Heather's family had lost a good deal of money on a business deal that went bankrupt and was close to dropping out of the privileged class. Once someone dropped out, they rarely, if ever, made it back in. The families had known each other for decades, and a hasty marriage was arranged between Heather and Mr. Benson, who had recently divorced wife number two. Heather felt little affection for Mr. Benson, but the deal secured her family's place in the social structure, at least for a little while longer. He was her best option—maybe her only option.

Heather had taken an interest in Jack. He scratched a certain itch, part sensual and part dangerous. She liked things a little dangerous. *Maybe too dangerous*, thought Jack. She was good fun, and Jack hoped to get some valuable information from her, but he would have to end the affair soon. *Not today, but definitely some time soon.* Heather was never content. She needed to up the ante, and Jack couldn't afford getting caught playing her games.

Heather's voice was soft and raspy. Jack could feel her breath hot against his neck. "I have a problem that I need you to fix."

Jack stole a quick glance. Heather wore a low-cut sleeveless black dress that ended midthigh. Even in the dimly lit room, Jack noticed a diamond and ruby necklace that must have cost a fortune. *She is likely going to be the death of me*, he thought. Without looking at her, he whispered, "I'm working right now, maybe we can arrange something later?"

Heather moved closer to Jack, sliding an inch behind his right ear, her voice barely above a whisper. "This can't wait. I have the information you want and to get it you will need to give me something in return." Heather blew hot air into Jack's ear.

Jack's heart pounded as electricity surged through his body. Heather knew how to make him crazy, and he really wanted that information. He scanned the ballroom looking for Wendy. She wasn't on the floor at that moment. *She was probably in the kitchen grilling the chefs.*

Worried about getting caught, Jack asked warily, "What do you have in mind?"

Heather sounded impatient. "They are going to play a stupid video. It's twenty minutes long. Doug droned on about it at lunch. We have plenty of time. No one will notice you're gone. Meet me at the room, if you want it."

Jack turned, but Heather was already strolling back to her table. He smiled to himself. *Can't get off the ride now.* Since he was not needed at the moment, he headed to the now vacant bar. David, his best friend, tended bar for the benefit.

David was a few years older than Jack. He had short blond hair with streaks of red mingled in, and was tall, tan, and good-looking. A new female bartender chatted him up. From the way she laughed and touched his arm, Jack guessed that David had made another *new* friend.

Upon seeing Jack, David moved to the end of the bar. "What's up, bro? Getting tennis elbow filling the water glasses?" David fidgeted with a small toy umbrella that he put into mixed drinks.

"Not yet, but I need a favor." Jack glanced around. They were alone, but he whispered anyway. "I need to use the room in a few minutes."

David's face lit up in a broad smile. "Man, you are playing with fire with that one. Are you sure?" David mischievously popped open the miniature toy umbrella with a smirk.

"Just this last time. She has something that I need."

David slowly brought his right hand down on the bar. "Don't get caught, bro. You can give it back to me tonight at poker." He lifted his hand, and Jack quickly palmed the brass key.

"I would never miss an opportunity to take your money. It's a gift that keeps giving."

Tonight was going to be a long one. The poker sessions usually ended after the sun came up. Jack quickly headed back to his section and made sure that everyone had a full glass of water for the start of the video.

CHAPTER

5

★ ★ ★ ★ ★

The lights dimmed, and the three-dimensional image sprang to life on the large white screen that silently dropped from the ceiling a moment earlier. No top-of-the-line benefit was complete unless it had a heart-wrenching, three-dimensional, high-definition video. For an event this important, Mr. Benson undoubtedly helped with the production.

Jack searched for Wendy who was stationed toward the front of the room beside Mr. Hoffman's table, wearing her forced smile, trying to look captivated by the video. Heather had already vacated her seat. Her chair was noticeably empty next to Mr. Benson who was involved in a heated conversation with the person seated next to him. *Convenient*, thought Jack as he smoothly strode toward the rear exit. He quickly scanned the room one last time to make sure that no one saw him leave. Everyone seemed focused on the video, except the redheaded singer who looked in his direction, her eyes focused on the exit door as Jack snuck out of the room.

The key felt heavy in Jack's back pocket. No one used keys anymore but the club. They liked the look and feel of the antique keys, and old was in right now. No one cared that the keys used the latest secure magnetic signature technology. They looked old and felt old and that was good enough for the club. Jack hustled his way up the nearest flight of stairs and headed for the east wing of the clubhouse toward the guestrooms.

Jack had no idea how David procured a key to one of the rooms, but it certainly came in handy. The guestrooms were never used. Most members probably didn't even know they existed, but Jack did and so did Heather. Every once in a while, they met in the small room for some *alone time.*

A lush, soft carpet covered the hallway. A white wooden chair rail split the walls horizontally. The top half was beige, and the bottom was painted a dark red. Pictures of popular politicians were periodically displayed along the top half of the hallway. Featured were, of course, old drawings or oil paintings of the founding fathers.[6]

Jack turned the corner and spotted Heather leaning against a wall, her right leg bent at the knee with a glass of champagne held lightly in her long fingers. Her blond hair tumbled passed her shoulders. Her eyes smoldered as she gave Jack her most seductive look. *I must be crazy*, thought Jack. "I thought you were working?" Heather spoke in a mischievous voice, licking her lips when she finished speaking.

"All work and no play makes Jack a dull boy." Jack smiled and inserted the key into the lock for room number 9 and twisted. When the door swung open, Heather quickly pushed past Jack and into the small room. The shades were drawn, the room dark.

Jack barely closed the door before Heather was all over him. Her lips crushed up against his, her tongue aggressively probing his mouth. He tasted fine champagne and had a hard time

---

[6]   No elite club or association in this time frame existed without prominent tributes to both the founding fathers of the country and the Constitution. The club was littered with them. The most prominent being the club's "Constitutional Room." The Constitutional Room was just off the main entrance to the clubhouse where a three-dimensional video featured a leading actor who dramatically read an abbreviated version of the Constitution on a forty-minute loop. The room was mostly forgotten by the club's members but was used at night as the unofficial home of the staff's crap game.

breathing as his hands wandered along Heather's back down her short black dress. In an instant, Heather pushed Jack away, shoving him hard against the door, a wicked smile crossing her face.

"I knew you couldn't resist me," Heather said as she backed up toward the bed. She slowly unzipped her dress and let it fall to the floor. She wore nothing underneath her dress, except for her diamond and ruby necklace. Even in the darkness of the unlit room, Jack could tell that her body was just about perfect, and although Jack knew she had some medical modifications done, who was he to complain?

"Well, are you just going to stand there gawking?" She motioned for him to come closer with one long finger. As Jack got within reach, Heather shook her head. He wasn't allowed to touch her just yet. Heather wanted to be in charge. She violently yanked his shirt over his head and, with a smile, unbuckled his belt. Unclothed, Heather pulled Jack down on the bed on top of her.

Jack was used to the routine with Heather. Sex with Heather wasn't about affection or closeness but was more of a physical act—almost like it was an extension of her workout routines. Jack once theorized that Heather used sex to hold on to her youth, something she couldn't hope to do with Mr. Benson, but whatever the reason, she liked it rough and hard, and Jack willingly played his part.

Jack pushed down hard on Heather's arms, and the two tumbled around, a jumble of arms, legs, and bodies. Tonight, Heather wanted to dominate, so she took control, which was fine with Jack, so long as things didn't take too long. Heather moved to her own rhythm, her eyes unfocused as if she was transported to some other place or time.

After an explosion of energy, Heather rolled off the bed, sweating lightly and breathing heavily. While Jack tried to catch his breath, Heather strode to the adjacent bathroom with her dress dangling in her hand. She reached the door and swung it closed, hard. The noise rang out in the small room, jolting Jack into action. He touched the lamp on the bedside table and soft white light flooded the room.

Jack quickly got dressed and glanced around the room. The bed was a mess. Even though no one used the room, there was no way he could leave it in this condition. As Jack straightened the pillows, his hand grasped something small and hard. Surprised, he pulled out the object and stared at a small black flash drive. *How did that get there?* There was no telling how long it might have been left behind. Intrigued, Jack pocketed the memory stick as Heather emerged from the bathroom, looking fabulous and holding an identical black flash drive. Grinning, she tossed the drive to Jack. "I think you will find what you want on this thing. Doug goes to bed early and left his tablet open last night. Be discrete. You didn't get this from me."

Jack smiled broadly. "Thanks."

As Heather reached the door, she spun abruptly. "You still owe me Jack," she said haughtily and quickly left the room, shutting the door behind her. The scent of her perfume still lingered behind in the small room.

Jack glanced at his watch. The entire episode took eighteen minutes. He took one last look around. The place appeared neat enough. Jack shut off the lamp and hurried out of the room, locking the door behind him.

Jack raced down the deserted hallway and down the stairs leading to the ballroom. He took a quick left into the employee area and charged into the bathroom. He needed to get his act together before his absence was noticed. He leaned against the sink, splashed some water on his face, and straightened his clothes. Checking his reflection in the mirror, he didn't like something he saw in the expression on his face, but he shook that off as a smudge on the glass. As he turned to leave, he felt the two flash drives uncomfortably rub against each other in his pocket and frowned. *What to do with them? I better take the one Heather gave me with me,* he thought as he pocketed one of the flash drives and stowed the other one in his duffel for safekeeping. *Maybe there will be something of interest on it? You never know what people leave around.*

6

Classical music rained down on Warren as sunlight streamed into his bedroom. The shades automatically parted; the recessed lighting started glowing with the latest "natural light," and the music from the hidden speakers slowly grew louder. This morning, it was Beethoven's Fifth Symphony in C minor. Warren rotated the classics on a random basis, never sure what music would awaken him. He rolled over and checked the time. It was eight. Quite a luxury to linger in bed this late, but last night's benefit ran late, and Warren's head ached with the aftermath of a few too many glasses of Scotch. He had been awake for hours with his eyes closed. He didn't sleep much, so he usually just lay in bed trying to calm his restless mind.

Warren swung his legs out of bed, grabbed his shorts, and opened the drawer in his bedside table. A row of glistening bottles and syringes greeted him like an old friend. Warren reached for the nearest one, filled the syringe, and injected the clear liquid in the vein behind his left knee. The injection stung for a moment, but Warren was used to it by now. As the fluid entered his bloodstream, he felt energy pulse and flow through his body, immediately feeling twenty years younger.

Warren couldn't help but grin. The fluid was the latest product from a large pharmaceutical company. They called it Enhanced Hormone Treatment. The company claimed that the treatments froze the aging process, but Warren found that if he increased the dose gradually, the aging process not only froze but reversed itself. Energy returned, and muscles regained old form. It was close to a miracle product, a very expensive and exclusive miracle product. The treatments cost a small fortune, and Warren was assured that the list of end users would be kept short. No more than a few dozen people knew about the drug, and it would stay that way. The money spent was well worth it.

Not for the first time, Warren grinned to himself about the reformed Food and Drug Administration as he glanced at a photograph of him shaking the hands of a senator whom he had convinced to vote his way on the bill. The government had no place regulating advanced medications like this one. Warren could judge for himself what he wanted to do with his body. Nowhere in the Constitution did it mention anything about regulations of advanced medicines. [7] Restricting people like Warren from getting drugs like these would be criminal.

Warren stretched as he got out of bed. The day's routine started with a few push-ups followed by stomach crunches—just enough activity to build a light coating of sweat and get the blood circulating. Warren finished strong and padded his way into the

---

[7]   The partial elimination of the FDA in the Safe Medication Act of 2025 was extremely popular with Originalist politicians. The FDA continued to regulate over the counter drugs, but had no authority over more advanced prescription medications. The Phoenix Corporation controlled the FDA, and made enormous money by *selling* the right to distribute over the counter drugs. After the act was passed in 2025, the drug companies greatly increased the variety of their prescription drug offerings. Unfortunately, the effectiveness of these medications was often defective, and within a few short years, the companies started to include highly addictive agents in their drugs. Even though the drugs were useless in combating illness, they were very expensive and very addictive. Of course anti-addictive medications were made and sold, which were also highly addictive and expensive. By this time, most consumers wouldn't purchase any drugs that weren't approved by the FDA prior to 2025 or approved by one of the governmental agencies in Europe or Mexico.

bathroom toward the mirror above the sink. Instead of glass, the new mirror was really an ultra thin flat screen that projected an image from the thumb-sized camera that was affixed to the wall above it. With a touch of the screen, Warren could either zoom in or zoom out the reflection in high-definition resolution. Staring closely at his own image, Warren liked what he saw. He was on the other side of forty, but his body looked better than anyone he saw in the gym. A nice six-pack had developed at his mid-section; his arms and chest were chiseled muscle. A few poses for the monitor wouldn't hurt. There was no harm admiring the hard work he put into his body. He already looked forward to today's session at the gym and his new young female trainer who, Warren was sure, was already obsessed with him. He could tell by the way she had been looking at him.

With his mood improving, Warren pulled on a silk T-shirt, wandered over to a small, gunmetal gray metal table beside his bed, and sat in the hard stainless-steel chair. Warren's house was a sprawling single-story contemporary-style home. Soaring windows at unusual angles kept the place interesting. The layout was open-spaced with few fixed walls. The two main exceptions were the specially designed media center and the suite of rooms in the basement with no windows that few people, other than Warren, knew about. The house was situated high enough on a hill that he had a fabulous view of the Hudson River. Sure he had to buy the two neighboring houses to tear them down, but it was worth the expense. The views were breathtaking, particularly the sunsets.

Seated at the table, Warren opened Michael's tablet. He expected to study it last night, but he wasn't in the mood after the benefit and the Scotch. He dismissed the lack of discipline as understandable. He felt poorly about losing an asset like Michael and needed a little time to unwind. The slight delay in reviewing the tablet would cause him no harm.

Warren unfolded the tablet and powered it up. The initial screen was locked. It asked for a user name and password in large, green, blinking letters. Warren smiled. The tablet was company-issued, and therefore, he knew the master user name and password that bypassed the security and would open the tablet. Typing in *Adams and Lexington*, the tablet burst to life. The explosive documents were still open, but Warren wasn't interested in studying them at this moment. There was plenty of time for that later.

Warren found the history function and clicked. A drop-down box filled the screen showing the latest activities that were performed on the computer over the past week. At the bottom of the list was the opening of the documents that Michael had showed Warren yesterday. Next up, only two minutes earlier, was something to do with an external memory drive. Warren started to see red, his vision blurring over angrily and his left eye twitching wildly.

Michael saved the documents onto an external drive minutes before he met with Warren. *Why would he do that?* Michael owed everything to Warren. He worshipped Warren. *How could he disobey me?* Warren flew into a rage and started pounding the metal desk with his right arm. *The treacherous little worm!* Blinded by his rage, Warren didn't realize what he was doing as the tablet jumped off the table, and the metal table twisted beneath his blows. In a fury, he lifted the table and bashed it violently against the floor. The metal dented, and the tiled floor cracked. Warren breathed heavily as the thunder in his head slowly quieted.

One of the side effects of the enhanced hormone treatment was increased passion. *So what*, thought Warren. Passion was real. Passion made life vivid, and he still had control when he wanted to. He sneered at the twisted metal table. He had grown bored with it anyway. The table was more interesting now. No harm was done.

Now that Warren's head cleared, he rationalized that Michael must have saved the documents on a flash drive to deliver it to him. No doubt Michael wanted to please him and wanted to be ready to hand over the flash drive if required of him. A smile crossed his lips. That made a lot of sense; Michael was a thought-ful person after all.

With a new sense of calm, Warren grabbed his cell phone. With a push of a button, Warren started talking to Steven. "Did you find any flash drives on the body?"

Steven's usually flat voice responded, "No, we did the usual search of the body and all the clothing. Nothing interesting was in any of the pockets or sewn into the seams of the clothes."

Warren didn't like the answer. His knuckles turned white as he grasped his phone hard. "How about the room? Did you do a full search?"

"We did not do a thorough search of the room. You told us to take care of the body, and because of the benefit, we had no time to linger. I thought discretion was more important than to search the room, but nothing was left in plain sight."

After a pause, Warren sunk back into his metal chair. "Yes, I know there was no time for a thorough search, but I need you to go back and search the room. Arrange the access with Bob. You should find a flash drive. It was created only minutes before I got there, and Michael didn't have any other opportunities to dispense with it. He must have hidden it in the room."

Warren didn't wait for a response. He disconnected the phone and threw it against the glass wall. The phone cracked open upon impact. Good thing he kept a few backups. Passion was good! He felt alive!

Every Saturday, Warren spent late mornings on the club's driv-ing range with the head pro. Golf wasn't Warren's favorite sport, but he spent enough time on the course with business associ-ates and colleagues that he needed to excel at it. Today, he was working with his driver. The ball wasn't jumping off the golf club lately, and consequently, he was losing distance. Nothing enraged Warren on the golf course more than being out driven by his playing partners. To rectify the situation, Warren had already made some modifications to his driver that weren't quite within the latest PGA rules. The results started to pay off when Warren's phone buzzed.

Warren signaled the pro that he needed to take a call and stepped away from the hitting area. Steven's voice came through the earpiece. "We took apart the room. There was no flash drive."

Warren kept his voice and demeanor calm. "It has to be there somewhere. Look again." He felt the passion returning in a rush.

"We did discover that the room was used by some other people during the benefit last night," Steven said.

"What are you talking about? Who used that room? That room was reserved for me." Warren's vision started to turn fuzzy and the noise in his head began escalating, but he fought hard to keep control, digging his nails into the leather grip on his golf club.

"A couple must have snuck in to use the room for some intimate moments. We found two sets of prints and other evidence of their interlude. It shouldn't take long for us to identify who they are."

"This is top priority. Call me back with the names." Warren disconnected the call. *Whoever used the room must have spotted the drive. They probably have no idea what is on the device yet. The damage can be contained so long as we act fast*, he thought.

Warren returned to the pro. The tall, lanky golfer spent a short time on the PGA tour but never made it big. He was considered a master instructor. In his usual low-key manner, he said, "Now remember, keep your hands out in front and make a smooth turn."

Warren stared at him with murderous intent and a snarl on his face. The pro instinctively moved back. Warren envisioned rapping the driver around his head but addressed the ball instead. He pulled back smoothly from the ball but swung through it with all his rage. The swing was errant, and he topped the ball off to the right. He laughed for the benefit of the other golfers on the range and brought the driver down hard on the pro's foot. "We are done here," he said, his voice charged with malice before stalking toward the golf cart. *Steven had better work fast,* he thought.

CHAPTER

7

★ ★ ★ ★ ★

Jack found himself in his old neighborhood. Last night's poker
session went late, very late. He slept over at Julian's apartment,
which wasn't surprising. Julian owned an old and lumpy couch
that was long enough for Jack's tall frame. By the time the game
broke up, the night sky had started to lighten, and there was no
reason to trek home. It wasn't the first time that Jack crashed at
a friend's house, but his back ached thanks to one loose spring in
the couch that jabbed him for hours, but he was the big winner,
and it felt good to have some cash in his pocket.

Jack had a place to go to. He had a room in his mom's apartment with his younger brother, but he infrequently stayed there.
It wasn't on purpose. He was just busy. There were an assortment
of women who soaked up his time, and a handful of close friends
with places he sometimes crashed. Jack kept enough clothes in
his duffel and his locker at the club that he didn't need to replen-
ish his supply more than once per week. One of the perks of
being a tennis instructor was the simple attire: shorts, white club
polo shirt, windbreaker, and white sneakers.

Jack pulled the Chief off the main road, stopping in front of
a small diner where he used to eat when he was a child. The sky
was cloudy, and rain had just started to fall in a light mist. It was
almost eleven o'clock, just enough time for breakfast before getting to the club for the afternoon lessons. Jack chained up the bike
and strolled into the small restaurant. There was enough room for
a handful of customers at any one time, including the seven stools

at the counter. The small place was almost empty. Only a young couple with a two-year-old girl sat at a table toward the back. Her brown hair was pulled into two pigtails that were tied with pink ribbons.

Jack sat at a table in the front with a view of the street so he could keep an eye on his bike. He breathed in deeply, the greasy smell of eggs and fried potatoes filling his lungs. It was like stepping back in time: the faded and cracked tiled floor, the long counter with the grill behind it, and the tables with uncomfortable metal chairs and small firm cushions. If he tried hard, he could remember coming here with his father when he was young. Every once in a while, Jack's dad took him out for breakfast alone, for some man-to-man time. Of course, he also took Tom to breakfast, but Jack knew his time with his dad was special. He told him so, right before he ordered the French toast with bacon. He always ordered the same thing. It was as predictable as the sunrise.

Jack's father died seven years earlier in an automobile accident. He drove home late from work at the club. The other driver was drunk and fell asleep at the wheel. The drunken driver crossed the line into oncoming traffic. Jack's father had just happened to be traveling at the wrong spot at the wrong moment. There was nothing he could have done. It was just bad luck, but it ended in a ball of flames. Both drivers died, and Jack's family was torn apart. It didn't take long before they had to sell the house. Truth be told, Jack's dad worked two jobs, and his mother worked one, just to hold on to the house before the accident. Without Jack's dad, the house became an impossible burden.

Jack vividly remembered the night that his mom told him and Tom that they would have to sell the house. It was in the dead of winter, two inches of fresh snow covered the ground, and the house was cold and quiet. Natural gas was expensive again, and the wind off the river made everything frigid. They had just finished dinner with the promise of ice cream for dessert. Ice cream was a luxury in those days, and Jack should have known that Mom was going to deliver bad news.

Jack was eleven, and Tom was nine. Mom started the family discussion in the living room. It was the only room in the house that had a view of the Hudson River, but in the wintertime, those views were stunning. She sat between her two boys on the couch facing the river with her arms draped over their shoulders. She tried to be upbeat and positive, pitching the move as a new adventure, but broke down in tears quickly enough as she stared out of the windows. They just couldn't afford to live in the house anymore. They would sell it to the real estate company that was gobbling up all the houses in the neighborhood. They could live in the house until school ended, but they would have to find an apartment elsewhere.

Tom took the news hard. He burst from the house red faced, tears flowing down his cheeks in little streams. He ran toward the small nature area that bordered the neighborhood. The house was close to the Hudson River, and through some weird quirk of zoning law, there was this oddly shaped piece of land that wasn't developed. Decades earlier, there used to be a small clay brick–making factory on the site, but now only the crumbling concrete outline of the foundation remained. If you looked hard enough, you could still find a few buried bricks with the company's name etched on them. Jack and Tom spent many hours in that nature area playing different versions of good versus bad. Tom always had to be the good guy. Jack usually won.

Jack ran after his brother, carrying his brother's coat in one arm. Jack found him sitting on the outline of one of the foundation walls of the old factory. "It's just not fair. None of it is fair," Tom said, voice cracking. He started to shake from the cold and the tears and the sadness that enveloped him.

Jack tossed his brother his coat and sat next to him on the crumbling foundation wall. "Fairness has nothing to do with it. Nothing is ever fair. We just need to make the best of it for Mom.

Someday, we will get our home back, but you can't be running off crying like a baby." Jack winced as he remembered the harsh words—what a jerk he had been. If only he could go back in time…but he could never get that moment back.

Tom dried his eyes on his sleeve and walked home with Jack in silence. He didn't speak to anyone for a week, but that was the last time Jack had ever seen him cry. The kid could be tough when he wanted.

Jack snapped back to the present when the waitress approached. He smiled brightly at the familiar form. "Hey, Abbey, what are you doing here?"

Abbey returned the smile. She was of average height, had short brown hair, and her cheeks were dotted with the beginning traces of summer freckles. The beige uniform made her look old, and Jack noticed some creases in the corner of her eyes that shouldn't have been there. "What do you think I am doing, Jack? Never the smartest one, was yah?" Abbey's voice sounded scratchy.

"I don't think I've seen you since sixth grade when we moved away. You were at the top of our class, what gives?"

"That was a long time ago, and I was never at the top of the class, you just thought so."

Jack pointed to the seat across the table from him. "Sit with me for a minute. There's no one else here."

Abbey looked around the restaurant. The couple with the toddler got up to leave and walked to the cook who also doubled as the cashier. "Okay, but only for a moment. I don't need to get into trouble."

"So how does a girl who was *just about* the top of her class end up waitressing here?" Jack's voice was soft and filled with sincere interest. There were worse jobs than waitressing at a small diner, but it was hardly anyone's idea of getting ahead.

"A year after you left, my grandfather died from the cancer. We took in our grandmother, but she'd been sick, and meds costs money. We could barely afford the expense, but what could we do?"[8]

Jack pressed on. "What about vocational school?"

"It still costs money. When I finished tenth grade, we just didn't have the money for further education, and I didn't place well enough in the assessment tests for a corporate scholarship. I figure I can work here for a few years and then attend a vocational school later. Maybe I can do something with computers? I always liked computers." As Abbey finished her story, a short silence hung in the air. They both knew the truth. Abbey wasn't going anywhere. She would make the best of the situation. Maybe work her way up to a cook, and hopefully find someone nice with a steady job to marry.

Jack lied. "There's still plenty of time. You can do it if you set your mind to it. Maybe one day you'll be featured on *Rags to Riches*."

Abbey laughed. "That would be something. How is your brother Tom doing? Remember the fight he had with Al? Al must've been twice his size, and it took three of us to pull Tom off him. Al still has a crooked nose. Or the game we played with the train? He used to scare me to death the way he waited until the last second to jump out of the way. I always turned away before the train passed. He was the wildest kid I've ever known."

Jack thought for a moment. It had been some time since he thought of Tom as being wild. Tom had thrown himself into his

---

[8] At this point in time, the government offered virtually no assistance for older citizens' medical costs. A legacy program named Medicare existed, but it was changed into a voucher program for private insurance companies two decades earlier. The voucher was only a small fraction of the cost of the insurance. Since the government subsidy was paid directly to insurance companies only after the senior first paid the balance of the premium, the program ended up being a subsidy for wealthy seniors that could otherwise afford the insurance. Two thirds of American seniors went uninsured.

studies so fiercely that he had little time for Jack. Tom was an all-or-nothing type of guy. Whatever he did, he made up his mind quickly, and went all in. Now his studies soaked up all his time. "Tom is doing well. He got all the brains in the family and is continuing with his studies." Jack saw no need to mention the corporate sponsorship with ICS.

Jack's phone buzzed. He recognized the number from the incoming call with a look of concern. Standing up, he told Abbey, "I need to take this outside. Can you get me some coffee and a donut? I'm going healthy today."

Stepping outside of the diner, Jack answered the call. "What's up?" Jack stood close to the door under the shelter of the tattered green awning to avoid the steady rainfall. The awning did a poor job protecting him.

Jack heard a familiar female voice. "This phone is not secure, so I have to be brief. I don't know what you did last night, but I am hearing some concerning rumors. Your name was floated around by some really bad guys. Be careful. These are just rumors at this point. Nothing has been confirmed. Be prepared to run, if I call back."

Jack's throat tightened. "I got something that could be interesting last night. If something happens to me, tell my brother that I will hide the information where home is." Jack disconnected the call.

False rumors floated around all the time. Maybe someone had spotted him and Heather leaving together? *Perhaps this had something to do with that redheaded singer?* There was a chance that this would blow over.

Jack went back into the diner. Abbey was waiting for him with a glazed donut and a hot cup of coffee.

"Can I have them to-go? I've gotta be heading out." Jack still smiled, but concern edged on his face.

Abbey studied him closely. "I hear you're teaching tennis at the Ronald. That's a good job. You were always pushing limits.

Don't mess it up." Abbey grabbed the cup and plate and went behind the counter.

I hope it isn't too late, thought Jack.

Jack walked up to the cash register and paid Abbey, giving her a generous tip. "It was good seeing you. Take care."

Abbey smiled weakly, touching Jack's hand before he left. "Don't be a stranger." Her eyes looked sad.

Jack left without looking back and jumped on the Chief. He had an errand to run before heading to the club.

CHAPTER

8

The rain fell down in sputters. The club had indoor and outdoor tennis courts, so lessons continued even during the worst weather. Jack looked at the time on his cell phone and realized that he was running late. *Why is it that I am always racing against time?* he thought as he weaved the motorcycle in and around traffic in an effort to speed up his arrival at the club.

Still pressed for time, Jack gritted his teeth and took a short-cut through the local streets. Something he loathed to do. This neighborhood wasn't one of the affluent areas or even one of the few middle-class districts left in Westchester; it was one of the growing ghettos. The ghettos housed the bulging lower classes in America where the majority of the inhabitants scraped by on the lowest end of employment: restaurant/service work, landscaping, and other manual labor jobs of the old economy. The ghettos operated as social/political structures of their own with their own sets of rules and their own forms of justice. Gangs dominated life in the ghettos, and it was a hard life rife with violence.

The government mostly gave up on these areas and the people that lived in them. Checkpoints were set up, restricting access to the affluent neighborhoods. Police checked vehicles and paperwork. Everyone was required to carry government-issued identification cards with computerized strips. Depending upon the need or the circumstance, access was limited to those people that *belonged*. Because of the club's location and Jack's unusual working hours, he had unlimited access to the affluent area surrounding the country club, but there were other areas in New York where he would be turned away. Residents were able to call their local police departments to permit access to certain individuals for temporary periods depending upon their needs. All these restrictions were adopted under the rubric of Homeland Security. Terrorism, both domestic and foreign, was never far from the lead stories on the news, scaring the population into submission.

Potholes and large cracks from years of neglect marked the road that entered the Lower Westchester Ghetto. The once-stately dwellings stood in disrepair. Victorian and large colonial houses dotted the street. Most of the windows were boarded up with plywood, and exposed wood siding rotted in the afternoon sun. Most houses held too many people for the structure; many leaned precariously one way or the other. Even at this time of the day, Jack spotted prostitutes and drug dealers walking the streets. Sometimes the rich sent their errand boys to pick up a treat for a party or to bring back a professional for some recreational time. Jack's family lived a few steps better than this. With his salary and what his mom earned, things were just manageable, and now that ICS paid Tom a stipend they were able to save a few bucks; however, Jack knew they were just one or two setbacks from the ghetto.

Jack zipped along, swerving around the cracks in the pavement, but a glance in the side mirror brought bad news. Two black sedans sped up behind him, closing in on him fast. They were private security cars. The privileged class used the private security forces as a specialized police department. They were heavily armed and functioned much like normal police, but they weren't bound by any governmental restrictions. No one messed with them if they could help it. Even the toughest gangs shied away from the "private police" as they called them.

Crap, thought Jack. Jack fought hard against panic. *It might be a coincidence.* Jack's heart started pounding. His hands were slippery from sweat as he twisted the grips on the bike. He couldn't help but glance back at the approaching sedans, his gaze drawn toward the danger like a moth to a flame. Jack almost jumped off his bike when he heard a voice through his earpiece. "Incoming call." Jack answered, and the same female voice from earlier whispered in his ear.

"Run, Jack."

Jack twisted the accelerator, pushing the Chief forward while sirens wailed on the private security cars as they sped up in pursuit. Jack raced his way through the mostly deserted streets looking for something, anything that could help when he heard a popping sound. *Crack, crack, crack.* The pavement sparked all around him as one of the officers opened fire with an assault rifle. He aimed low, trying to take out the bike's tires. Jack pushed the bike even harder, but the roads were slick, and there wasn't much room to navigate.

Jack needed a plan, and then he heard a church bell chime. It was twelve o'clock. This might be the break that he needed. Each ghetto had one large government-run food distribution facility. For the most needy in the neighborhood, the government provided one hot meal per day and usually a small take-home snack. Each facility opened its doors at twelve sharp and stayed open until they ran out of food for that day. They were supposed to be able to supply all that was needed, but often they ran out of food before serving everyone. At this time of day, there would already be long lines of people milling about. Jack swerved quickly to the left as he heard another round of pops. *The facility must be around here somewhere.* Usually they were centrally located on a main street.

A quick right and Jack heard the crowds before he saw them. *Good, they sounded particularly unruly this afternoon.* Perhaps it was the hot weather or the rain or just pent-up feelings of despair and frustration, but whatever the cause, Jack could use it. One more turn and hundreds of people came into view. Shocked, Jack slammed on the brakes and lost control of the bike on the slick pavement. The bike skidded on its side to a stop ten feet before the masses, ripping up Jack's leg in the process. Jack heard the sedans slam on their brakes behind him and smelled the unique odor of burning rubber. With no time to check for injuries, Jack bolted to his feet and raced toward the lines of people, glancing back to see the private security officers jump out of their sedans. They were dressed in all black, wore armored clothes, and carried assault rifles.

Jack dove into the mass of humanity, leaving the officers behind. He heard warning shots fired in the air, but they would have no luck dispersing this crowd as the facility doors opened. These people were desperate. Jack pushed through the crowd as if he waded through a mud pit, apologizing as he went, working his way desperately to the other side of the facility, jostling against arms and bodies. The stench was overwhelming. It burned Jack's sinuses as he reached up to cover his nose with his hand. The few faces he saw were hollow, the cheeks sunken, the eyes lifeless. Then all at once, he broke free of the crowd and ran forward, pushing his legs hard. Fresh air filled his lungs as he turned left off the main street.

He wasn't safe yet. He knew the officers would be close on his tail. He needed to get off the street as fast as possible. He tossed his cell phone, worried that it could be used to track him. Up ahead, he spotted a prostitute loitering on the stoop of an old yellow Victorian house. Jack lurched to a stop. Voice sputtering, he breathed hard, "Can I have a date?"

The woman responded, "Sure, sweetie, if you have the cash, we can party."

"No problem, I have enough. Let's go inside." Jack moved toward the door.

The woman grabbed his arm. "It's going to cost extra if we go inside. There is an alley out back if you would rather." She smiled seductively.

"I'll pay, let's go inside." Jack stepped inside the door. He looked back down the street, expecting to see the worst, but the street was still empty. He got inside just in time. The foyer of the house smelled of old urine and rotting garbage. The wood floors were cracked. The paint peeled off the walls in long strips. The walls might have been painted brown at some point, but that was a long time ago. Now there were more bare spots than color.

"Okay, the second door to the left. Just open the door and push hard."

Jack pushed open the old wooden door with a heave of his shoulders. The door had swelled in the moist April heat and opened only after Jack gave it some effort. The room was no more than a twelve-foot square. On one corner, there was a queen-sized futon with an old, stained, beige sheet. Next to the futon was a small table. On the table was a lamp with a red lampshade and a digital clock radio displaying the wrong time in dim blue numbers. The lamp was lit, casting a red glow into the room. There was one window with a drawn shade that hung crookedly and didn't quite go down all the way to the window ledge.

Jack turned and smiled at the woman. It was hard to tell how old she was. She could easily be Jack's age or twice that much, but it was difficult to tell with the extreme makeup that was caked onto her face. Stress lines were etched into her forehead and in the corners of her eyes. She was very thin, probably too thin to be healthy, and wore a cut-off white T-shirt and pink shorts, her complexion a sickly ash white, her brown hair stringy, and she looked like as if she hadn't had a proper shower in some time. Her eyes were dilated, and Jack saw old injection marks on her right arm. It was hard to imagine who she really was underneath the drugs, dirt, and stress of a hard life on the streets.

With a shove of both hands and one foot, she managed to shut the door. Turning to Jack, she said, "You are a cute one! What would you like?" She smiled and licked her lips in an exaggerated motion that was meant to be sensual but struck Jack as more comical than anything else. A dense cloud of cheap perfumed enveloped Jack. He coughed as the perfume stung his lungs.

Feeling cornered, Jack said, "How about we talk for a while." Jack peeked through the dusty window, looking at the alley running alongside the house. He got the uneasy feeling that he had made a mistake.

CHAPTER

9

Warren's phone buzzed. He answered it quickly before it could vibrate a second time, anxious to get an update from Steven on Jack. "Do you have him yet?" He was annoyed with the delays.

Steven's calm voice responded, "We know where he is. He still has his citizen card on him. We are moving in now."

"Make sure you take him alive. I need that flash drive, and we need to figure out what the kid knows and who he's spoken to. You know what to do when you grab him?"

"Yes. Do you want us to snatch Heather?"

Warren smiled, his voice light, and laced with amusement. "Not yet. I'm meeting with Doug Benson in a few minutes at the club. It's going to be a fun conversation. Once he learns what Heather was doing with the young tennis instructor, we will have all the cooperation we'll need." Warren disconnected the call. He knew Benson reasonably well. They played golf together from time to time when either one needed a favor. When Warren called, lunch was set up immediately. Warren's face lit up with a satisfied grin, and he felt a surge of power ripple through his body. Benson was a powerful media mogul, but when Warren called, he jumped.

Benson made most of his money in television. He owned and produced the nation's most popular television show, *Rags to Riches*. It was a weekly reality show that pitted two worthy adversaries against each other. Both contestants typically worked at large corporations where their talent and accomplishments stood out from their peers. The show profiled each contestant, and the nation voted on a winner. The winner had his debts forgiven and his contract satisfied with his corporate sponsor. Once a month, the show spotlighted some remarkable person that had made it out on his or her own, someone who moved from the middle class into the privileged class based upon nothing but his or her own merit, hard work, and talent.

The show was great propaganda. Each week, the nation sat riveted to the television, watching the American Dream play out in high-definition color, proving to the nation that it was still possible to move up, proving that the system still worked, and proving that America was still great. The biggest stars all made appearances one way or another on the show. Schools made it required viewing for current events.[9] All the major network stations played the show at the same time. Warren recognized it for what it was—a great way to control the masses. As long as people believed they could climb the economic ladder, they were pliable. They might understand that the system was rigged against them, but if they believed that they might make it to the top, they let a lot slide. It was that hope and belief that the government needed to nurture. Truth was not important. No one wanted to know that the country had greater percentages of poor people than ever,

---

[9]   The Originalists passed federal legislation mandating that every school in the country incorporate *Rags to Riches* into their curriculum for each year of schooling from second grade, up. When discussing the constitutionality of the legislation, the decisive argument came from a particularly righteous congressman from Texas who produced an original letter from George Washington extolling, "Americans to meet at coffee houses around the country to proclaim our freedom, liberties, and free-market Capitalist way of life lest they be taken away and be replaced by tyranny." The letter was an obvious forgery. Washington never drank coffee. He was a well-known tea addict, but it should be noted that the congressman's main financial contributor owned an international chain of coffee shops. Any school principal that failed to follow the law could be tried for treason.

or that America ranked toward the bottom on upward mobility among developed nations. The country watched the American Dream come true for someone each week, and if it could come true for someone, why not for themselves?

Warren sauntered into the grillroom with a bounce in his step. He thought it would be better to take a private table in the less formal dining area, away from the usual prying eyes that roamed the dining room on Saturday afternoons. The grillroom was furnished casually: exposed wood, two fireplaces, large screen televisions showing either golf or financial news, large cushioned chairs, and a long bar with a mirrored wall.

An attractive hostess rushed to meet Warren as he stood in the doorway. She smiled sweetly while holding a few thin-screened tablets that functioned as menus. "Do you want a table in the main room or in the Library?" The Library was quieter and smaller. It was adjacent to the grillroom. There were no televisions, and it was rarely used.

Warren slowly ran his eyes up and down the hostess. She was in her early twenties with long, straight blond hair with streaks of blue and red; she was full-figured with a small beauty mark on her left cheek that looked genuine. She was new and obviously attracted to him. He noticed that ever since he started the treatments, women, regardless of age, were immediately drawn to him. He wasn't surprised. Even before the treatments, most women were pulled toward him. They sensed his power and importance, but now he must overwhelm them. Maybe he would take this hostess up on her desires at some later point; right now he was busy.

"I'll dine in the Library. I'm meeting Mr. Benson." Warren strutted toward the more secluded room with the hostess in tow.

Smiling broadly, the hostess said, "Mr. Benson is already waiting for you."

Of course he is, thought Warren as he turned the corner and entered the Library. The décor in the Library was slightly more sedate than the larger grillroom. The chairs were all leather. The bookshelves were filled with hard-cover books, items of the past but a luxury that was appropriate for the setting. Doug sat in the corner at a small table large enough for two. He wore a yellow golf shirt, a navy sport coat, and tan slacks. A drink stood in front of him on the table. The drink was undoubtedly a vodka soda, Doug's usual drink.

Doug spotted Warren as he approached. He made a motion to stand, but Warren waved him off. Smiling, Warren sat down in the chair opposite him. The hostess handed Warren a menu and left the two men alone. Warren didn't notice her haste to leave. As she turned, her face lost the friendly veneer and retained a tight, slightly disgusted expression, as if she had just eaten something unexpectedly tart.

Warren opened the conversation. "Thanks for meeting me so quickly, Doug."

Doug's jaw clenched tight, and he folded his arms defensively across his chest. Despite the air-conditioning, a few beads of sweat formed along his brow. He sounded anxious. "I came to the club to play doubles later anyway. I don't have much time, so I already ordered lunch. We can wave over a waiter if you're hungry?"

Warren didn't want lunch. He wanted to see Doug squirm, the powerful media mogul bent to his will, and he wanted it quickly. He had to move rapidly to contain any damage. *Doug wasn't the man he used to be*, he thought. *Clearly he had lost his edge with age.* His body had gone flabby, and his wife cheated on him right under his nose. Warren's expression couldn't quite hide the contempt with which he looked at his companion.

"I am not here for lunch, I'm here to discuss your wife. We have a problem." Warren forced a light smile on his face.

"What does Heather have to do with you?" Doug's lips pinched together, his voice sharp and slightly raised.

"I hate to tell you this, but she has been carrying on with a young tennis instructor named Jack." Warren paused. He enjoyed the look on Doug's face: part surprise and part humiliation.

"What does that have to do with you?" he said, irritation wrapped around the words.

Warren glanced around the room. They were alone except for a waiter who stood nearby.

"Normally nothing," said Warren as he shrugged his shoulders. "I would just pass on the information as a courtesy, but she met this Jack in one of the private rooms of the club last night during the benefit. I've come to learn that there was a flash drive left in that room earlier that evening. It will be extraordinarily damaging if the drive landed in the wrong hands. I had my people sweep the room this morning, and it's gone." Warren looked at Doug impassively, letting him make his own conclusions.

"So there is no proof that Heather took anything. Maybe this Jack discovered the flash drive? Do you have him?" Doug's eyes narrowed with hate. His voice was louder than it should have been.

"My people have found him and will collect him by the time you finish lunch, but I can't stress enough how important the information on the drive is to our way of life. We can't take any chances that it gets out." Warren's eyes bore down on Doug.

Doug sighed and sunk deeper into the cushion on his chair, his shoulders slumped downward. "You want to take Heather into custody and interrogate her?" The comment was more of a statement than a question. Doug took a long drink from his glass.

Warren didn't respond to Doug's question. Instead, he continued to stare silently at Doug, letting the silence do all the work for him. Time ticked away slowly; Warren's smile was slight, almost imperceptible. Doug would cave in to his request. He had no choice. Her infidelity with the young tennis instructor was damaging to a man in his position. *Even if Doug was fond of Heather, he had no choice; Doug was weak and I am strong.*

Doug looked away from Warren's piercing gaze, and said, "I assume you have authority from the highest levels?"

Warren nodded even though he had told no one about the flash drive but Steven and now Doug.

Doug fixed his eyes back at Warren. "She is at home. A piano teacher is scheduled to give her a private lesson at one o'clock. I will make sure that my security team permits your men access, but I don't want her hurt. Only interrogate her if the boy doesn't give you want you need. Even then, I want to know before you touch her. *Am I clear?*"

Warren stopped listening after Doug told him he could take her at his house before one o'clock. The rest was irrelevant. Warren recognized the anger in Doug's face, but he thought he detected admiration underneath the raw emotion. *Sure Doug must be furious with Heather, but he obviously admires me. He can sense my power. Amazing how effective these treatments are.* He wondered what would happen if he increased the dose just a little more. Perhaps he would take an extra injection before he interrogated Jack and Heather. The thought made him smile.

Warren's private thoughts were interrupted by the presence of a waiter who brought Doug a seafood Cobb salad. An attractive-looking dish, the colors leaped off the plate, but Warren wasn't hungry. His appetite wasn't what it used to be, and he had a mess to clean up.

As the waiter left, Doug said, "Well, if you aren't hungry, I am sure you are quite busy."

"Absolutely." Warren stood, turned, and left the room. Doug watched him leave. His face still filled with hatred as he pushed away the plate of food in disgust.

"Incoming call. Ronald, National Country Club. Urgent." Tom buried his head under his pillow, trying to drown out the sound, but he could not ignore the urgent nature of the call. Groggy from lack of sleep, he fumbled around his bed, looking for a phone. He grabbed something hard and started talking into it, but it was the remote for his stereo. Tossing it aside, he found the phone buried under a pile of dirty clothes.

His voice sounded husky. "Yes?"

John answered. He sounded more than a little annoyed and spoke quickly. "Tom, where is Jack? It is already well past twelve, and there is no sign of him. I can't get him on his cell."

Tom sat up, pushed aside various clothes and books, and tried to rub the sleep from his eyes with little luck. "I don't think he came home last night. Give me a minute."

Tom grabbed some sweatpants and wandered around the apartment. It felt empty. His mother had left early for work. Tom stayed awake late last night. He worked on a chemistry paper and went for a four-mile run sometime right before the sun came up. The run allowed Tom to reset his mind so he could slow it down for sleep. It took four miles before the equations, variables, and implications of the chemistry project faded and were replaced with the monotonous repetition of his strides. He was scheduled to work at dinner tonight at the club, so he was hoping to get some rest before the long night. He was definitely not a morning person. He liked to extend the night and cut short the morning if at all possible.

Tom wandered into Jack's room. His bare feet felt cold against the ceramic tile floor. Jack was the neat one. There was no sign that he came home last night or this morning. His bed was still made, and nothing looked out of place. "John, he didn't come home last night. There is no sign of him. I'll call around and see what's up."

"He is always on the edge, but he has never been this late before. I'm going to kick his ass! Tell him to call me when you find him." John abruptly hung up.

Not good, thought Tom. Jack needed the job at the club. It was perfect for him, and pissing off John was a good way to get fired.

Shaking the cobwebs from his head, Tom stumbled his way into the kitchen. The apartment had three bedrooms, one living room, two bathrooms, and a kitchen. All the rooms were really small, especially to Tom and Jack. Like Jack, Tom was tall. He had similar curly brown hair, but he kept his long, almost at shoulder-length, and let it fall where it wanted to. Even though Tom was two years younger than Jack, Tom was thicker in the shoulders, chest and arms due to years of intensive workouts, mostly to clear his overworked mind.

Tom smelled coffee and silently thanked his mom. She left a pot on the coffee maker with a handwritten note in her unique cursive style. She prided herself on her handwriting—something she felt was a lost art.

> Tom, will be working late tonight. Try to get a ride with Jack to the club. Give me a call if you can't get a ride home after work.
>
> Love always,
Mom
>
> PS: If you could clean up the Lab before the landlord kicks us out, that would be great.

The *Lab* was what they called Tom's room. It was always in a state of organized chaos, or so he told his mother. Truth be told, from time to time, things got away from him in there.

Tom poured a cup of coffee and popped it in the microwave. He drank it black. Sugar and milk were both pricey at times, so he had trained himself to drink it black. It took a month of discipline, but now he didn't mind.

Tom grabbed the hot cup from the microwave. What was he going to do about Jack? Where to start? He reached for the phone on the table. Tom was good with numbers. Usually they just stuck in his mind. *Let's try David first.*

Bam! Bam! Bam! Three strong raps on the front door startled Tom. He spilled a little coffee from his cup, burning his fingers. *Did Jack forget his keys?*

"I'm coming! No need to break down the door!" Tom shouted from the kitchen as he shuffled his way to the front door still holding his coffee cup.

Three more loud raps on the door greeted Tom as he reached the front. "Open up, Tom, it's me, David."

What's going on? thought Tom. *Is Jack really in trouble?* He swung the door open. David quickly barged through the door, accompanied by a girl who swiftly followed him. Tom immediately noticed her long, wavy, red hair. He momentarily forgot how to breathe. It wasn't that Tom was necessarily shy around the opposite sex. It was just that he hadn't had time to figure them out yet. They seemed so different, and Tom spent all his time on his studies or working out. He was the last chance his family had of making it up the ladder. Getting the scholarship was only the first step. He needed to take a lot of steps before he earned some measure of financial security for his mom and brother. Without his dad and with Jack's limited options, he felt a lot of responsibility and pressure.

The girl had a thin figure, light complexion with a number of golden brown freckles dotting her face, and emerald green eyes that sparkled brightly. She wore a gray pullover sweatshirt, tan cargo shorts, and plain white sneakers. David wore a beige V-neck T-shirt advertising Cuervo Tequila, blue cargo pants, and brown shoes. Both looked wet, from a steady rain falling outside.

Tom shut the door and turned toward David. "What's going on?"

David's usual relaxed and go-lucky demeanor was replaced with dark storm clouds full of concern and anxiety. Tom's stomach churned. Something was definitely wrong.

David asked anxiously. "Have you heard from Jack?"

"No, John just called. He's late for work. Did you try his cell?"

David glanced at the girl, sharing some type of unspoken communication. "Tom, Jack's in trouble. He's gotten himself into something really nasty. We think he might have been taken by some really serious dudes."

Tom looked from David to the redhead. They were both very serious. If this was a joke, they had easily fooled him. "What do you mean *taken?*"

The girl spoke, her voice confident and authoritative. "We don't have much time. We have got to go." Tom thought he smelled roses and a hint of cinnamon, and he liked it.

David turned toward Tom. "You know that Jack is my best friend. You need to trust me. I will explain everything later, but right now, we have to leave and go quickly. It won't take long for them to show up here. They're probably on their way as we speak." David pushed Tom toward his bedroom. "Hurry, grab a few things."

Tom trusted David. He had known him for a few years, and he was always a standup guy. Tom hustled back to his room now fully alert, and threw some miscellaneous clothes into a duffel bag. He didn't have much, just his work clothes for the club and loose-fitting T-shirts, sweatpants, and jeans. He opted for comfort over style. Besides, comfort was a lot less expensive than style. His sneakers were the only extravagance for his wardrobe, but they contained science, the latest micro cushions that propelled the feet. He noticed that he wasn't wearing matching socks but didn't think it was worth the time trying to find a matching pair amongst the chaos. They were close; both were mostly white. Just as he was leaving, he spotted his shoebox full of childhood mementos. Without thinking about it, he grabbed it and jammed it into the bag with the rest of the stuff.

The redhead held out a strange-looking metallic box. "Put your cell phone and identity card in the box."

Tom reached for both. "Why? What is it?"

"It is a wave jammer. This way they won't be able to track you." Tom dropped his phone and his wallet in the box. He wasn't sure why he trusted her, but he would jump off the roof of the building if she said he had to. His head swam, but two questions cut through the fog. *Who are they and what did Jack get himself into?*

11

Jack had a bad feeling. His stomach turned sour, and the hair on the back of his neck stood on end. It was the same feeling he got when he faced match point in a competitive tennis match. He spun around the room looking for something useful, but he was alone with the woman. He needed her cooperation. "So what is your name?"

The woman pursed her lips. "They call me Red because of my red hair." She batted her eyes playfully.

Jack's eyebrows rose in a question mark. "You have brown hair."

Red chuckled. "Not that hair, silly. You want to see?" She lifted her hand to unbutton her shorts.

Jack's face reddened, and stopped her with a wave of his hand. "Not just yet." Jack heard the feint sound of children playing and laughing. "Why do I hear children?"

Red frowned, "That's the nursery. It's upstairs. What do you think we do with the little ones when we're working?" Red's eyes narrowed slightly. It was obvious that she was a little annoyed.

"How many children?" Jack asked.

"Must be three dozen, but they won't bother us."

A bottle broke in the alley. It sounded like a boot had kicked it. Two private police officers carefully stalked into the alleyway, assault rifles drawn at the ready. They looked serious, and it was no coincidence that they had chosen this alley so quickly. Somehow they tracked Jack to this building. He had thought that the old Victorian house would make a good hiding place. He had needed to get off the streets, but now he realized that he had made a serious mistake. What seemed like a safe hiding place a moment earlier closed in on him.

Jack wrenched opened the door slightly and saw the stairs leading to the second floor. *If I could make it to the second floor, maybe there is a fire escape behind the house.* But as the thought entered his mind, he heard giggling and laughing from the nursery. If he tried to escape through the second floor, the private police would chase him, and those children would be put at risk. All it would take would be one over-anxious security officer with an assault rifle, and that was not a risk he could take. He shut the door and studied the small room more closely. "So, Red, tell me, is there a trapdoor somewhere or some other way out of the room besides the door or the window?"

"This ain't no palace with hidden doors. What you see is what you get. How much money you got?" Red started tapping her right foot impatiently with both of her hands on her hips. Her face swung from seductive to angry in a flash.

The front door creaked open. He was out of time, and there was nowhere for him to run. Slowly he pulled out the wad of bills that he had won during last night's poker game. It was his best night since the regular game started. Red's eyes widened in anticipation.

Jack handed the entire stack of bills to her. "It's all yours, Red. Spend it wisely." He figured the money would do him no good now.

Red greedily took the handful of bills. She quickly counted the money and tucked it away somewhere in her shorts. Jack hoped it was a good hiding spot.

Jack raised his hands. "Better lift up your arms, Red, and kneel down on the bed. Try to stay still."

"Sure, sweetie. Whatever you want." She knelt down on the futon playfully.

Jack stood still as the door was kicked in. Wood splintered everywhere. The crashing sound rang loudly in his ears. Red screamed. Three men barreled in the room with guns drawn. "No one move. Hands up." The guns swept across the small room.

Jack stood motionless as Red curled up on the futon in a fetal position. An older man followed the three private police officers into the room. His helmet was off, revealing short straight black hair peppered with gray. "You are going to have to come with me, Jack." His voice was flat; his blue eyes sharp and intelligent. He ordered the nearby officer to cuff him.

As Jack was roughly pulled out of the room, he heard Steven's voice again. "Search the prostitute and the room fully. We are looking for a small flash drive."

Red screamed, and Jack winced as he heard the sound of a steel-tipped boot hit bone.

CHAPTER

12

David popped open the trunk to his car. It made a metallic clanking sound as it sprung open. The car was custom-built; the trunk expanded into a false backseat. Tom could barely make out the contours of the hollow seat as he peered into the dimness of the trunk. David grinned and pointed, making it clear where Tom was headed. He cautiously crammed his long frame inside the metal box. David said there was room for two people in the trunk, but Tom was big and the roads were bumpy. He did a quick calculation in his mind. Based upon the cubic square feet in the trunk plus his own size, there would only be enough room for someone shorter than five feet and weighing 100 to 110 pounds depending upon the person's muscle-to-fat ratio.

Despite a thick layer of padding around the false trunk's edges, something hard jabbed into his back. The hot April day felt twice as hot in the trunk. A soft breeze circulated from inside the car, bringing with it the greasy aroma of old French fries, and within a few minutes, Tom was already slick with sweat. He had a hard time making out what David and the redhead said in the front seat. The voices came back as nothing more than garbled sounds; however, he was able to figure out one important piece of information: Mary was her name.

David explained that for security reasons, Tom needed to travel hidden in the trunk until they could figure out if *they* were after him. Tom had no idea who *they* were, but presumably, *they* were the same people who had taken Jack. David assured Tom that everything would be explained when they got to wherever they were going. It was one of these "trust me" situations, and Mary's green eyes were clear and honest. Tom could get lost in the contour of her green eyes.

Tom cleared his mind and focused on Jack. *What in the world did he get himself into?* He must have left some clues, but Tom couldn't think of anything out of the ordinary. A wave of guilt washed over him. Just last night, Jack mentioned something about poker, inviting Tom to join him and his friends for a late-night game. He should have thought about that before. *Wasn't Julian hosting the game?* Tom was too busy with schoolwork for that. *Actually, to think of it, I've been too busy with schoolwork for quite some time,* Tom thought miserably. The tires screeched, and the car stopped abruptly. Tom's head bumped against the metal partition between the trunk and the passenger compartment. David garbled an apology from the front seat.

When the trunk finally popped open, Tom breathed in deeply, freed from the hot, metallic box. He didn't realize it before, but it seemed like he had been holding his breath for the entire ride. David reached down to help Tom out of the small space. With a heave, Tom managed to get his legs out of the car and lurch onto the pavement, stumbling a bit. Cool, refreshing rain fell steadily. It felt good after being stuffed in the trunk for the whole ride.

Mary handed Tom a pill. "Take this." Tom looked suspiciously at the small yellow pill. "What does it do?"

Mary moved closer to Tom. Her closeness made him nervous. He smelled her perfume. It was something light and sweet. The scent of cinnamon returned. Her lips were naturally red and moist. "It won't harm you. It acts as a marker and will permit us to wipe your memory from this point on if need be. It's a necessary precaution."

"What's it made of? I don't like ingesting something when I don't know what's in it. There are so many dangerous things out there."

"I don't have a clue. You're going to have to trust me." Mary stared at him, unblinking with those emerald eyes.

Tom took the pill. Something happened to Jack, and this was his only chance to figure out what was going on. "There's no other way?" Tom questioned.

"This is the only way to move forward. We are wasting time as it is." She whispered. Tom felt her breath against his face. He reluctantly swallowed the pill. His family was small, but it meant everything to him.

"Good, let's get going."

The ground was familiar. Tom recognized it almost immediately. "This is the aqueduct above the old Sleepy Hollow Cemetery. I used to come here with Jack when we were kids. There is a dirt bike trail that we would use."

David smiled. "It's one of the oldest cemeteries in the country. A few rich and famous people are buried here. It is one of the reasons why it is so well-maintained and seldom used."[10]

Tom trudged behind David and Mary, kicking up leaves, branches, and twigs as he went. They hiked along the cemetery's eastern border along one of the aqueduct trails. The small path was crowded with trees, low green plants, and a small creek off to the right, which swelled with fast-moving water. The ground was slick with mud and wet leaves. An old metal chain-link fence separated the aqueduct from the cemetery. They walked parallel to the fence for five hundred yards until Tom noticed a small break in the fence up ahead. David darted for the opening, and peeled the metal fence backward so Mary could clear it. Tom glanced warily at David. He looked more like his usual self—tanned, confident, and relaxed with his blond hair soaked by the

---

[10]   Because of the Urban Renewal Act of 2025, many cemeteries were closed and sold to private investors for redevelopment. "Historical" cemeteries were excluded from redevelopment. Gardening in any of these developments was a risky proposition. No one wanted to dig too deeply.

rain. There was still a trace of concern on his face, but his eyes twinkled. "Time to go down the rabbit hole, Tommy."

"Great," muttered Tom as he followed Mary. They were in the oldest part of the cemetery. It was constructed in the early 1800s. The tombstones were unevenly spaced apart and haphazardly arranged around trees and rock outcroppings. They took a sharp right turn behind a large rock formation and Mary stopped at the tombstone of Samson Burr who died in 1845 at the age of seventy. The tombstone was hidden from the rest of the cemetery. If Mary hadn't guided him here, there was no chance that Tom would have found it on his own.

The tombstone was relatively large and laid flat on the ground. The grass surrounding the stone was tramped down more than the others. With a quick glance around, Mary knelt and pushed down on the "o" in *Samson*. Tom heard a latch click, and the tombstone rose up slightly. One last glance around and she lifted up the side of the stone marker. It swung on a large heavy hinge with the help of a hydraulic hiss. There was enough space for someone to walk down into the grave. Dim lights illuminated the way. Without hesitation, Mary disappeared into the earth.

Tom turned to David. "Am I the only one who thinks this is a little creepy?"

"Hustle it up, Tommy. I promise there are no zombies. We don't like using this entrance during the day as it is." Tom smelled moist musty air as he plunged down the dark staircase after Mary. His wet sneakers slipped on the stone steps, throwing him off balance. Falling forward, his hand shot out to grab the railing, but his fingers missed badly. Off balanced, he stumbled down a few steps trying not to fall, and crashed into Mary, sending both of them tumbling toward the bottom of the staircase. Tom twisted his body underneath Mary at the last second so she safely fell on top of him. Tom's back crashed hard into the edge of the last step of the staircase, sending searing pain shooting through his body.

David rushed down after them. "Are you guys all right?"

Mary quickly stood, grumbling to herself. Tom couldn't quite make out what she said, but he was certain that she called him a clumsy oaf. Tom grimaced and sat up, his face turning red from embarrassment as his hand absentmindedly rubbed the sore spot on his back.

David shook his head and grinned. "Welcome to the Fourteenth Colony."

Tom stood. He was a little sore, but nothing was broken. He sheepishly apologized to Mary. She turned her back on him and entered the tunnel. Tom noticed the words *Fourteenth Colony* written in red spray paint sprawled across the rough stone tunnel wall. Something about the handwriting was familiar. The tunnel was faintly illuminated from a string of exposed white lightbulbs that hung along the right side of the tunnel and stretched into the distance.

The tunnel wasn't particularly wide or tall. Tom had to stoop down a bit to avoid hitting his head. Mary quickly moved down the line without looking back. David squeezed past him, tapping him on the back as he went. "Follow us, Tommy."

What did Jack get himself caught up in? thought Tom as he plodded behind David. *What is the Fourteenth Colony?*

CHAPTER

13

Xavier entered the private elevator and pressed the only button available to him, *PH* for penthouse. When the doors closed, he started slowly pacing nervously. The inside of the elevator was made from dark cherry wood and gray slate tiles. Two mirrored panels framed in cherry hung on each of its three walls, and the elevator door was clean stainless steel. When he caught his reflection in a mirror, Xavier noticed dark circles under his eyes and the trace of stubble on his face. He was so anxious last night that he didn't sleep and forgot to shave this morning. Acid churned in his stomach as the elevator smoothly rose to the top of the building. He had to meet with Sheppard. It was his only chance at saving the situation.

The luxury glass apartment building rose fifty stories into the heavens. The penthouse consisted of the top two floors of the building; however, the elevator only stopped on the first of the two for security reasons. Sheppard owned the penthouse. He installed a twenty-foot circular reflecting pool in the lower floor of the apartment to go with the expansive living space, media room, dining room, and kitchen. The second floor housed bedrooms, offices, his study, and a private gym.

The apartment was spectacular. It was one of the finest properties in New York City and undoubtedly the best private residence on the Upper West Side. On clear days, the floor-to-ceiling windows afforded views of three of the area's airports. Central Pepsi Park stretched out regally in the near distance. The apartment had every conceivable luxury, yet somehow, it still felt tasteful. Most of the gadgetry was hidden from sight.

Xavier had been to the apartment on two prior occasions, both work-related. Sheppard periodically hosted events for small groups of the most talented members of his staff drawn from different areas of his company. He believed that a relaxed social atmosphere combined with diversely talented people brought about a cross-pollination of ideas. At least that was what he said. However, Xavier suspected that he enjoyed the social aspect of the gatherings as much as anything else. Plenty of wine flowed to help smooth the conversation. A few of the company's most profitable concepts and businesses traced their roots back to a social gathering at Sheppard's apartment.

The bell rang, announcing Xavier's arrival to the penthouse. The elevator door opened with a quiet swish, revealing the bright green front door to Sheppard's apartment. It was the only door and an unnecessary precaution since no one gained access to the elevator without Sheppard's permission, but Sheppard liked having an entranceway. Xavier waited patiently, the small camera above the door whirled to life, focusing in on Xavier's face, the door swung open, and a smiling Charles Sheppard appeared in the doorway.

Sheppard was in his late sixties. He had shockingly white straight hair cut on the longer side and parted neatly to the left. His skin was tan from a recent trip to the Caribbean. He was average height, had a thin wiry build, sharp angular facial features, and brilliantly bright sapphire eyes. His laugh was warm and infectious. He wore loose-fitting navy blue pants with a sharp crease, a crisp white linen shirt, a cordovan-colored belt with matching cordovan shoes, and a navy sport jacket. Xavier noticed an antique gold Rolex on his wrist. Sheppard smiled at Xavier, revealing perfectly white teeth, and waved the younger man to enter.

The front door closed, and just like his first two visits, Xavier was struck by the open expansive feel of the apartment. Sheppard patted Xavier on the back, "Come in, Xavier. Can I get you something to drink? How about a glass of wine? I just opened a fabulous Cabernet from Napa Valley. It comes from one of the company's finest vineyards." Sheppard led Xavier into the cavernous living room. The exterior walls of the apartment were constructed of glass. At a touch of a button, they turned clear or opaque. Sheppard reached for a keypad, and they turned a dark gray color. Privacy was important for today's meeting.

Xavier's body was tight with anxiety. "No, thanks, Charles. I don't think I could stomach it right now. Are we alone?" Sheppard was a very private person. Little was known about his personal life. He was once married, but some type of mysterious tragedy took his wife twenty years ago. Rumors always circulated around Sheppard's private life, but in reality, not much was known about his personal habits. Even a causal observer could tell that he was an extreme workaholic, but there were times when he vanished for weeks at a time and was almost impossible to reach. No one knew where he went or with whom.

Sheppard smiled reassuringly. "Yes, Xavier, we are alone in all this space. I am not expecting anyone else for some time." Sheppard's eyes were bright. Curiosity seeped into his face. He led Xavier past the reflecting pool with its sparkling, blue water and toward a couch in the living room.

"We have a very serious problem, Charles. Last night I was looking over the documents we assembled on Operation Phoenix, and I noticed a glitch. Someone hacked us and downloaded them from our server." Xavier rubbed his hands across his head. Very little of his brown hair remained and what did stood on end. "I don't know how they could have gotten past our security, Charles, but someone did."

Unexpectedly, Sheppard showed no concern. In fact, he smiled broadly. "Interesting, when do you think they were taken?"

"I think it was yesterday, probably midday." Xavier's voice had a hint of panic in it.

"Do you have any idea who might have taken them?"

"None. The hacker came from a foreign server, but I can't trace it beyond that. It could be anyone." Xavier sunk despondently into the white leather couch.

Sheppard paused for a moment, lost in thought. He checked the time on his antique gold Rolex wristwatch. Xavier had seen that look before. Sheppard was hatching a plan. *It had better be a good one*, thought Xavier, *or all would be lost*. Sheppard was one of the most powerful people in the world. His power and influence spread across the globe. His parents had money, but he had increased his holdings tenfold over the last four decades. Undeniably brilliant, he had a talent for persuasion like no one else. His charms were legendary and virtually irresistible. A few minutes alone with a person and he could change the strongest conviction. Not only would the person change his position, but he or she would also become an avid supporter of whatever Sheppard was advocating. Many times the unsuspecting victim had no idea what had just happened. Xavier saw it unfold on numerous occasions, but it never failed to amaze him.

"Sometimes, Xavier, it takes a push to start the train moving downhill. Maybe this is our push. We knew the risks when we started this project. We were close to ready anyway. I will arrange a meeting for tomorrow afternoon. We will need to be persuasive, but our time has come. We must set the wheels in motion before others figure out our plans on their own. After all, we are just saving them from themselves." Sheppard beamed a bright smile. There was no hint of anxiety or concern. Relieved, Xavier felt his body relax for the first time since he had learned of the theft. A sharp pain stabbed through his shoulders from the tension that had built up from the long night before.

Sheppard walked over to the bar and poured two glasses of wine. Handing one to Xavier, he said, "We have time to enjoy a glass of wine. I really want to know what you think of this vintage."

Xavier took the glass and smiled despite his worries. Sheppard was truly amazing. Everything he built was on the verge of ruin, but he seemed as relaxed as if he was on a beach enjoying a sunny day. Xavier swirled the wine in his glass and breathed in the aroma deeply. He paused and took a sip of the dark red liquid. "It is remarkable, our best vintage yet. I particularly like the hint of cherry."

"I was thinking the same thing." Charles swirled the wine in his glass. "Oh, one other thing. We need to know who took the documents. Call Clint and put him on it. I trust him completely, and if anyone can trace it, he can."

Sheppard took a sip of wine. It took years of patience to create wine this good. He didn't have time for that type of patience with this situation. He hoped Clint could work his magic quickly. It would not be a good idea to go into the meeting tomorrow without knowing who knew what.

The concrete tunnel gradually began to climb upward. As Tom ran his hand along the side of the tunnel, small bits of concrete flaked off the walls. The walls were damp and brittle, which was not a good combination for an underground tunnel. "How old is this tunnel?" Tom asked David, his words echoing softly. If he knew the age, the depth, the thickness of the concrete walls, and the moisture level of the tunnel, he could determine how much time the tunnel had left until it crumbled. Without the inputs, he was helpless. To Tom, life was a series of calculations. All he needed were the inputs and then he could calculate the rest.

David's voice bounced off of the tunnel's walls, reverberating in the small space. "It was built in the early 1800s by the original owners of the property where we're headed. They wanted an escape route if need be."

They walked mostly in silence. David wasn't in a mood to answer questions, claiming that their leader, Rachel, would know more than he did. Mary just seemed annoyed. She walked with a crisp pace, giving the impression that she wanted to leave the tunnel and Tom behind as soon as possible. Tom couldn't help but feel disappointed that he hadn't made much of a first impression. He knew it was silly, but he kept trying to think of something clever to tell her, a joke or some insight about Jack, but cleverness was never his strong suit. Deciding it was better to stay quiet than to make a fool of himself, Tom mostly heard the sound of their footsteps as they trudged on their way. He was sure he might have heard a rat scurry here or there, but he wasn't concerned about that. That seemed like the least of his worries. At random points, he noticed concrete patch, which made a weird type of piecemeal design. He tried to visualize a pattern out of the repairs. At least it took his mind off the foul smell and Mary's frosty attitude.

Finally, the end was in sight. The string of lights climbed up a small metal staircase. An old wooden door that looked as if might have been original to the tunnel marked the end of the staircase and was dimly lit in a green hazy light. Tom tried to figure out where they were. They had been walking for twenty minutes—probably enough time to end up in the national park, but that made little sense.

"Where are we going?"

David chuckled. "I thought you were the smart one? You should have figured that out by now. We are headed to Kykuit. The tunnel was built with the original structures as their escape route."

Tom was right; they were headed to the National Park. "Kykuit? The historical place open to visitors? I went there on a school trip when I was in elementary school. I don't remember any tunnels."

Mary's voice rang out sharp and piercing in the quiet tunnel. "Everything isn't always what it seems." Tom heard a note of rebuke in her voice. For the first time in a long while, he wished he was Jack. Tom tried to think of a catchy comeback, but his mind was as blank as a new smartboard. Jack was always the one with the witty comments.

Mary, first to arrive at the door, placed her palm up against a glass screen. The screen flashed green, and the door creaked open. She moved inside, leaving the door ajar. David quickly followed, and with a deep breath, so did Tom.

The first old wooden door opened to a small hallway, which led to another door. This one looked secure. It was made of heavy steel and had a small square glass window at eye level. Mary pressed a button on the doorframe and waited impatiently, tapping her left foot in agitation. A few seconds later, Tom heard the metallic clinking sound of a latch releasing, and the heavy steel door swung open with a *whoosh*.

A bright white light burned Tom's eyes. His pupils were unaccustomed to the stark white light after the long walk in the dark tunnel. Squinting against the light, he adjusted to the new surroundings, and as his vision cleared, he saw a large rectangular room with three long wooden tables with computer screens and communication equipment evenly spaced upon each. The tables were made of coarse wood, appearing like something that might have been used at a picnic station, but the equipment looked new and high tech.

A dozen or so people mulled about, most of them in their twenties or thirties. The room was obviously underground; there were no windows, and the walls were made of unfinished concrete blocks. Tom heard air circulators and felt a faint breeze. All the eyes in the room turned toward Tom, David, and Mary as they stood in the room by the door. Tom felt the weight of their collective stare. He had the feeling that it was highly unusual for newcomers to emerge from the tunnel.

David, noticing the attention, smiled broadly and bent at the waist in a low bow. Tom heard a few murmurs and some arms waved in their direction, but eventually everyone went back to what they were doing before they arrived. David turned to Tom. "Welcome to headquarters. Rachel will want to see you right away. She should be upstairs in her office."

Mary climbed a short circular metal staircase that led to a wooden trapdoor in the ceiling. The light above the trapdoor was green. She pushed the door open and stepped through, leaving the underground high-tech equipment behind, and entered a part of America's past—the ground floor of an early-1800s empty wooden barn. The walls, ceiling, and floor were made of oak with sawdust haphazardly spread across the floor. The building might have served as a small carriage house or a barn at one time. Large double doors at one end of the building were wide enough for a team of horses that might have pulled a carriage for an important visitor. Now, it was just old and filled with dust and cobwebs. The vaulted ceiling was constructed of exposed wood beams with a small hayloft on one side of the structure. Basically, there wasn't much to look at. David closed the trapdoor, and it seamlessly fit into the floor. Only upon close inspection did Tom notice a gouge in the wood that could be used as a handhold to lift the door. Anyone that didn't know exactly where to look would never find the trapdoor.

Mary led them to the west end of the room, hunched down, and placed her palm against a small glass plate hidden toward the corner of the wall. There was another green flash of light, and a secret wooden door swung smoothly open on modern stainless steel hinges. Mary walked in trailed closely by David and Tom. David swung the door closed behind them.

This end of the building had a false wall. It looked exactly like the rest of the structure, but the door led to a hidden room beyond it. The secret room was a very neat narrow office with smooth white walls. A light-colored carpet covered the floor. It felt soft and spongy to Tom's feet and oddly out of place, a bit of luxury in an otherwise sparse setting.

Toward one end of the room, there was a huge antique oak desk with three flat panel computer screens, a new holographic video monitor, and two narrow paper files that were placed on opposite ends of the desk. The office had no personal effects in it, no family photographs or mementos. The only items that gave a glimpse into the personality of the occupant were a framed 1973 New York Knicks' jersey and an old AFL-CIO Union poster. Tom was a Knicks fan, and recognized the championship team, but he had never heard of the AFL-CIO.[11]

---

[11]   It is not surprising that Tom was unfamiliar with unions. In 2022, Congress passed the Freedom in the Workplace Law, which made

A large video projection brightened the long exterior white wall, which was split in eighths. Each smaller square depicted a live feed from a security camera. The squares kept changing. Tom noticed the outside of the tombstone where they entered the tunnel, a long shot of the tunnel, and a number of other scenes that he did not recognize. On one end of the room was a long gray couch made from a soft microfiber that could easily double for a bed in an emergency. Facing the couch were two small, plain, wooden chairs. A small oval-shaped antique cherry wood cocktail table separated the chairs from the couch.

Behind the desk sat a woman in her early sixties with long black hair streaked with gray that was pulled back in a ponytail. She had a rich tan, soft features, and a small black mole on the left side of her chin. She looked matronly, but pretty and authoritative. She wore a white button-downed shirt, smiled warmly at Tom, and spoke with confidence and authority, her voice rich and textured. "Welcome, Tom. My name is Rachel. I know all this must seem unreal to you. Please sit on the couch so we can have a chat."

Tom looked at the couch but hesitated. He wanted information. He needed data. "What is going on with Jack? Where is he?"

"We will get to all that in a moment." Turning toward Mary and David, she said, "Mary, I need you back downstairs. Try to find out any information on Jack's whereabouts." David waited

---

all unions and collective bargaining illegal. This spurred a brief time of violent unrest until Congress passed the Undesirable Treaty with the European Union. In the treaty, all union leaders were exiled to Europe where unions were still accepted, and Europe, which was going through a moralistic phase, exiled all its political leaders that were convicted of sexual scandals to the United States. No official records are available, but it is widely believed that Europe got the better of the deal. The treaty was repealed in 2052 when the ability to collectively bargain was reinstated and the Celebrate Union national holiday was created in recognition of the important contribution unions have played in America's development.

for instructions while Rachel decided what was best for him to do, the look on her face uncertain as if she wrestled with a number of bad choices. Finally, she told him, "You go with Mary and see if you can help her."

Mary shot a look at Rachel, and before the two left, Rachel changed her mind. "On second thought, David, instead of helping Mary, would you mind working with Susan. She's close to figuring out the latest atrocities that our esteemed governor will propose in Albany to clamp down on the ghettos. I'm sure she could use a little help."

"If I have to." David smiled broadly. He had a thing for Susan, and spending a little time with her was anything but a chore. Rachel waved her hand, shooing them out the door.

As Rachel approached Tom, she pointed to the couch. She moved gracefully. "Sit down, Tom, let's talk."

Out of options, Tom flopped on the couch, desperate for data.

15

"What's Jack gotten himself into and where is he?"

"It's hard to say exactly, Tom. Jack's been a member of the Fourteenth Colony since he was sixteen. Over the past few years, he has gathered information for us. Nothing dangerous, just things he heard at the club, but he said he was onto something *big*. He wouldn't tell me what it was until he had some proof, so we don't know for sure." Rachel exuded sincerity, trust, and confidence. It was easy to see her as a leader. Tom believed instinctively that she was being truthful. "We're trying to figure out what's happened to him, but maybe we should start at the beginning."

Tom's mind spun, searching for a logical starting point. "Okay, what is the Fourteenth Colony? I've never heard of it before."

Rachel smiled, suddenly sounding youthful and energetic. "The Fourteenth Colony[12] is an underground movement aimed at restoring America to what it once was. We started the movement twenty years ago. Your father actually came up with the name."

Tom sunk deeper into the couch. He felt as if he had been punched in the stomach and the air knocked out of him. The handwriting he identified in the tunnel was his father's cursive. He still remembered it from the long letters he inserted into

---

12   The Fourteenth Colony was the predecessor to today's Colonial political party.

every birthday card. He had a few of those letters in his duffel with him. "My father?"

"Yes, the name was his idea. At first it was sort of a joke. A play on the Thirteen Colonies of the Revolutionary War, but over time, it stuck. He was one of our founding members and a great patriot. We officially started the movement when Congress voted to grade voting rights by the amount of taxes paid by individuals. I remember the vote vividly. We all sat around a flat screen in my house and watched as our elected officials sold our votes. The final vote ended at one twenty-three in the morning. The room had the feeling of a funeral, but to be honest, the movement really started well before that day. The signs were all there. First, the privileged class made voting more difficult for poorer people, requiring citizen cards that were difficult for them to acquire. Then, unemployed people were excluded—if they didn't contribute to the treasury, then they shouldn't have a say in the country's finances. That was what they argued.

"The country was still reeling from the effects of the Great Recession, and there were so many fears about the country's finances and the changing nature of our demographics. Fear is a terrible agent; fear can cause the unthinkable to seem reasonable, maybe even practical. Finally, they enacted today's system— four grades depending upon the amount of taxes paid by the individual."[13] Rachel shook her head; anger momentarily flashed across her face.

---

[13]   Actually, the four-grade system was not the initial proposal. The initial proposal had votes weighted based upon actual income taxes paid (one vote for each dollar paid). Ironically, this met with fierce opposition from those in the top 10 percent. At this point in American history, income was so concentrated in the top 1 percent of earners that they could have determined any national election on their own. For example, only five people voting together would have been enough to elect the senators from Arizona. After extensive negotiations, the four grades were determined as a sliding scale based on

Tom still looked confused. "We learned about that in school. It was the start of the *Originalist* political party. 'No Taxation without *Adequate Representation*.' It was unfair to have everyone's votes count the same when some people contributed much more in taxes than others. The founding fathers would have never supported a system so unjust, so we changed it. It is all laid out in the textbooks."

Rachel grinned. "Of course they would teach you that in school. History is always written by the victors. Anyway, the change in voting rights was really just a culmination of a political movement that started decades before it—viewed in its best light, a belief that unchecked capitalism was the best system of governance. It became more like a religion to many than a political belief."[14]

"But that's what our country was founded on. Isn't that what makes us special?" Even as Tom spoke, he knew the words sounded hollow. It was something they told him so often in school that he failed to give it any thought on his own. He preferred the sciences

---

percentage of a person's gross income. Four votes went to the top 5 percent, three votes to 5 to 10 percent, two votes to 10 to 20 percent and one vote to everyone else. This entire system was repealed and replaced in 2050 with today's universal vote, giving each citizen an equal vote.

[14] Rachel was probably speaking literally. Starting in the 2030s, a charismatic preacher developed a new religion that blended the most conservative Christian fundamentalist views with a belief that select founding fathers were prophets sent by God. The Constitution along with many letters written by the chosen founding fathers became sacred texts. The religion enjoyed an explosion of popularity until its leader predicted that the world would end on May 1, 2045. The preacher's belief in his prediction was so strong that he spent the one-year leading up to the end of the world selling all of the church's assets and spending the money. He essentially went on one amazing drug and orgy filled party for twelve months. When the sun rose on May 2, 2045, he and the religion were bankrupt and disgraced. He lived his remaining years as a blackjack dealer in Tahoe.

to social studies. In the sciences, every action had a predictable and repeatable reaction. Social studies was filled with shades of gray and shadows of meanings.

Rachel responded patiently as if she was a schoolteacher explaining a simple concept to a poor student. "Not really, Tom. For over two hundred years, America was governed under other principles. Sure, capitalism was center to our way of life, but the government always had a role to ensure fairness and opportunity for those who were not on the top economic rung of the ladder. America was once a place where anyone had a chance to move up if they worked hard enough and had enough talent. Sure, it was always easier if you had the right connections, but the opportunity was still there. Now it is virtually impossible to have that opportunity unless you are born into the privileged class, and what was once a great middle class shrinks every year. Soon there will only be the rich and powerful and the poor and subservient." Rachel paused.

Tom thought about what Rachel's had said. The words rang true, but they were very different than anything he had learned in school. He would need time to think it through. Still, he had a hard time believing his father was involved in this movement. He couldn't recall his father being interested in politics, but he was young when he had died. Maybe he just didn't think Tom would have understood. His face reddened slightly.

Rachel continued, "This is a conversation that I would love to have with you in more detail at some other time, but now we need to focus on your brother. I only ask that you keep an open mind. Accept the possibility that there is a better way."

It was hard not to trust Rachel. She had a way of making things seem simple. Tom agreed and said, "So what was Jack doing for you?"

"Our movement is a lot bigger than you can imagine. We have a number of people working at the club that are friendly to us. They pass on information as they discover it. The rich often forget that others are around. They don't notice the waiter who is standing within hearing distance, or the bartender, or for that matter, the tennis instructor. Jack, along with a number of other members of the group, have been providing beneficial information to us. I believe that Jack was on to something important. He must have gotten what he was looking for, and that scared some very important people. We began hearing his name pop up in communications earlier today. I warned him to run, but I fear it may have been too late. He was heading to work when I last spoke to him, and we haven't heard from him since."

"John called this afternoon looking for Jack. He was pissed that Jack was late. It wasn't like him to be that late. Jack is always pressed for time, but he has never been late for tennis lessons before," Tom explained, his anxiety rising.

"Exactly, Tom. He gave us a message when I spoke to him earlier today. We could only speak briefly because we were not on a secure line. He said he had gotten the information he was looking for. He told me that if anything happened to him, to tell you that he left it *where home is*. Do you have any idea what he meant by that?"

Tom considered it for a moment. *Where home is*. It could mean anything. He shook his head. "I'm not sure. Jack didn't come home last night, so it probably doesn't mean the apartment, although I can't be positive. He spent most of his time at the club, so that would be where we should start looking."

Rachel leaned back in her chair, looking a little disappointed, her shoulders slumping back slightly as she closed her eyes. "This information is the key to getting Jack back. I think you're right. It probably has something to do with the club, but it will be dangerous for you to return. We have to assume that whoever else wants this information will stop at nothing to get it. They won't hesitate to grab you or your mom if they think it will help them find it or help persuade Jack to tell them where it is."

Tom broke out in a sweat, fear jolted through him. "What about my mother? She isn't safe. I need to get her." Tom was so busy worrying about Jack he hadn't thought about the danger that his mother might be in.

Rachel raised her hand, stopping Tom for getting up. "She is fine. We spoke to Maggie earlier today. We are picking her up at the law firm and will take her to a safe house."

Relief flooded over Tom like a wave at the beach, and then he focused more closely on Rachel's words. "My mom knows about the *Fourteenth Colony?*"

"Of course, Tom. She introduced me to your father."

Tom felt another shot to the stomach. Suddenly, Tom didn't really know his parents that well after all and his head swam. *What other secrets did they keep from me?* Rachel smiled pleasantly, but there was steel behind those eyes. She was not someone who should be messed with.

Rachel hesitated before continuing, "Tom, I know this comes as a big shock to you, but I am going to be honest with you. This situation is dangerous. We are literally at war with the ruling class. Other parts of the country have turned violent. It hasn't been widely reported in the media, but we are close to a full revolutionary war. My hope is that we can change things nonviolently, but we are at a boiling point. I think the best chance we have at getting the information and your brother back safely is for you to go to the club and figure out what Jack's message is about. The message was for you, so there must be something you know that others do not." Tom heard the reluctance in her voice. "If the wrong people find you, it might prove fatal. This is a terrible risk for you to take. I would understand if you didn't want to do it."

Tom's face turned hard with anger and resolve. "I will do whatever it takes to get my brother back. Whatever it takes."

Rachel closed her eyes for a second in thought. She had watched Tom from afar since he was born. The boy was talented, but he was so young. She had no doubt that he would do his best, but was she asking too much from the boy? Rachel had agreed with Tom's mother that they would not involve him with the Fourteenth Colony until he turned eighteen when he could make the decision for himself. Everything was different now. He was the only chance they had to get Jack back and to get that flash drive. It was easier with Jack. He didn't have a scholarship or another path out. *How much could be expected from one family? First, Tom's father, now Jack, and maybe Tom; that was a lot for any one family to sacrifice, but this was war and Jack risked his life for something that he thought was important.* If she only knew what was on that flash drive, then maybe she would know if it was all worth it. Sometimes you had to guess. Rachel would have to trust her instinct and hope Tom would get lucky.

CHAPTER

16

Charles Sheppard needed to take a risk. He had a carefully procured reputation as a risk taker, but that was mostly smoke and mirrors. Most of the big bets that he was famous for were very carefully calculated and taken only after the outcome was certain. This time, it was different. Everything was on the line, and the variables were too many to know the outcome for certain. In truth, Charles was worried that he had lost his nerve. Without this emergency, he might never act on Project Phoenix. Just to make sure he was fully committed, Charles crafted no alternative plans. There was no alias in South America and no valuables stashed away if he failed. No, if he failed, he would sink. He needed that pressure.

The big meeting was set for tomorrow morning with five extremely wealthy and powerful business leaders. He knew them all personally and knew that they would be sympathetic or, at the very least, receptive to his argument; but he would be asking a lot from them. And they were not used to being asked for much. The timing was extraordinarily tight for people so powerful and busy. They all had calendars jammed up for months, but no one refused him. They made the time. Even among some of the wealthiest and most powerful people in the country, Charles stood out.

The meeting, as important as it was, was the least of Charles's concerns at the moment. If the stolen documents were released to the wrong hands and linked to him, then all his wealth, connections, and talents would fail to save him. He would be branded a traitor and, the repercussions would be immediate and severe.

Surprisingly, Clint smacked into a dead-end. Clint was a large man in his early fifties who grew up in a rural town outside of Atlanta. Technology, more specifically, computer hacking, was his entire life, and he was a master at it. Charles had met Clint thirty years earlier after Clint had hacked into the Sheppard Group's main server. Nothing was stolen and no harm seemed to have been done, but he had left Charles a message so he would know that he had been hacked. The incident intrigued Charles. Through a good deal of luck and far superior equipment, he traced the breach back to a very ordinary-looking farmhouse in Clint's rural town. Armed with a small, heavily armed security detail, Charles paid Clint a visit. He found a tall, large-boned, beefy, shy man in his early twenties sitting behind a row of computing hardware that was, at least, two generations behind the latest versions. He lived in a small farmhouse with his parents. If Charles's memory was accurate, he recalled that they grew peaches in a small orchard that stretched behind the farmhouse.

Instead of seeing a risk, Charles saw an opportunity. He took Clint to the local diner where they talked technology for hours. Clint had no education above high school, but he had a talent and passion for computers and hacking. Charles convinced Clint to join the Sheppard Group, which was not the easiest thing to do. He often commented on how that was his hardest sale. Clint had never left Georgia, and relocating to New York was a stretch for him, but Charles worked his magic, finally cracking the resolve of the young man. Under his watchful eye, Clint got access to the latest equipment and instruction. Within four years, Clint headed up the Sheppard Group's Technology Security Group, and Charles estimated that he was among a handful of elite hackers in the world.

Charles knew he was in trouble when he spoke to Clint a few moments earlier. A youthful buoyancy usually laced the timbre of

Clint's voice, but he spoke with a weary monotone. After a few hours tracing the source of the security breach, Clint was unable to come up with anything concrete. He tracked the breach to a server in Singapore, but the trail went cold after that. Clint would not give up, but it would take time for him to figure it out. He was confident he could crack it, but it would probably take days—well past tomorrow's meeting.

Charles had a problem. He could ignore the situation and hope that whoever copied the documents had no immediate plans to use them, or he could take an educated guess and try to thwart any damage before tomorrow's meeting. Charles decided to take a chance. He had enemies, a number of people would love to dig up dirt against Charles, and even a few had the resources to pull off the job. Among the list, one name stood out above the rest—Carl Robinson[15] from the Phoenix Group. Robinson had been a fierce business rival for forty years.

Charles left his apartment building alone and felt surprisingly liberated. He rarely went anywhere without one of his bodyguards, which had become a necessary evil in the current dangerous climate, but today, he needed to slip into the anonymity of the great city. He had to meet Robinson alone.

The clouds had scattered, and the afternoon sun fought its way through the gaps. The sun felt good on his face, warming his skin and his spirits. The wet city streets were slick and dirty from

---

[15]   The Sheppard-Robinson feud had become legendary. Historians dispute the origin of the feud. Sheppard and Robinson were classmates at college. It is widely known that Sheppard met and started dating his wife in his junior year. What does not seem as well known was that Robinson had dated the same woman the preceding two years. Other historians believe the dispute started when Robinson, acting as the school's mascot, was nearly hospitalized when someone laced his bear outfit with a potent heat cream. In agony, Robinson ripped off the furry suit at a basketball game. Unfortunately, he wasn't wearing anything underneath. Video of the incident is still available. Sheppard denied any responsibility for the incident.

the rain and the usual city debris. His destination wasn't far. He headed north to a bar a few blocks from the condo.

The bar was not the most sophisticated or exclusive place on the upper west side, but at this time on a Saturday, it would be mostly deserted. Perhaps a few basketball fans would be watching the afternoon games—the perfect place for a secret meeting, right there in the open for anyone to witness. Robinson, who also lived on the upper west side, readily agreed to meet his longtime adversary on short notice. He couldn't resist the urgency in Charles's voice, like a shark that smelled blood.

The bar was essentially a dark, medium-sized rectangle that was divided into two separate rooms by a copper metal railing. The right side of the restaurant housed a dozen evenly spaced tables used for dinner or lunch. On the left side, there was a long wooden bar with flat screen televisions hanging at both ends. Further into the restaurant, past the bar, stood a few small tables capable of sitting four people comfortably. The place was almost empty. There were a total of six different customers—all men and all clustered at the near end of the bar watching a Nets game on one of the flat screen televisions. They all seemed to know each other. Everyone had a pint of beer, and there were two large plates of partially eaten chicken wings on the bar. Two bartenders manned the bar while one bored hostess leaned against a podium near the front door.

Charles arrived before Robinson. He smiled affably at the hostess and asked for a table toward the rear of the bar. She gave him a quick once-over, sizing him up in the way all good big-city hostesses size up their customers. She apparently judged that he might be a good tipper and smiled broadly at Charles. Encouraged, she said, "Of course, will anyone be joining you?" She gently touched Charles on the arm, giving him a flirtatious squeeze and headed for a table in the back.

Charles followed closely behind her, passing the televisions and the bar. "Yes, I should be joined by another man shortly. Did I hear a hint of Eastern Europe in your accent?"

The waitress smiled. "You did."

"I'd guess Russia."

"Yes, but Russia is a big country," challenged the hostess.

Charles settled into his chair. "Sounds like St. Petersburg," Charles wagered.

The waitress looked surprised. Charles smiled. "The community where I was raised had a large Russian population. I spent a good amount of time talking to them with my father." Charles ordered a vodka martini, tipped the hostess twenty dollars, and sat at the table facing the bar and the doorway.

Within minutes, Carl Robinson lumbered into the bar. Charles suspected that he had been watching the establishment from outside, waiting to enter only after Charles had arrived.

The hostess brought Robinson to the small table and took his order, a Whiskey Sour. Charles greeted Robinson with a nod and managed to say, "You are looking fit, Carl.[16] Thanks for meeting me on such short notice." Robinson was of average height but massively overweight. His body creaked under the strain of all that extra flesh, but if Charles looked closely, he could still find the prickly, thin, arrogant man that he knew in college. His eyes were the same. Born of privilege, Robinson felt entitled to everything that he had and everything that he wanted. He never competed fairly. Charles had to admit that Robinson was clever; everything he did was slight of hand. Sheppard despised him.

---

[16] Carl Robinson had a dire battle with his weight for most of his adult life tracing back to the unfortunate mascot incident. His weight was known to fluctuate by as much as a hundred and fifty pounds from its two extremes, however he seemed to lose all desire to reduce his weight after purchasing a Swiss chocolate company. This meeting took place during one of Robinson's large phases.

Robinson was amused and a little cautious about the meeting. His eyes darted around the room as if Charles might have hired a hit man to sneak out of the shadows, and his face was lined with a sly smile. "What can I do for you, Sheppard? You sounded very *disturbed* on the phone." Robinson spoke as he stuffed himself into the chair opposite Sheppard. Robinson breathed heavily from the exertion, the chair groaned in protest, and Charles wondered whether the legs of the chair might snap under the pressure.

Charles smiled pleasantly. "A matter has come up that I thought we should discuss."

The hostess returned with Robinson's drink. She winked at Charles and quietly returned to her solitary position by the front door. Robinson took a sip of the Whiskey Sour. As he replaced the glass on the table, he glared at Charles, unable to disguise his feelings for his rival. "What could we possibly have to discuss? You don't like me, and I certainly don't like you." Robinson sounded whiny.

"Well, all that might be true, Carl, but I've learned that some computer documents were recently stolen from someone who works for me." Charles paused, studying Robinson carefully. "And I would like them returned."

Robinson laughed derisively. "So what do you want from me? Are you accusing me of the theft?"

Charles grinned, but his eyes were sharp and angry. "If someone working for you has stolen them, I expect them back immediately."

"And why would I do that?" The statement was more of a challenge than a question as Robinson leaned forward.

It was time for Charles to gamble. "Let's say I have some information about your dealings with International Lodging Group that you would rather stay secret. I would hate to be forced to reveal something so inflammatory." This was the bluff. There were rumors that Robinson had been stealing from ILG for some time. The Phoenix Group was one of their biggest food suppliers, and they were rumored to have been overbilling ILG with the help of some very friendly ILG middle managers. If it was true and it came out, it would devastate the Phoenix Group and Robinson personally. Charles gambled that Robinson was insecure enough to think that he had the evidence.

Charles stared defiantly at Robinson. Robinson angrily pushed back his drink, splashing some onto the table. "Baseless accusations, Sheppard. I wouldn't repeat them if I were you." The two men glared at each other for a few moments, locking eyes in a silent tug of war. Neither one backed down until Robinson said, "I will see what I can do to help you out of your little problem, Sheppard. I would expect a favor in return."

Robinson rose from the table, squeezed out of his chair, and slowly plodded toward the door, bumping into a few stools as he made his way past the bar.

Charles called after the big man. "But you didn't finish your drink. I thought we could share some lunch." Robinson didn't turn around as he strolled past the hostess and out of the restaurant.

Charles smiled to himself. He wasn't sure that Robinson was behind the theft, but his bluff worked. Robinson was scared enough that he would think twice before he used any information he might have acquired. In the end, Project Phoenix was too damaging to Sheppard for Robinson to resist using it, but he would hesitate and make sure that his plan was solid, and that would buy Charles time. And time was really all that he needed.

Charles chuckled as he heard a collective moan from the guys watching the Nets[17] game, and then an idea bobbed into his mind like a buoy in the ocean. Maybe he could turn the situation around to his advantage? He glanced at his watch, and wondered if Clint would have the necessary time.

---

[17]   Sheppard was a well-known Knick fan and minority owner in the franchise. No doubt he chuckled at the Nets' misfortune because the Phoenix Group was the principal owner of that basketball team.

CHAPTER

17

Robinson left the bar angry, his mouth still bitter from the badly prepared whiskey sour. *What kind of proof did Sheppard have on me? How many times did he mess something up for me in the past?* He thought about returning to the bar and strangling him. He actually hesitated before he continued down the street, imagining his large beefy hands squeezing the life out of Charles's scrawny neck.

Robinson started sweating, his body uncontrollably heating up. Even after all these years, Sheppard could still get to him. He could still press those buttons. Robinson reached for his phone. With a snarl on his face, he pressed one of his speed dial numbers.

"What are you doing?"

A flat voice responded, "I'm cleaning up a mess for Warren. I am on my way to his place right now."

"What in the world has that psychopath gotten himself into now?" Robinson's mood wasn't getting any better.

"I'm not sure. We are trying to retrieve a flash drive that was stolen from him. I would have thought that you had been briefed on the matter."

Robinson thought for a minute. Warren was becoming increasingly erratic, and his appearance was deteriorating quickly. It looked like he had aged a dozen years over the past six months alone. He had lost a lot of weight recently, and there was an unnatural gleam in his eyes that frightened Robinson. Robinson didn't like the sound of this problem, but he was still hot from his meeting with Sheppard and had more important things to worry about. "Tell him to call me. I can't have him running around creating problems for me. Anyway, I have more important things for you to do."

"Yes, sir."

"I want you to take out Sheppard tomorrow. We know he jogs in the park every Sunday. We already have a plan. I want it done!" Robinson's face heated up as he spoke, his voice rising.

Sheppard jogged in Central Park every Sunday at seven thirty in the morning. He entered the park at Seventy-Second Street and ran a loop of varying distances before heading back to his condo. Only one bodyguard joined him for the run. It was like clockwork—very predictable and very bad for his security.

Steven spoke slowly, "I don't know if he is in the city. He travels frequently. Obviously we need to figure out where he is, and the time frame is very short to get this done."

Robinson laughed. "Well, he isn't traveling. I just had a drink with the bastard. I don't care about the time frame. We have a plan for this, and I want it done! Is that clear?"

"Do you want us to take him or kill him? That was never decided."

Robinson considered his options. It would certainly be nice to kidnap Sheppard. After all these years of interfering with his plans, Robinson would enjoy getting his hands on him, watching him sweat, hearing him beg for mercy. It would be sweet. Robinson realized that he was holding his breath. He remembered his yoga training. He breathed in and out slowly and let oxygen flow throughout his body, feeling a little lightheaded.

Robinson continued walking north, the sun temporarily ducking behind a cloud. "I want him dead. Do it quickly and take out the bodyguard also. I won't tolerate failure." Robinson didn't want to take any chances. If he kidnapped Sheppard, the lucky bastard might just find some way to escape.

"I understand completely. I will take care of it personally."

Robinson disconnected the call and smiled to himself. He still had to figure out what Sheppard knew, but the world was suddenly a nicer place. He felt a weight being lifted off his shoulders, and he had a sudden craving for a nice chocolate truffle.

18

Tom's internal clock ticked loudly, reverberating like a hammer banging against a steel drum in his head. Time was running out for Jack, and Tom knew it. With each passing moment, the chance that he would see his brother alive again decreased, and Tom's worry increased. He needed to do something, but he was in unchartered waters. He only had a few facts to go on. He knew that Jack was missing. That much was clear. David was Jack's best friend, and as far as he could tell, a standup guy. The graffiti at the tunnel's entrance looked suspiciously similar to his father's handwriting, but he really didn't know anything about the Fourteenth Colony, Rachel, or Mary. He had a gut feeling that they were trustworthy, but he didn't have a whole lot of experience relying on his gut. For that matter, he didn't have a lot of options either. He decided to trust Rachel, but he reminded himself that it wouldn't hurt to be a little cautious also. Rachel's priorities weren't fully clear.

"You must know something about what he was working on. There has to be a clue." Tom asked Rachel urgently, stress filling his voice.

Rachel was about to respond when her phone rang. With an apologetic smile, she answered the call. Tom heard her side of the conversation. "That's good work, Mary. Faster than I expected. Grab David and come up here so we can brief Tom… Yes, you have to bring David."

Rachel returned her phone to her pocket and faced Tom. "Mary and David will be up in a minute. She has the latest information. It isn't much to go on, but it's a start. Let's wait until she gets here before we continue." Rachel smiled reassuringly at Tom, but it had little effect on him.

Tom sat restlessly on the couch, bouncing his left leg up and down anxiously. The room was hot. There were no windows, and the one standing fan was doing a poor job circulating the hot air. Based upon the size of the room, the width of the fan's blades, and the speed in which the blades revolved, three fans would be ideal for the best relief from the heat. Tom calculated the optimum placement for each fan. His mind had a habit of working that way. When he saw a problem that could be solved through math or science, he dove right in whether or not he really wanted to swim through the calculations, as if compelled by an unseen force.

The heat didn't seem to bother Rachel. She looked cool and calm, but Tom perspired heavily as he was buffeted by waves of anxiety. He tried to figure out what Jack meant by his message: *It is where home is.* It would help if he knew what he was looking for. Jack always called his locker at the club his home away from home, which was probably the place to start. Jack might also have some space at the locker room at the tennis facility. That would make some sense too. Neither he nor Jack had any fondness for the apartment so that probably wasn't a likely hiding spot.

As Tom's mind sorted through the possibilities, Mary and David arrived at the office. Mary had a stern look on her face while David sported a guilty grin. Both of his hands were stuffed deeply in his pockets, looking like he had just been reprimanded.

Rachel addressed David. "David, explain for Tom what we know about Jack's last movements starting at the benefit last night."

David stepped around Mary, gently bumping into her with his elbow. Tom was sure he nudged Mary on purpose, and noticed the scowl on Mary's face deepen as David described the events of the prior evening. He hesitated when he reached the point where he gave the key to the guestroom to Jack, but he continued when Rachel urged him on.

David wrapped up his story. "He mentioned something about Heather giving him some important information, but I don't know what that was all about. I asked him about it later, but he just smiled and said he needed to check it out first. Anyway, the rest of the benefit was uneventful. After the benefit, a bunch of us went to Julian's apartment for poker. Nothing special. We took some leftovers from the benefit and had a few beers. I left late. Jack was the big winner. He was still there when I left. That's just about everything until Rachel called."

Mary added, "Heather left the benefit early. She didn't look very pleased."

Tom looked surprised. "You work at the club? I don't remember seeing you there before."

"I was singing with the band last night. It was my first gig at the club." Mary smiled thinly.

Rachel interrupted. "Mary will become a regular at the club, Tom. She also sings at some of the other elite clubs in the area. Mary, why don't you continue with what you learned just now?"

Mary leaned forward as she held the top of the empty chair. Her face turned serious, and her eyes narrowed. "I spend a lot of time with the computers and the surveillance equipment. Earlier today, I intercepted a cell phone call. It was garbled, but I am pretty sure that I heard Jack's name mentioned and a plan to grab him—"

"That was when I called Jack," interrupted Rachel.

"After the initial call, I kept searching, and I intercepted part of a second call. It seems like someone is looking for a flash drive that was left at the club. For some reason, they believe that Jack has it. There are reports from some of our friends in the lower Westchester ghetto that a team of private police officers chased someone riding a motorcycle. The driver ditched the bike and took off on foot. The private POs gave chase, and it appears that they might have snatched him in a local apartment building. I can't know for sure, but the description fits."

"What type of bike did the guy ditch?" Tom's heart raced.

"A red Indian Chief." Mary looked away, avoiding the expression on Tom's face.

Tom sank into the seat. "They may have Jack, but it sounds like they need that flash drive. They need to keep him alive until they get it. If we can get it first, then we would have something we could trade for Jack." Tom sounded as if he was trying to convince himself as much as anyone else in the room.

Rachel agreed. "That flash drive is the key, Tom. We need to find it."

"Do we know who's after Jack?" Tom asked hopefully.

Rachel shook her head. "The calls were all garbled. I know one of them was received at the club."

David interjected, "Whatever is on the flash drive is probably connected to Heather. If we can get to her, maybe we can find another way to save Jack?"

"I thought about that, but Heather Benson has gone missing. My informants tell me that she missed her piano lesson earlier today, and no one knows where she is." Rachel sounded a little weary.

Rachel certainly seemed to be connected, thought Tom. *How far did her connections reach?* "Is there anything else I should know?" Tom glanced around the room. He had a feeling that there was more, but everyone shook their head. "Okay, so I go to the club and search for the flash drive, and if we hear anything else about Heather, we can make a run at her also." Tom popped to his feet, anxious to get started. He needed to do something.

"Mary, have you or any of the other analysts heard Tom's name mentioned yet? Is anyone looking for him?" Rachel asked.

Mary shrugged. "So far, nothing. It doesn't mean that much, but if they had a full-out alert, I would probably have heard something."

"True, there is no way to be sure. Everything depends on Jack and Heather. If they are indeed captured and they turn over the flash drive, there would be no need to go after Tom, but I think Jack is too smart for that. Once he turns over the information, there is little need for him, and he will vanish the way so many people vanish these days. I think Tom and David should get to the club as soon as possible, but you are going to have to be pre-pared." Rachel rose and walked behind her desk. "David, I assume you are volunteering to help Tom and go back to the club."

"Of course, Jack is my best friend." David looked angry, a look that Tom had never seen on his face before. Tom felt a wave of affection for him. *At least I'm not going alone*, he thought.

Rachel returned to the couch carrying a small black metal box. She carefully opened the box. Inside were two very small guns. Rachel handed one each to Tom and David. "Tom, do you have any experience with firearms?"

"No." Tom felt blood flush on his face. He must look like such a novice to Mary and that thought stung him. He knew how guns worked and could calculate the range and velocity of the bullet with only a few bits of data, but that wasn't the same thing.

"I wouldn't expect you to, Tom. This is a very simple weapon." Tom noticed a series of four-numbered buttons on the side of the handle. Rachel pressed four numbers and handed the gun to Tom. "You are right-handed, correct?"

"Yes." Tom gingerly took the black, lightweight weapon. It was no larger than the size of his hand.

Rachel said, "Grasp the gun in your right hand and hold it firmly. No need to put your finger on the trigger right now. The gun will instantly read your DNA much like the access panels we use. There is no safety. Only you will be able to fire the weapon. You must use your right hand to activate the gun."

Tom held the gun firmly. The plastic handle flashed green.

"Great, Tom. This gun has explosive ammunition. It looks small, but each round will do extensive damage. You have only six bullets loaded in the gun. I will give you another replacement clip. David can show you how to load the gun. All you need to do is point with a steady hand and squeeze the trigger. The gun has a small kick, so expect it. Hopefully you won't need to use this, but we are at war and the other side is very determined." Rachel gave Tom a stern look. "Don't hesitate to use it if you must."

Rachel handed the second gun to David who confidently took the weapon and pocketed it. Rachel also handed him two replacement clips, which he put into one of the cargo pockets in his pants.

Rachel removed two antique bulky mobile phones from the metal box, handing one each to Tom and David. Tom looked curiously at the phone as if it was made from alien technology. It was larger than anything he was used to and had a flip top. There was no multicolor touch screen. "These are semi-secure phones. They utilize an older technology than we use today, one that is not so easily traced because it is mostly forgotten. You can use them to call me if necessary. Just speed dial the number 14. Even though they're harder to trace, they're not fully secure. Only call in case of an emergency. Keep the conversation short, no more than two minutes."

One last item remained in the box, a small, round, unusual-looking timer that Rachel handed to Tom. It looked tiny in his large hands. "Tom, we are putting a lot of trust in you. Your family's service demands this of us, but it was not an easy decision. The timer is set to go off in approximately twenty-two hours. There are two hidden compartments within that box each containing one pill. To access it, you must squeeze both sides of the clock at the same time." Rachel demonstrated for Tom, and the two compartments popped open. "The blue pill will dissolve the trace that Mary gave you, and you will remember everything. The red pill wipes your memory clean from the moment you took the trace. You will not remember anything about the graveyard or what you have done since then. In all likelihood, your memory of some of the events earlier in the day, before Mary gave you the trace, will be hazy and appear dreamlike. When the alarm rings, you have to make the choice. If you take the blue pill you become our newest member, and there is no going back. You already know too much. If you take the red pill, then life as you knew it would return with no memory of us or the Fourteenth Colony. If you are about to be taken, you must swallow the red pill. This will automatically wipe your memory. It is necessary for both your protection and ours."

Rachel gave Tom a piercing look. "Do you understand how important this is?"

Tom nodded. "I understand completely. I won't jeopardize what you are doing here." Tom took the device and stuffed it into his front pocket.

Rachel smiled. "I know this is a lot for you to come to grips with, Tom, but sometimes, reality confronts you all at once. You can do this."

Glancing at David, Rachel said, "Mary will be singing at the club later tonight. Meet with her before she starts performing to get the latest information or to pass on anything that you've learned back to me through her. She will know how to reach me."

David glanced at Mary, winking playfully at her. "No problem."

"Good luck, gentlemen. I will keep Tom's phone and citizen card here. It is likely that they will be looking for him shortly, and they can trace through either one pretty quickly. Be careful. I suggest Tom stays in the trunk until you get to the club."

Relieved to get going, Tom nodded at Rachel and Mary and followed David out of the small office and into the old carriage house. Jack needed him, and Tom swore he would do whatever it took to get him back.

19

Rachel frowned at Mary as David and Tom left the office. She touched Mary lightly on the shoulder, restraining her before she could leave. "Come sit down and tell me the rest of what you've discovered." Rachel sat in one chair and pointed to the other.

Mary smiled softly as she sat next to Rachel. "How do you always know what I'm thinking?"

"It's my job to know my most important people, Mary. Now tell me what else you have learned that you did not think was appropriate to share with Tom and David." Rachel's stare was piercing, but the rest of her demeanor was calm and patient.

"We received a report from Daniel Johnson. He works as a waiter at the club. Apparently, he was working at the Library earlier today and noticed Benson and Warren Scott sitting together at lunchtime. He described the meeting as short and tense. Benson ordered lunch, but Scott did not. Scott left quickly, leaving behind a very angry Benson. He was almost certain he overheard Jack and Heather's name mentioned." Mary spoke evenly, as she simply reported the facts that she had uncovered.

Rachel's hands were clasped together in her lap. She looked composed, but Mary could tell that her mind spun quickly, digesting the new information. After a few silent minutes, Rachel sighed. "This is not good news. Warren Scott is a very dangerous man. I don't understand why he is involved in this mess. He would be the last person that Benson would turn to if he discovered Heather's infidelity with Jack, or if he needed to retrieve some information that Heather may have stolen from him. He has plenty of resources of his own, and it would be dangerous for him to turn to a character like Warren Scott."

Mary said, "I have been giving it some thought. There are a couple of likely possibilities. Perhaps Scott discovered the affair between Heather and Jack and delivered the news personally. His involvement may have nothing to do with the flash drive, but that theory has some holes. Scott and Benson had lunch *after* Jack was taken. It doesn't make any sense that Benson first found out about the affair after he had Jack kidnapped. Alternatively, the flash drive could contain information that is important to Warren Scott. Heather must have delivered the flash drive to Jack when they met during the benefit. Scott learned about that meeting in his search for the flash drive. It can't be a coincidence that Heather went missing after this lunch meeting. Scott might have been looking to Benson for approval or help in taking Heather."

Mary paused for a second and continued, shrugging her shoulders, "Of course the flash drive could be unrelated to Heather and Doug Benson. I wish we knew what was on it. It's possible that Jack stumbled upon it by accident while he met Heather and Scott is tying up loose ends in his search."

Rachel twisted uncomfortably in her chair. "I hope it is nothing more than Scott confronting Benson with the embarrassing bit of gossip, but based upon what we know so far, I fear that Scott is involved. Scott is ruthless, and the speed with which Jack was taken from the ghetto reeks of his particular evil. If that is true, we don't have much time. Jack's really gotten himself in deep trouble. I'll need you to try and get some satellite surveillance on Scott's house."

Mary nodded. "That won't be easy, but I might be able to manage something with the new Chinese satellites."

Mary shifted forward and was about to get up when Rachel stopped her with a look. "What do you think about Tom now that you've met him?" Rachel's voice was calm, almost soothing, but Mary knew Rachel well enough to know that this was more than an innocent question.

Mary was uncomfortable. Her gaze shifted around the room. She spoke without looking directly at Rachel. "I read his dossier. From the report, he is undeniably brilliant, but I still have my reservations about involving him at this point."

Rachel smiled. "You are the only person I am aware of that scored higher on the tests.[18] Jack's situation forced me to reach out to him. If he found out that he could have helped Jack, but we kept the information from him, he would never forgive us or trust us in the future." Rachel paused for a moment and then encouraged Mary. "I can tell there is more, what else are you thinking, Mary?"

"There is something unsettling in his eyes. They burn fiercely. I saw it when we first told him that Jack was in trouble, and again, when I gave him the trace pill. He has no training for any of this. I'm worried that he won't be able to control himself and will act recklessly. He could put us all at risk." Mary's face clouded with genuine concern. This was the second time she had discussed concerns about Tom with Rachel. In their first meeting this morning, when Rachel first sent David and Mary to retrieve Tom, Mary quietly questioned the wisdom of involving Tom so directly. She was met with an icy stare and dismissed.

"You have more on your mind than that. Some people have warned me about that same look on your face." Rachel chuckled. "He is a good looking kid, don't you think. His hair is a little long for my taste. I think you're about the same age."

"I really hadn't noticed. He seems a bit clumsy to me." The words came out quickly, Mary's voice strained.

---

[18]   In all likelihood, Tom was given the IQ test secretly by his mother. The test that Rachel is talking about should not be confused with the college assessment test that Tom took the prior year, which has been proven to be particularly ineffective on assessing intelligence or collegiate success.

Rachel studied Mary, amused at her distress. She noticed the slightest trace of color flush around her cheeks. "It never hurts to notice these types of things, Mary. Anyway, your concerns are duly noted, but my decision is final in this matter. On a different topic, I think you need to give your brother a break. You seem to be riding him awfully hard these days."

Mary shrugged. "I worry about David, that's all. He acts like his luck will never run out. That life owes him because of what happened to Mom and Dad running out on us, but these are dangerous situations. He needs to take them more seriously."

Rachel stood and stretched. "We all hide our insecurities differently. Some use confident bravado while others fall back on cool logic." Rachel shot Mary a knowing look. Mary had lost a lot in her young life, her mom to disease and her dad to immaturity. She was very protective of David and otherwise kept a brick wall around her heart to keep from getting burned.

Rachel continued, "Whatever is on this flash drive has really stirred up a hornet's nest. We need to find out what it is. It may be our last chance to prevent an all-out war. Tom and David are our best option to find it. We have no other choice. David's a lot smarter than you give him credit for. I just hope we haven't already lost Jack."

Mary rose, resignation evident in her body language, her shoulders slightly slumped and her gaze fixed toward the floor. The discussion was over. "I better get started on the satellites."

Rachel added, "You were right not telling Tom and David about Warren Scott. We don't need them going off picking a fight with him and planning an ill-conceived rescue attempt. We need them focused on the flash drive until we know more." Mary nodded and left the room.

Alone, Rachel started pacing. Sweat materialized on her brow. Every conceivable path was full of risks. What if Tom takes the red pill? The technology behind the memory-modifying drug was still experimental. There was no telling how his mind would react if he took it. Everything could work as designed, but more likely, Tom would lose a substantial amount of his memory—much more than she had told him.[19]

Rachel continued pacing. Mary was right, as usual, to express her concerns about Tom. Tom was mostly an unknown and untrained quantity that Rachel had now trusted with very sensitive and damaging information. If he proved untrustworthy, or perhaps just unlucky, the damage to the Fourteenth Colony could be extensive.

Rachel frowned, her confidence in Tom was based, in large part, on intuition—a *gut* intuitive feeling that Tom was essential to the Fourteenth Colony's future. More particularly, Tom and Mary together were essential to the future of the country. There were times when she just *knew* what needed to be done—when she first dated her husband or when she started the Fourteenth Colony. She wouldn't go as far as to say they were premonitions or ascribe some type of paranormal reasons for her certainty, but

---

[19]   Many people mistakenly believe that this memory-erasing technology was first developed for military applications. In fact, a large Wall Street Investment firm was the first to develop the technology, believing that it would come in particularly handy when selling IPOs or structured products. The technology could liberate them to emphasize the positive aspects of potential investments while downplaying or ignoring altogether the potential risks involved. If the investment went south, a small pill could erase all the unsupported promises that the bank may have made when selling the investment. The plan was exposed when the firm's CEO accidentally ingested a pill, erasing the last ten years of his memory. He woke up the next morning believing he was still married to his second wife instead of his current (fifth) wife. Taking advantage of the situation, the second wife was able to tap into large portions of the CEOs assets before the scandal became public. The firm never publicly admitted anything, but they were forced to halt development of the drug, which was deemed too unstable to be effective anyway. The pills that Rachel gave Tom were developed decades later by the underground movement.

she still felt it. Every time she followed her intuition the results worked out, and she felt as strongly toward Tom as she had in any of the other instances. The die was cast. There was no going back at this point.

As Rachel chased away her doubts, her mind gravitated toward Warren Scott. How was he mixed up in this? His involvement changed the dynamics completely. This situation was very dangerous indeed. It might be time to reach out for some additional help. She looked at the video monitor and saw David and Tom enter the tunnel, hoping that she had not become a silly old fool and placed everything that she had worked for in jeopardy.

Tom and David retraced their way back through the tunnel toward the cemetery mostly in silence. The return trip seemed to take half the time as the first one, now that Tom had a purpose. Tom spent the time focused on the club and possible hiding places for a flash drive. *Couldn't Jack have given me a better clue?* A flash drive was so small it could fit almost anywhere. As they reemerged into the fresh air, Tom's mind snapped back to the present.

Tom asked, "How long have you been part of the Fourteenth Colony? I've never heard of it before."

David laughed lightly. "It wouldn't be much of a secret underground movement if everyone knew about it, would it? I've grown up with the colony my entire life. My parents were both members. My mom died young, and Dad couldn't cope without her. Rachel stepped in and in some ways she took their place."

"Rachel seems very impressive. What's her deal?"

"Don't let her looks fool you. She's one tough lady. Without her, we would be lost. I don't know how she gets her information, but she seems to know everything." David pulled back the fence for Tom as they both crossed outside of the cemetery and onto the aqueduct trails.

"I can't believe Jack never told me about the colony. He's my brother. How does he leave me out of something like this? Why didn't he trust me?" Tom's voice reflected the rebuke that he felt from his brother as he kicked a branch off the trail.

David grabbed Tom's arm, stopping him as they reached the street. "Whoa there, Tommy. You got it all wrong. The colony's work is really dangerous. When you got the corporate contract with ICS, Jack was so excited we partied for days. He was going to tell you about the colony, but he wanted to wait until you were ready for college. He wanted you to have the opportunity to choose your path. You had a different way out, and he didn't want you following him just because he chose the colony. Jack is very proud of you."

Tom roughly shook off David's arm. "I am old enough to make my own choices. When we get him back, I'm gonna kick his butt."

David slapped Tom on the back as they approached his car. "Listen, we'll both kick his ass, but lets find him first. Where do you think we look?"

"First place has to be the locker room. After that, we need to get creative," Tom said. As they reached the car, Tom asked, "So what is the deal with Mary? Do you know her well?" His skin suddenly felt clammy, his implied question hanging in the air.

A stern look crossed David's face as he popped the trunk. "Looks like we made it to the car, Tommy. Jump on in. I'll try to avoid some of the potholes."

CHAPTER

21

Warren was irritable; the passion lingered close to the surface. He had to keep it in check, fearing that it might get the best of him. He missed his usual workout with his new young female trainer. A cold smile crossed his lips as he imagined the disappointment she must have felt when he canceled the training session. *It probably ruined her day.* She was the third trainer he had this year already. They just couldn't seem to keep up with him. *After a few months they burned out, probably obsessing over me,* thought Warren.

Warren felt sluggish now that he missed his afternoon session at the gym. The blood just wasn't pumping through his veins the way he liked. Steven and his men had finally corralled Jack and Heather. Both were tucked away in the secret rooms in his basement, waiting for Warren to question them. He looked forward to the interrogation with a childlike anticipation. This was something that he would enjoy, but first he needed another injection of the Enhanced Hormone Treatment.[20] Without the workout, he

---

[20] The exact nature of Warren's "treatments" is unknown. Based upon Warren's diary, the mostly likely possibility is an experimental concoction derived from orangutan sperm and cocaine. At this time, one large pharmaceutical company had conducted extensive tests involving orangutan sperm in an effort to stop the aging process under the mistaken belief that an ancient African tribe had achieved longevity by eating orangutan meat. The researchers thought they could replicate the results with the sperm. Most medical professionals believe that the changes in Warren's body and emotional state were

needed a little pick up, something to get him going so he could operate on all cylinders.

Warren crossed the doorway into the master bathroom suite, which had a separate room for the toilet and large whirlpool tub, and a smaller glass enclosure for the shower. Gray slate slabs covered the entire floor. All the fixtures were clean, stainless steel, and polished to a high shine. Warren sat on a metal stool facing the newly designed high-definition mirror. A row of bottles and needles were neatly arranged in his black leather case on the counter in front of him. Just a small dose was all he needed, but if he took a full one then he would feel better, sharper, younger.

Warren felt the familiar surge of power as the chemicals entered his bloodstream. His blood flowed faster, and his mind cleared with a sharp lucidity. An image of his father flashed in his mind. Sometimes the treatments brought back memories of his father, Franklin Scott.

Warren's father used to beat him regularly—most often with his fists, but sometimes with a belt or a wooden spoon or once with a metal chair or really anything that was handy. Nothing Warren did was good enough for his father. In Franklin's mind, Warren was useless, stupid, and lazy. It didn't matter if he was at the top of his class or accepted into the best universities. Any success was always met with derision. If only Warren would have been more

---

consistent with results associated with this research. However, some experts point to the absence of strange orange back hair (a typical side effect of the sperm treatment) and believe that the "treatments" were most likely a common mixture of sugar water and caffeine. They believe Warren's physical and mental changes were byproducts of his psychopathic/delusional mental state hastened by the placebo nature of the sugar water and caffeine injections. It is interesting to note, as designer prescription drugs, either "treatment" could have been legally sold to Warren as the FDA was limited to testing only over-the-counter medications at this time.

like his father, he might amount to something. Unfortunately, to Franklin, Warren was hopeless and nothing like him.

Franklin's sour feelings for his son started from the very beginning, from the moment he arrived into the world. Warren was a large baby, and his delivery was long and arduous. It seemed like even from the beginning, he had to fight for his place in this world. The difficult delivery left Warren's mom, Harriet, barren. Something that Warren's father unreasonably blamed on him and told his son many, many times. During most of those occasions, Franklin was drunk or high when he raged at his son but not always. Sometimes he was cold sober. Those were the worst times for Warren. Warren grew up strangled under the heavy burden that he was the only son that Franklin Scott would ever have, and his father's belief that his very arrival into the world screwed everything up for the entire family line.[21]

Warren's father grew up in a small town in northern New York. His family owned and operated a salt mine going back for generations. The revenue and the value of the salt mine made his family practically royalty in their small community. They were the town's most prominent citizens. The local high school was named Scott High School after Franklin's parents donated a generous sum to replace the football field with an expensive man-made alternative. Franklin had been caught cheating on a math final in eighth grade, and the gift went a long way toward resolving the problem. The superintendent for the school closed the file with a happy shrug of this shoulders, saying, "Boys will be boys. We wouldn't want something like this to be added to the boy's record."

Franklin was an only child. He was completely average-looking in almost every aspect, except his exceptional eyes. He had extraordinarily, wide, round eyes that were as black as night. They

---

[21]　In reality, Franklin Scott is believed to have fathered four illegitimate offspring—three sons and one daughter.

brought charm to his face and transformed an average-looking man into something else, something much better.

Franklin suffered intense scrutiny in his small community as the only heir to the Scott holdings. He rebelled at small town life and felt claustrophobic without bright lights and big cities, fleeing the first chance he got. He went to college in California at the farthest school he could find that was willing to accept him. Finding academic pursuits tedious and reveling in his newfound freedom, Franklin began exploring the world of drugs and other illegal vices. Franklin's parents enabled their son with a generous living stipend, which unwittingly supported his growing habits. Using a mix of natural ability, bribes, and extensive cheating, Franklin managed to graduate from college in the middle of his class.

He was drawn to New York City as if he was a sailor that got swept away by a siren's song. The big city offered an impossibly wide variety of illegal pursuits for the young and wealthy. Having no real ambition, he studied at a third-tier law school in an effort to put off finding a real job for as long as possible. Upon graduation, five years later, he got a job with the help of his father at a large New York law firm.

Practice at a large law firm did not suit Franklin. He believed that long hours and rigorous work wasted his talents, whatever they might be. Within a year, the job became more like an expensive camp where Franklin's father paid the law firm enough in extra fees to cover Franklin's salary and expenses, plus a tidy profit. In return, Franklin was assigned to a "special projects" division where he reported to the office a few times a week and worked on "long-range" assignments that never progressed very far.

This new arrangement suited him. He enjoyed all the recreational activities New York City had to offer with the façade of a high-charging and high-paying career. Franklin's most difficult responsibility was to make sure that his expensive habits (i.e., drugs, gambling, and prostitution) did not cost more than the generous salary he took in from the law firm, which he routinely failed at, often requesting bonuses from the law firm to cover unforeseen expenses. Franklin's parents, through the law firm, always satisfied these requests with little fuss, enabling the young man's downward spiral.

Life was easy (if not empty) for Franklin until his mother and father died during a burglary at their estate in mid-December when Franklin was thirty-one years old. The alarm was triggered, and the local police found both of his parents dead, shot at point-blank range. After an extensive manhunt, the person(s) responsible for their death were never identified. Everything changed from that moment on for Franklin. The job at the law firm disappeared, and Franklin faced the responsibility of his family's business back home in his small, rather dull, town. The transition did not go well for him. Luckily, a very capable, solid, loyal, and trustworthy family associate managed the business. Nonetheless, as the months crept by, Franklin fell into a steep depression.

At Franklin's darkest point, he found himself lying on the floor in the lady's restroom of one of the three bars in town. The cold porcelain toilet pressed against his forehead as vomit still clung to parts of his cotton shirt. He had no idea where he was when he saw the fuzzy headline of the local newspaper: the congressman who represented his district had died of a massive heart attack. Franklin literally saw the opportunity as a sign from God. He cleaned the vomit from his shirt, splashed water on his face, brushed his hair back, staggered to the stage, and sang a very well received rendition of God Bless America (it was karaoke night), and went home to start planning his political ambitions. Franklin had never been interested in politics, but a few of his long-term assignments over the years dealt with political lobbying campaigns, and the Scott name was still well regarded in his district.

Franklin met with a professional political operative who readily agreed to run his campaign for the special election.[22] For the first time in his life, Franklin found something that excited and interested him that he didn't buy in a form of a pill, injection, or sleazy one-night stand. Franklin focused on his campaign with an energy and interest that he had never shown anything else in his life up to that point. Christian conservatives dominated Franklin's district, so Franklin publicly embraced those beliefs, painting a picture of himself as a pious, hardworking person that no one who had previously known him could have recognized.

Franklin's campaign was well run and extremely well financed by his holdings. More importantly, Franklin had found something that he was finally good at. He was charismatic and able to repeat the views that his campaign manager handed him. His popularity as a fictional, righteous, hardworking, small-town politician exploded. The fact that he held very few political positions of his own only enhanced his standing with local special interest groups. They found someone they could support and influence, creating a perfect political marriage.

Franklin enjoyed campaigning, and for a short time in his life, he limited his usual vices. He met his future wife, Warren's mother, during the campaign. Harriet was a young staffer that fell in love with the charismatic politician. For the first and only time in Franklin's life, he felt at peace, immersed in the campaign, and amused by the affections of his young assistant.

The election produced a landslide victory. Franklin won by such a wide margin that, for a short time, he became a darling of the national party. Within months after the election, after consulting with his campaign manager, and a near scandal involving two strippers, cocaine, and a horse in Washington, DC, Franklin

---

[22] At the time of the meeting, the political operative was working as a used car salesman at a Hyundai dealership. After Franklin's successful campaign, he became the head of the RNC.

married Harriet. The relationship started off well enough. Harriet lived in Franklin's hometown in upstate New York with Franklin making frequent visits back home from Washington. On one of those visits, Harriet became pregnant with Warren.

Franklin took the news of Harriet's pregnancy poorly. All of a sudden, the responsibility of fatherhood felt like a noose tightening around his neck, he could practically feel the rope burns. Franklin began staying in Washington for longer periods and lapsed into his prior vices with a renewed vigor. Warren's birth only accelerated his father's decline.

Throughout Warren's life, Franklin stayed in Washington for substantial periods, earning Franklin the unjust reputation as a hardworking and dedicated representative. Franklin discovered that he had very little talent or interest in governing, relying on staffers to do the work for him, but he was a gifted campaigner and had a talent for throwing extreme and lavish parties. The campaigns kept him going as he won one reelection after another, and the parties bought him favor with other members of Congress.

Franklin was an original member of the famous "Gang of Eight." These eight representatives sold themselves as the staunchest conservative Christians in Washington, living together in a town house that they unofficially called the "Rectory," as one of the eight was an ordained minister. The Rectory became famous for its "private parties," which revolved around drugs, orgies, and gambling. Congressmen of all parties competed fiercely to get invited to the affairs. The guests were unaware of the sophisticated surveillance equipment that was installed in the bedrooms. The Gang of Eight was the most influential members of the House of Representatives during their time.

Warren, however, grew up in a loveless household. Harriet, being deeply religious, never considered leaving Franklin; and Franklin, who crafted a very elaborate public reputation as a staunch Christian conservative, could not afford to divorce

Harriet. Besides, the arrangement worked well for Franklin as Washington offered him many opportunities to indulge in his two favorite vices—drugs and prostitution. Harriet subconsciously blamed Warren for her husband's frequent absences, which led to an overwhelming tower of resentment toward her son. In many cases, they didn't speak for most of the week except in preparation for the Sunday visit to church.

Warren had mixed emotions about his father's infrequent visits back home. In equal parts, he both dreaded and looked forward to his father's arrival. He desperately wanted his acceptance and love, but was inevitably met with disdain and abuse, both physical and emotional. Warren fed off his father's contempt, using it for motivation. He worked extraordinarily hard to prove his father wrong, not only achieving the highest academic awards in his schooling but also learning how to be cold and calculating with his relationship with others. Unable to connect with other people, he fostered acquaintances that he thought were valuable from time to time, but he was unable to make any real friends. There was just no one that he trusted or bonded with.

As Warren's graduation as valedictorian from college approached, he decided to give himself the one graduation gift that he most desired. He planned to kill his father. Franklin was busy in Washington and would not attend his son's graduation ceremony. The night before graduation, Warren drove down to Washington, a six-hour drive, snuck into his father's room in the Rectory, and found him passed out with a hooker lying next to him.

Warren stared down at his father for a long moment, savoring the opportunity to end his father's life. He resisted the urge to wake him up and make one last attempt at connecting with him. Instead, Warren focused on his father's neck. Quietly and purposefully, Warren reached down, wrapped both of his hands around his father's bloated neck, and squeezed. For a brief moment, Franklin opened his wide charismatic eyes, and for the first time in his life, Warren believed he saw respect and affection in his father's gaze. Franklin didn't even struggle as the light left his face. The prostitute never woke up. Warren thought back with satisfaction upon that night and the next morning when he gave his valedictorian speech, praising his father's influence on his life.

The police investigation was quick. No one suspected Warren's involvement in his father's death, and, fearing a scandal, the other members of the Gang of Eight influenced the investigation, forcing the police chief to rule that the death was a simple heart attack. Warren briefly considered running for Franklin's newly opened representative's seat but decided he was better suited for more important pursuits.

Still, as Warren looked into the mirror, he could see his father's face staring back at him. The usual look of disdain and hatred filled those black eyes. He looked tired and old. Trying to wash away the image, Warren splashed water on his face, adjusted the mirror's scope outward, and refocused his vision. Suddenly, he appeared youthful and healthy again, his eyes returning to their true form.

Warren emerged from the bathroom feeling refreshed and found Steven and two of his men waiting for him in his kitchen. All three men were dressed ominously in black. Steven had a holster with two sidearms while both of the other men slung assault rifles over their shoulders.

Steven was closely examining the dented metal table and shattered tile floor in Warren's living room. He glanced at Warren with a piercing look and asked, "Was there something wrong with the table?" Steven couldn't help but notice an ugly-looking red welt on Warren's right arm. It looked fresh, and infected.

Warren waved at the wreckage of the twisted metal table, dismissing it. "I never liked it. I like it better this way. It is unique." Still, there was something in Steven's stare that unnerved him, forcing him to break eye contact.

Steven spoke quietly. "I got a call from Robinson earlier today. He would like to have a word with you."

Warren felt his blood boil. He fought back the passion with all his willpower, biting down hard on his cheek. The pain helped him stay in control. He tasted blood. *Robinson had called. What did that fool know? Better to deal with him later once everything will be wrapped up.*[23]

---

[23] Warren worked for Robinson and the Phoenix Group. Their business relationship went as far back as the sale of Warren's family business, which he sold to Robinson. There are no records that identified

Warren spoke calmly, "I'll talk to him after we interrogate these two." Warren felt the weight of Steven's gaze assessing him.

"Shall we wait for the interrogation doc to arrive? I spoke to him a moment ago, and he's only thirty minutes away. He should have no problem getting the truth out of them." The doc would bring his extensive collection of pharmaceuticals, and Jack would be powerless to resist him.

Warren laughed shrilly. "No need to wait. I am sure we can crack these two quickly enough." Warren shuffled to the coat closet near the front door of his house. Steven noticed his slight limp. Warren didn't notice anything and certainly didn't feel any pain in his knee. He felt strong and rejuvenated and eager to deal with Jack and Heather.

Once Warren reached the coat closet, he pushed aside two long trench coats and dialed a series of numbers on the keypad affixed to the wall behind them. A light on the keypad flashed green, and the back of the closet swung out, revealing a well-lit hidden staircase. Warren led Steven downstairs, leaving the two gunmen behind.

At the bottom of the stairs, there was a short hallway, just long enough to connect two doors. A small metal stool sat unused between the two doors. The floor and walls of the hallway were made from rough concrete. The doors were constructed of steel and contained a small rectangular glass window at eye level made of thick bulletproof glass. Warren led Steven to the door on the left, and they entered a small, rectangular room. White overhead fluorescent bulbs supplied harsh white light. It more closely resembled a man-made cave than a room. One small vent

---

what Warren actually did for the Phoenix Group, but from Warren's personal papers and some references to Warren in Phoenix Group newsletters, it seemed like his time was focused mostly on political lobbying and stealing trade secrets from other companies. Ironically, it is more than possible that Warren's career was helped with some surveillance tapes he might have absconded from his father.

hummed near the door, providing a small amount of fresh air that did little to combat the oppressive heat. Heather Benson sat rigidly upright in a plain metal folding chair. Her rigid posture projected anger and defiance. Her hands grasped the edge of the small table in front of her firmly, her knuckles white from the effort. Two other chairs were in the room, one next to Heather and one across the table.

Warren smelled Heather's fear as he lingered in the doorway, and he liked it. *Heather would crack easily enough,* he knew. Warren sneered at her as he walked into the room. She was physically beautiful, but her weakness and vulnerability sent his blood racing. *Maybe I could have some fun with her before I return her to Benson?* The idea turned his sneer into a horrifying, cold, thin smile.

Warren settled into the chair opposite Heather on the other side of the table while Steven stood, arms crossed, beside Warren. Heather spoke, her voice loud and laced with contrived anger, doing her best to show a false bravado. "You are making a serious mistake. My husband is Doug Benson! You are messing with the wrong people. Let me go and maybe Doug will let you live." Heather's voice cracked. She hesitated for a moment, looking back and forth from Steven to Warren, but her gaze eventually fixed on Warren. She saw something in his face that frightened her and started crying uncontrollably. It sounded like music to Warren. He fleetingly thought about recording it, wondering if his mornings would be improved by replacing the classical music with the sounds of Heather's distress. The idea intrigued him, but he needed answers quickly.

Warren spoke in a low voice barely above a whisper. "I know who you are. We've met on a number of occasions. I'm surprised that you haven't recognized me."

Heather squinted, her vision marred by watery tears. Realization dawned on her face. A new wave of fear and anxiety rolled through her. "You're Warren Scott. I remember you. What are you doing? Doug is going to have your head!" Heather was more frightened now than a few moments ago. She never liked Warren. He looked different than she remembered—thinner and older and somehow more sinister. He turned her stomach, and now he had her.

Still whispering, Warren said, "I think Doug is going to understand. I had lunch with him a few hours ago. He seemed a little surprised that you've been having such a close relationship with the young tennis instructor, Jack." Warren smiled cruelly.

The color drained from Heather's carefully crafted tanned face. "It's all a misunderstanding. I don't know what you are talking about. This is crazy." Tears started flowing again. They looked real enough to Warren. They would not soften him. As usual, he enjoyed it.

Warren's voice turned loud and sharp. He banged the table hard with his right hand. A loud thud rang through the small interrogation room. "I don't care what you have been doing with that punk! You could be screwing around with the entire staff at the club as far as I care. I only care about what you and your little boyfriend found in that room last night."

Heather flinched from the twisted fury in Warren's face. She didn't know what to do or say. *They didn't find anything in the room. Was this about the information she took from Doug? Why would Warren care about that?*

Heather started breathing slowly, trying to regain a measure of control. Her voice sounded small and mousy. "I don't know what you are talking about? We didn't find anything. The room was empty."

Warren rose from his chair, its metal edges scratching the concrete floor as he stood. A cold smile froze on his lips. He slowly crossed behind the table, and stood uncomfortably close to Heather. She sobbed uncontrollably, unable to look at him. Warren smelled the fear mixed with sweat and the remnants of her perfume. He hadn't felt this good all day. He leaned close to her, close enough that she could feel his breath on her face.

Deliberately he reached down and gently touched her chin, lifting her face toward his. "You are going to tell me what I want to know. One way or the other, *understand?*" Warren increased the pressure on Heather's face as he finished speaking.

Heather tried to recoil her entire body from Warren's touch, but she could only press backward against the back of the chair. The room was intensely hot. She saw the dark circles under Warren's eyes, and the tightness of the skin against his skull, making his face look almost skeletal. His cruel black eyes leered into hers. The coarseness of his fingers rubbed against her chin. Heather tasted bile in her mouth as she choked back the urge to vomit.

As Warren released her, she stammered, "I didn't find anything in the room. Ask Jack! He was there after I left. Maybe he found something? I would tell you if I knew. I would give you anything. Please let me go!" Another round of sobs racked through her.

Warren nodded to Steven who left the room to fetch Jack. "Let's see what your little boyfriend has to say. I hope he is more useful than you've been, for your sake." Warren chuckled to himself as he settled back into his chair.

Steven and another guard roughly dragged Jack into the room. His eyes went wide when he saw Heather's tear-streaked face. His surprise was replaced with anger as he was deposited into the empty chair next to Heather. "Are you all right?" Jack's hands were bound behind his back by a plastic restraint, his curly hair soaked with sweat. The left leg of his jeans was torn from when he ditched the bike and smeared with dark-crusted blood.

"No, Jack, I am not all right! Just tell them what they want to know!" Heather broke down into another bout of tears. Her head hung low on her shoulders.

Jack turned to Warren. Recognition dawned on him. He knew Warren from the club. He avoided him if he could. There were never any good stories involving Warren Scott among the staff.

Warren leaned forward in his chair. "Welcome to our little party, Jack. I think you have met Mrs. Benson before. Are you ready to return what is mine?"

Jack worked his hands against the restraints. They were tight, but with some effort, they loosened. The metal chair had a sharp edge that he used as a wedge. Jack quickly scanned the two armed men in the room with him. One guard held an assault rifle, but Jack knew that Steven was the deadlier of the two. His omniscient eyes looked as if they didn't miss a thing, and even though he wasn't a large, muscle-bound man, he looked as lethal as a coiled cobra ready to strike.

Jack stared defiantly at Warren. "You are looking very well, Mr. Scott. This is really a very nice house you have here. I like how you've decorated it."

Warren didn't appreciate the insolent tone in Jack's voice. He slapped Jack hard across the face. Still, he wanted to teach the boy a harsher lesson, one that would really hurt. "I never realized this before, Jack, but you resemble your father. He was a nosey, annoying, little man like you. Tell me where you hid the flash drive!" Warren pounded the table for emphasis.

Jack's face hardened. "You don't know anything about my father. He was twice the man you will ever be!"

Warren stood and leaned against the table. His voice was low, and his face animated. "I killed your father. I caught him sneaking around the member locker room late one night. We were alone. I thought he might have gotten into my locker. He denied it of course, but I knew better. I grabbed a five iron and beat him with it across his head. Oh, it was wonderful! His head bled so much when I cut it."

"My father died in a car crash! You're a liar!" Jack strained more intensely against the restraints. They loosened as he ripped them against the jagged portion of the metal chair.

"You believed that little nonsense, Jack. I stood over him with my five iron as he begged for his life. He had a wife and two kids,

JEFF ALTABEF

little Jack and Tommy—blah, blah, blah. I laughed as I struck him again and again." Warren's face lit up as he relived the moment. There was no denying the truth in his words.

Rage powered Jack's body. He thought of Tom and his mom and the tears they all had shed. He launched himself across the table. His hands came free from the restraints. He reached the other side of the table, only inches away from Warren, when Warren swung his metal chair at a terrible force, hitting Jack squarely on the face.

The blow landed hard, and Jack crumpled to the ground unconscious. The sharp edges of the chair cut his head. Blood sprayed on the concrete floor. Warren's body shook furiously. He lifted the chair over his head to bring it down a second time, but Steven was too quick. He reached Warren just in time, grabbing the chair before he could hit Jack. Warren kicked Jack instead, snapping his head back. Heather screamed. For a moment, Warren's eyes locked with Steven's. He still shook with anger, but Steven's neutral expression calmed him. He let go of the chair.

In his rage, Warren cut a new gash on his forehead when he struck Jack with the chair. Heather's shirt and face were splattered with blood, and her screams blended together, forming one long high-pitched screech.

Steven checked to see if Jack was still alive. There was a lot of blood, but there was still a pulse. Steven doubted that he would make it. He looked at Warren, who let out a bone-chilling laugh. Steven wasn't sure, but he thought he heard Warren muttering something about Jack's eyes, full of hate and disdain before he turned and left the room.

CHAPTER

23

Robinson relaxed in his private library. The air-conditioning was turned on high, and a nice silver tray of chocolates spread out attractively in front of him. He sat in his favorite chair, an oversized, down-stuffed, microfiber recliner with just enough support for his large frame.

Half of the two dozen chocolates were eaten when Robinson picked up his phone. He preferred a handheld unit as opposed to the more common earpiece. With a click of a button, he said, "George, we have a problem I need you to look into."

George Waterbury was the head of the Phoenix Group's Technology Department. He was in his early fifties, just over five feet tall, and an avid equestrian. He placed fifth in the nationals last year for show jumping and hoped to do better for the upcoming Olympic trials. "Yes, Mr. Robinson, what problem are you referring to?" George had a Southern accent, being born and raised on a horse farm in Kentucky.

Robinson eyed a chocolate-covered macaroon with murderous intent. "It seems that someone working for me may have hacked into Sheppard's computer system."

"Wouldn't that be a good thing, Mr. Robinson?" George was understandably confused.

"Under normal circumstances I would agree completely, George, but something unusual has come up. I need to know who did the hacking and what they may have gotten." Robinson's words came out slightly mumbled as they competed for space with the half-eaten macaroon. Luckily, George was able to figure out the brunt of the message.

"We have a big organization, Mr. Robinson. Do you have any suggestions to narrow down the search? If you will forgive me, it seems a little like looking for a needle in a haystack."

"The information seems very important to Sheppard so he probably had a ton of security on it. Start with the most talented and experienced hackers." A chocolate-covered caramel caught Robinson's attention. It practically screamed his name.

"Well, that should limit it some. When was the goose cooked?"

"Sometime yesterday." Robinson was about to hang up the phone when an idea popped into his mind.

"George, you should also look into anyone who might be working with Warren Scott."

"Warren Scott, sure, will do. I suppose you need the answer by yesterday?" There wasn't much question in George's voice.

"Yesterday would be fine George. Call me back with the name." Robinson hung up. George would find the answer if someone in the Phoenix Group was responsible.

Robinson operated the remote control audio system. Beatles[24] music filled the room. Robinson closed his eyes and imagined tomorrow's events in his mind's eye. He could see the park and Sheppard with his smug face jogging along the Central Pepsi Park loop, wearing shorts and a tank top. He imagined the surprise on Sheppard's face when Steven runs up next to him and shoots him in the head. Robinson particularly liked the part

---

[24]   Robinson was a well-known Beatles fanatic and listened exclusively to Beatles music. Each year, Robinson would throw an extravagant birthday party for himself where he hired the best Beatles impostor band he could find. One year, the lead singer messed up the words to "Let It Be." He was never seen again.

when Sheppard's body collapses to the ground, blood covering his white hair.

I wonder if he'll know that his death comes at my hand. I hope that his last waking moment will be filled with the knowledge that I beat him. Robinson's mind floated on a wave of chocolate-induced euphoria as he took his late-day nap.

CHAPTER

24

Steven wandered through Warren's expansive house. An old rusted plaque reading *Quaker Meeting House* in script caught his eye.[25] It looked out of place as it sat on the shelf above the fireplace. The house had a cold, unlived-in feeling. There were no family photos and no personal effects except for a few items on the shelf above the fireplace, which showed holographic images that hovered in the air as if they were ghosts. Most dealt with legislation that successfully passed Congress, some announced business transactions. There were two framed photos: one picture that Steven recognized as Warren's father at a campaign event and a different photograph of what looked like a young Warren giving a speech at his college graduation. The two photographs were on opposite ends of the shelf.

Warren's house made Steven's small apartment look like a closet in comparison. The views of the Hudson were stunning, the sun sparkling off of the wide river. Steven suddenly felt old and tired. *If I could just spend my days fishing*, he thought.

---

[25]   There are no property records indicating that Warren Scott owned any property in Westchester County. This particular house was most likely owned by the Phoenix Group. Property records do show that they owned the "Quaker Meeting House," which was a historical landmark in this vicinity. Most likely, they bulldozed the historical site, erected this house, and somehow the local authorities didn't notice, keeping its tax-free status.

Warren emerged from his bathroom. Steven's jaw dropped. He prided himself in his ability to mask his thoughts, but even he couldn't hide his surprise. Warren had cleanly shaven his head. The gash he received from the chair had left a three-inch jagged mark stretching above his left temple toward the top of his head. Warren applied a clear liquid bandage skin sealer, which would close the wound over time but did nothing to conceal the ugly-looking cut.

Warren smiled widely. "I haven't gone clean shaven since I was a freshman on my college's swim team. I like it." Warren rubbed the top of his cleanly shaven dome affectionately.

The wound on Warren's arm appeared worse; the red nasty bruise looked like it had bubbled up with an infection. Steven asked, "Do you want the doc to look at your arm? It doesn't look so good."

Warren lifted his arm and turned it to inspect the ugly forming red infection. "It's nothing. I don't even feel it. I can't remember how I got it." Warren waved his arm in the air to prove that it worked and that he felt just fine.

"What does the doctor say about Jack?"

Steven shrugged. "He doesn't know if Jack will make it. He lost a lot of blood, and there could be some internal injuries. He stitched him up the best he could and is giving him some fluids, but he gives his chances no better than 25 percent."

Warren's face flushed with anger. Steven saw the veins in his newly shaved head pulse with his increased blood pressure. "I don't care if he lives! I just care if we can wake him up to question him!"

Steven kept his face neutral, but he widened his stance and brought his hand closer to a small club he kept at his side in case he needed something solid to use as a weapon. Warren was always somewhat volatile, but he had never seen him this explosive. "The doc says that if he survives, he won't be conscious for days. He really has no chance of regaining consciousness if we don't take him to a hospital."

Warren's eyes grew cloudy. He smiled as if he didn't hear Steven at all and was lost with his own thoughts. Suddenly, he spun around and stalked off to the kitchen. Steven followed a good distance behind. Warren opened the refrigerator and took out a glass bottle of water.[26] Steven peered into the refrigerator while the door was open. All he saw were lines of neatly stacked water bottles, one glistening bottle after the other.

Warren turned to face Steven. "It's a shame that the boy is so weak. It's so hard to predict these types of things. Still, I need that flash drive. Have your men searched his apartment?"

Steven glanced at his watch. "They should be finished shortly, but they haven't reported anything to me. It doesn't look promising." Warren increased the pressure on the bottle. His hand started shaking slightly as he smiled pleasantly at Steven.

Warren sounded strained. "We need to take his family and find out what they know. Maybe the kid passed the flash drive to his brother or mother."

---

[26]   The Americans for Environmental Purity Act in 2021 disbanded the EPA. The AEPA repealed all federal environmental laws with the intent that a group of industrial leaders would remake the laws balancing the cost of regulation with effective environmental safeguards. The committee met for years, creating long unreadable reports but never promulgating new environmental regulations. Eventually the committee outsourced its job to a large law firm, which was more than happy to bill the government as it created one long unreadable report after another. When the EPA was essentially recreated, no one was able to identify the then-current members of the committee to notify them that their service was no longer needed.

One of the many disastrous results of the AEPA was a dramatic drop in water safety. By this date, no sane person drank public drinking water in the country unless they were forced to. Most people drank cheap beer instead while wealthier people imported most of their drinking water from Canada.

"It might help me if I knew what was on the drive. Maybe the contents could offer me some clue as to its location," Steven suggested.

"You do not need to know what is on the flash drive!" Warren spoke in a low growl. It looked almost as if he was barring his teeth in a threatening manner.

"May I suggest we take Jack to the hospital. We can put him in a private room with one of my men watching him. This way, if he wakes up, we can question him, and if we need additional leverage over his family, Jack's life will be hanging by a thread."

Warren smiled and gulped down some water. He drank quickly with some of the water splashing over the edge of the bottle and onto his gray silk shirt. "I like it, Steven. Either way, we kill him, but that can wait until after we find the flash drive."

Warren shuffled from the kitchen back toward the living room. Steven gave him plenty of space to pass as he trailed behind. Warren's limp had gotten noticeably worse.

"What about the girl?" asked Steven. "I don't think she knows anything. Jack must have found the drive after she left the room. I'm sure that Benson will want her back as soon as possible."

Warren laughed, and it sent a chill down Steven's back. It was a high-pitched shrill laugh, almost inhuman. "She is really lovely. I like the way she smells. Let's keep her here for the time being. I think we might have a future together. You can tell by the way she leers at me that she wants me. Leave one of your men behind to watch her. I need to go out."

Steven looked quizzically at Warren. "Where are you headed?"

"I'm going to the club. I want to show off my new haircut, and I have a feeling Jack hid the flash drive somewhere at the club. It's the last place that we know the drive was for certain." Warren gulped down the last of the water. He slammed the bottle down on the marble counter forcefully, breaking the glass and cutting the palm of his hand in the process.

The ride to the club was hot, cramped, and bumpy but otherwise uneventful. Tom was more than a little relieved when David pulled to a stop and turned off the engine. David parked on the south end of the employee lot away from the other cars. He smiled as he opened the trunk, his eyes twinkling mischievously. "Sorry about some of those bumps, Tommy. Couldn't be avoided."

Tom uncoiled from the trunk with a grunt, and stretched his back and legs. The parking lot was deserted; late afternoon was not a typical time for a staff change. The cars in the lot were old and beaten up. Most were small compacts, although Tom noticed the usual two or three pickup trucks. Few people could afford new cars these days; however, Tom couldn't help but think how different the member lot looked.

Tom said, "Let's get to the locker room. It's our best chance to find that drive."

"Lead the way, Tommy. If anyone asks, you're working tonight's event. Wendy called you in early to help wash dishes. Make sure you mention that she isn't paying you for that. Everyone will believe you." Tom smirked and headed to the clubhouse at a fast walk.

The clubhouse was a massive wooden, three-story white building. It featured a dome in the center of the building reminiscent of a miniature capital dome with a golden rooster weather vane affixed on top.[27] Two white beams crisscrossed the sides of the dome and intersected straight through the rooster's perch, offering texture to the structure. The front of the building sported eight Corinthian Greek columns, four evenly spaced apart on either side of the arched entranceway. The columns supported a second floor porch, which was used as a casual drinking area during the summer months.

A horseshoe driveway, ringed by Belgium Block stones, led to the front of the building. Members left their cars for the parking attendants under the covered entranceway. The driveway cut through a lush garden featuring thirty yards of Kentucky Blue Grass. Award-winning rose bushes,[28] which had already sported flower buds due to the warm weather, bordered the entire front of the building. Six large, ten-foot-tall, divided-light windows spanned both sides of the arched doorway along the entire length of the building providing light and views inside the clubhouse.

Six long steps constructed of different colored river stones formed a half circle that led to massive double-entrance doors. The doors were famous. They were rumored to have originally

---

[27] The rooster was originally made of twelve-carat gold; however, shortly after the disastrous Operation Atlantis, the family that then owned the club took it down in the dead of night and replaced it with a gold-plated replica. No one would have known about the switch except that they inadvertently installed the new weather vane reversing north and south. The mistake still exists today.

[28] These rose bushes are said to be the product of Niles Greenburg. Mr. Greenburg was a world renowned botanist who pioneered many plant varieties we currently have today, using advanced genetic engineering. Unfortunately, Greenburg is mostly known for his foray into animal gene splicing. He spliced the genes of a duck and an ostrich, hoping to create a larger version of the duck for commercial uses. He fell in love with his creation and was killed when the six-foot ducorich pecked him to death while watching a game show on television. No information is available as to what happened to said ducorich after the unfortunate incident.

been used in a sixteenth century Belgian monastery, and were constructed of dark brown wood with a hint of red mixed in and curved at the top to perfectly fit the arched entranceway. They had large, black, sturdy, metal handles. It was easy to imagine the doors holding back hordes of medieval invaders. They were exceptionally heavy and were always propped open, even in the dead of winter. Modern glass doors stood behind the wooden ones that were usually closed and manned by a Club security guard.

The clubhouse was only one of many structures on club grounds. There was also the golf-pro shop, the tennis facility, the riding area and stables, the pool house, and a clay shooting range that was seldom used. All the buildings were painted bright white and were magnificent in their own right, but none equaled the grandeur of the clubhouse.

The employee parking lot was on a lower level safely out of sight behind the clubhouse. There were no antique Belgium wood doors for employees. Tom and David made a beeline for the small, simple, white employee door that led inside the basement of the club. The distance seemed longer than usual as Tom continued his mental wrestling match with the possible hiding places for the flash drive, his sense of urgency increasing with each step.

Tom reached the white metal door first and pushed his way inside with David following close behind. The door opened to a poorly lit hallway. To the left led to a series of small administrative offices, and to the right was the employee locker room. Tom led David toward the right. Oddly, the way seemed foreign to him. He must have gone this way dozens of times, but today, the place had a surreal quality about it. Tom noticed cracks in the plaster, posters that were placed crookedly on the walls, and an unpleasant, damp, musty smell that he had never noticed before. Details popped out in vivid relief as he looked for clues everywhere, his mind racing wildly. The short hallway led to a set of double doors with a wood sign that read "Employee Locker

Room—Authorized Personnel Only." The staff called the place the Dungeon.

Tom hesitated at the door. David urged him forward. "Come on, Tommy, we need to be quick, bro."

Tom breathed in deeply and pushed his way into the Dungeon. At all times of the day, people milled about in the Dungeon. Today was no exception. David led Tom toward Jack's locker, nodding and smiling at people he knew. The locker room was huge, with over seven hundred lockers for employees. Both genders used the facility with different bathrooms and showers for each. Although the lockers were half the size of the member's lockers, they were large enough to hold clothes and some equipment.

There were ten narrow rows with thirty-six beige-colored aluminum lockers on each side with a bottom and a top locker at each slot. Together, the metal lockers were seven feet tall, leaving a five-foot gap between the top of a locker and the ceiling where people could place bags or things that didn't fit in the lockers themselves. This practice was frowned upon at the club, so the space was rarely used.

Jack's locker was a top locker, three from the end on the row furthest from the showers and the bathrooms. David hastily turned a corner and bumped into Johnny who was coming from the other direction. Johnny was a longtime employee at the club who was in his late fifties, short, only five-foot-six or so, thin, with white thinning hair. He had a crooked smile with dingy gray teeth, a few of which were missing, which created a pronounced lisp when he spoke, which he did constantly.

Few members of the staff liked Johnny. Most thought that he was an informant for management. He was known to run errands for members, often going to the ghettos where he purchased recreational drugs on behalf of clients. Johnny liked to put on an air of superiority among the employees as he hinted at a close relationship to members from time to time. Most people laughed it off as large talk from a small man, but there was something there.

He was not to be trusted. Jack had warned Tom about Johnny before he worked his first day at the club.

Johnny bounced off David, and careened into a row of lockers. David smiled apologetically, catching Johnny before he hit the ground. "Sorry about that, Johnny. We're in a bit of hurry."

Johnny's face turned red as his small beady eyes focused on David and Tom. He looked like he was going to say something nasty but thought better of it. The sour look was replaced with a forced nervous smile. "No harm done, boysss. I am in a bit of a russhh myself."

David and Tom watched as Johnny scurried his way down one of the locker corridors toward the door. Tom whispered to David, "I don't want to be paranoid, but that was strange."

David continued toward Jack's locker. "Don't worry about it. Johnny's always a little strange." When they got to Jack's locker, no one was in sight.

Tom looked at David. "Better open it and see what he has in there."

David looked puzzled. "Dude, I don't know the combination. I thought you did." Tom's stomach dropped. All the lockers had combinations consisting of six numbers from 0 to 9.

"He never told me the combination. You know Jack, he is such a pain in the ass about his privacy." Tom's pulse quickened. He realized that there were one million possible locker combinations and groaned.

"It has to be a date. Everyone uses dates," said David.

"Okay, let's try some." Tom's hands were sweating. He punched in Jack's birthday, his mom's birthday, and his birthday. Each time, he got a red light in response.

"Come on, Tommy, think about something that was important to Jack that wouldn't be so obvious." David's voice had an edge to it as he nervously looked around.

"Do you know what day Jack started working here? Maybe he used that one?" Tom asked.

"Sure, he started working events on Thanksgiving Day five years ago. That was the first time that I met him. We both bussed tables." Tom fumbled with the numbers, but at the end, he got another red light.

"Did he ever give you a hint?" Tom asked, desperately.

"There was this one time when I tried to get it out of him. He frowned and told me to go pound sand, but I could tell that he was remembering something sad. I never bothered him about it again." David shrugged with a weak smile.

Tom's mind spun. What could mean that much to Jack that he needed to remember the date, and then an idea flashed into his mind. "Let's try 05-25-35." Tom punched in the numbers and the locker flashed green. The door opened with a metallic clicking sound.

"What's that date?" asked David.

"That's the day dad died."

CHAPTER
26

Jack's locker swung open with a creaky groan. The locker was a lot tidier than Tom would have guessed. Jack was a neat person by nature, but the locker was operating room clean and organized. The top shelf had miscellaneous things neatly stacked in size order, and the main portion of the locker had shirts and pants properly hung on hangers. The floor of the locker was filled with sneakers—one black pair and two white ones.

"You take the top shelf, and I'll go through the clothes," declared David.

Tom busied himself by taking out one item at a time, inspecting it and dropping it on the floor in a pile. He went through baseball-style caps, toothpaste, a toothbrush, a small bag of weed, a small flask of Scotch, tennis magazines, condoms, snack bars, etc. With each item, Tom's heart soared and then fell back down in disappointment. David did the same thing with the pants and shirts, careful to check all the pockets. Eventually, there was nothing left but the sneakers on the floor of the locker.

David grinned. "There's no way I'm going through those, bro. You can smell them from here."

As Tom reached down to inspect the footwear, they heard the door to the Dungeon crash open loudly. Tom's heart stopped. He concentrated hard on hearing what was going on. The door didn't sound right. It was forced open too roughly. It was followed by the unmistakable sound of someone being roughly tossed into the side of the metallic lockers, the metal creaking against the weight. They heard a low voice snarl, "Get out of here, now." The door swung open, and sneakers squeaked as people hustled through it.

They were trapped in the Dungeon. The only way out was through the doors that they came in, and that was no longer an option. Whoever was after them would be on them in minutes. Tom fought back the panic that hit him like a bucket of ice-cold water. David motioned for silence as he looked furtively around for some type of hiding spot.

A plan popped into Tom's head. He saw the gap on the top of the lockers and the ceiling—just enough space for him to perch and swing down if he took the right angle. He smiled at David and pointed up. Without hesitation, he smoothly climbed on top of the lockers using the handle as a foot wedge. As he laid himself flat, two private security guards entered their row. With assault rifles menacingly held out in front of them, they turned down the corridor toward David.

They shouted, "Hands up! Don't move!" They looked dangerous and serious, their eyes pinched together, and their jaws clenched tight. Tom was convinced that they would pull the trigger at the first sign of trouble.

David lifted his hands. "Just doing some spring cleaning. I don't want any problems."

The two gunmen approached warily. One was short and broad, five-foot-seven inches or so, and the other one was six feet and leaner. The shorter one led the way, squatting down, gun pointed in front, finger resting uneasily on the trigger. They were both thick with muscle and very sober. "Where is Tom? We know he's in here." So far, they hadn't seen Tom on top of the lockers. If they looked up, Tom and David would be lost. "We don't need you. We're just looking for Tom."

David tried to look innocent. He smiled disarmingly and shrugged his shoulders. "I don't know what you're talking about. I'm just going through my stuff. Trying to do a little spring cleaning." David nonchalantly pointed to the pile of Jack's stuff on the floor at his feet.

The taller gunman growled loudly. "There is no way out, Tom. We've got someone by the door. We'll kill your friend if you make a run for it. Come on out with your hands up, and no one will get hurt." The duo continued their slow, cautious progress forward.

In a few moments, they would pass right by Tom. He could see them in detail now. Both were white: the shorter one had a beard. Sweat rolled off of the taller one in waves. He looked nervous. His eyes constantly swept from one end of the room to the other. His trigger finger twitched anxiously, sweat glistening off the hair on his knuckles. David kept his eyes fixed on the two men, careful not to give Tom's position away with a look.

The duo crossed right below Tom. He had to fight through the panic, and move now, before they got too far. Tom summoned up his courage, put pressure on his hands, and swung his body over the top of the lockers. He caught them by surprise, crashing hard into the taller man, sending him stumbling into the shorter one. The taller gunmen reflexively squeezed the trigger, sending a volley of bullets into the air. Tom heard the shorter guy groan in pain. David rushed forward.

Tom landed softly on his feet. He pounced on the taller guard, grabbed him by the shoulders while he was still off balance, and rammed him hard into the lockers, making a loud thud as his big head smashed into metal. The guard cursed. Tom quickly swung his legs out from under him with a leg sweep that sent him plummeting to the ground. The assault rifle flew off his shoulder. Tom brought down a vicious right forearm to the man's head as he struggled to get up. He put all his weight behind the blow, knocking the guard out.

Breathing heavy, Tom turned toward David and the shorter gunman. The guard was shot in the shoulder. Blood smeared across his shirt, but he still held onto his rifle. David grabbed his arms and grappled for the gun. The guard might have been short, but he was powerful, with thick legs and biceps. Just when it looked as if David might topple him, the guard brought the butt of the assault rifle around, hitting David hard on the temple. The blow sent David stumbling backward.

Tom knew it would be bad to give the man space. He would fire the rifle and that would be serious trouble. Tom moved on instinct. He faced the guard and launched a right hook to the guy's midsection, which bent him forward, knocking the wind out of him. Tom grabbed the back of the guy's head and drove his knee upward. He heard the man's nose break as blood gushed out of his face. The assault rifle dropped to the floor.

Still, the guard lunged forward, grabbing Tom around the waist. He pushed off the lockers and took Tom down, falling heavily on top of him. Tom's head hit the ground hard. He saw stars as he looked into the bloody face of the private security guard. The man's mouth bent into a smile; he reared his right arm back, blood from his nose had gotten caught in his beard. Tom tried to shift out of the way, but he didn't have enough leverage to budge the powerful guard. Tom tensed for the blow, wondering if his nose would break and suddenly he heard a hollow clunk. David had brought around the butt of the loose assault rifle forcefully on the man's forehead, cracking the rifle on the man's hard skull. The blow bent him back, knocking him completely out, hand still clenched into a tight fist.

Tom heaved the man off him. David grinned. "I forgot that you did karate. That was awesome." Tom grabbed David's outstretched hand and pulled himself to his feet, his head still aching dully.

Tom whispered, "Actually, I've studied jujitsu since I was five. It's really all about angles, leverage, and math. What about the guy they left at the door? We better go check on that." David led the way forward with the assault rifle held out in front of him. This time, Tom grabbed the gun Rachel had given him and pointed it in front with his hand trembling slightly. They reached the end of the corridor and turned quickly, guns swinging out ready for action. Johnny yelped in surprise. He lifted up his hands in surrender. "Don't s-s-shooot. I didn't know . . ."

Tom and David advanced with their guns still firmly trained on Johnny. David spoke, his voice hard and angry, "You didn't know what, Johnny?" Johnny was shaking. Tom saw a wet stain spread across the crotch of his pants.

His voice stuttering, Johnny said, "That they were s-s-s-so serious. I th-th-th-thought they jus-s-st want-t-ted to talk to-to-to-to you."

"Right," David said. Tom's blood boiled. He measured the distance to Johnny, spun forward, and landed a right roundhouse kick against Johnny's head. A tooth soared in the air as Johnny fell to the ground unconscious. *Too bad*, thought Tom, *Johnny really couldn't afford to loose any more teeth.*

CHAPTER

27

David dragged Johnny's unconscious body back to Jack's locker and joked, "I think Johnny's small enough to stuff him in."

"I doubt it, but I wouldn't mind trying. What are we going to do with these three? As soon as we leave, they will either wake up, or if we tie them up, someone will free them. This place will be crawling with goons in no time." Tom didn't like the defeatist tone in his voice. "We need a plan." The Dungeon was still empty, but Tom guessed that it wouldn't stay that way for too long.

David smiled broadly. "Don't worry, I have an idea." He led Tom to the corner of the locker room to a small, dingy, gray metal door with a few dents toward the bottom. David punched in a series of numbers in the keypad, and the door sprung open. The small closet had a mop, bucket, and some cleaning supplies. It would be cramped, but it was big enough for all three men.

Tom shook his head. "How do you know the combination?"

David grinned. "It's my thing. I collect keys, bro." David and Tom took the phones from the three men, used the guards' plastic restraints to tie their hands, dragged them to the closet, and stuffed them in. The closet looked like a jumble of body parts. David pushed hard on the door to get it closed while Tom took the butt of one of the rifles and smashed the keypad. "This won't keep them locked in forever, but it will take some time before anyone figures out how to get them out."

Tom strode back to Jack's locker. He looked disappointedly at the piles of Jack's stuff. His spirits sank. "I was really hoping we'd find the drive."

"Nothing is that easy. At least we know it *isn't* in his locker." David reached down and grabbed the bag of weed. "I don't see any good letting this go to waste." He slipped the bag into one of the pockets of his cargo pants.

Tom took one last look at the locker. Jack had wedged a family photograph in one corner against the sharp metal edge of the locker. The picture was shot before their dad had died with all four members of the family smiling in the small nature area near their house. Frosty white snow surrounded all four of them. *Dad must have used the timer*, Tom thought. Everyone was happy back then, before Tom's father died. Tom reached out and snatched the picture. He wasn't sure why, but it didn't feel right to leave it behind.

"Let's toss this stuff back and get out of here." Tom haphazardly tossed the piles of stuff into the locker.

"Where do you think we go next?" David eyed the small bottle of Scotch with larcenous intent.

"Let's go to the tennis facility. Jack probably spent more time there than anywhere else." Tom's voice had small traces of hope mixed in with a large dose of doubt.

David clasped Tom on the back. "We'll find it, Tommy. Sounds like the best place to go." Tom noticed David pocket the small bottle of Scotch. Caught in the act, David shrugged his shoulders. "Well, when we get Jack back, I'm sure we're going to want to celebrate."

"Definitely, what do we do with these rifles? We can't go wandering around the club looking like Rambo." Tom surveyed the Dungeon, looking for a good spot to ditch the weapons.

"I have an idea," David said. He marched quickly to the showers and tossed both rifles in one of the stalls, put on the water, and closed the curtain. "I hope they aren't water proof." Based upon the design, Tom knew that water would do little damage but figured there was no reason to tell David.

David led Tom to the door and out of the Dungeon. No one was in sight. Tom wasn't surprised. It rarely paid off to be around when the private security guards showed up. Tom hoped that word would spread quickly to avoid the Dungeon for as long as possible, but he knew they didn't have much time.

28

Rachel waited anxiously for Mary to arrive. She was fifteen minutes late. The time felt a lot longer to her than it really was. She was not looking forward to this conversation.

As Mary entered the office, Rachel's face broke out in a wide smile. "Mary, you look stunning! That dress looks lovely on you. I knew it would." Rachel was sincere and full of genuine affection. She now understood why Mary was late; she needed the extra time to dress for her performance.

Mary wore an old dress that Rachel had given her for the evening. It was a dark green, formfitting silhouette that ended mid-thigh. The sleeveless dress had two thin shoulder straps, and silver sequins that ran across the front of the dress, forming a V shape that ended conservatively high on Mary's chest. Mary's light complexion, red hair, green eyes, and thin figure were all enhanced by the striking green color of the dress. She wore a light application of makeup with just enough silver sparkles to catch the light.

"Thank you, but I would rather be wearing sweatpants and a T-shirt." Mary's lips turned up slightly. Most people would have missed it, but Rachel knew Mary very well; Mary was embarrassed by Rachel's compliments.

"I'm sure you would, but that would not be in keeping with your character as the lovely jazz singer. The members of the club will undoubtedly request you for all their upcoming benefits."

Rachel's eyes sparkled. "Tell me what you found out from the satellite surveillance."

Mary stayed on her feet. Her face turned serious, her eyebrows creased, and her eyes narrowed. "The weather hasn't been a lot of help today. The clouds keep coming in and out, but I did have a clear shot just before I came up here."

"From the look on your face, the news is not very good. Please, what have you learned?"

"There's a lot of activity at Scott's house. I counted three large black sedans, no doubt from Robinson's private security force, and there was one ambulance on site."

Rachel sighed heavily as she leaned back in her chair. *So Warren Scott was involved in this mess.* They needed to catch a break. "Were you able to see if anyone was loaded into the ambulance?"

"Impossible to tell. I only had a clear shot of the house for a minute or so, and then the clouds obstructed the view. I couldn't hold the satellite any longer. That's all we have." Mary's voice was flat, but Rachel could hear the disappointment and sense of failure in it.

"There is nothing you can do about the weather. You must learn to worry about only those things that you can control." As Rachel spoke, she wished she could follow her own advice. "Were you able to identify the ambulance? If we know what hospital it is associated with, then maybe I can find someone that works there who is friendly to our cause."

Mary paused for a minute. Rachel could tell that she was recalling a mental picture of the satellite feed. Mary had a near-perfect photographic memory. It was very rare and very valuable. "The markings on the side said it was from Westchester Hoffman Hospital."

"Westchester Hoffman Hospital. That's not surprising. If Jack is injured and they want to take him someplace, they could keep him hidden there in the premium wing." Rachel grinned.

"I assume you have friends at that particular hospital."

"Oh yes, we have some friends that will come in very handy if they take Jack there, but I'm sure that they will have him under heavy guard. In the meantime, you need to get to the club. Don't tell David and Tom about our suspicions concerning Warren Scott or Jack's condition. Be careful. I will call you in an hour with the latest information from our intelligence analysts for you to pass on to David and Tom."

Mary started to turn for the door, but Rachel would not have it. "Hold on a second." Rachel raised her right hand, stopping Mary from leaving the room.

Mary stopped cold. Her body tensed as she turned and looked back at Rachel. Rachel's expression was all business.

"You need to be extremely careful. This is a highly dangerous and volatile situation. Take this with you." Rachel held a very small pistol and thigh holster made from a tan stretch micro-fiber in one hand. She held the weapon and holster steady as she pushed them toward Mary.

Mary hesitated, looking at the gun with a mixture of revolt and disdain. "I would rather not have that thing. You know how I feel about guns."

"I know, Mary, I share your feelings, but this is an explosive situation and you need to be able to protect yourself.[29] This gun has only three bullets in the chamber. It is as small a weapon that exists, but don't let the size fool you. The ammunition will prove deadly if it finds its target. But you already know that. Do you remember how to use it?" Rachel gently placed the gun and holster in Mary's hands.

"Yes I do. Do you think this is really necessary? I hate these things." Mary looked down at the gun as if she had just cleaned up after the neighbor's pet.

---

[29] Although Rachel became known as an outspoken proponent of non-violent change, at least three deaths are directly linked to her.

"Yes, Mary, I am sorry, but I think it is wise for you to be prepared to defend yourself if necessary. Don't hesitate to use it. These people we are dealing with won't hesitate to use *extreme* violence." Rachel watched closely as Mary examined the gun. She checked to make sure that it was loaded properly and that the safety was on before she strapped on the holster. *Good for you*, thought Rachel.

There was one more thing Rachel needed to talk to Mary about. It was a delicate subject, and she felt a wave of anxiety about bringing it up, but there was no choice. "Please sit down for a moment, Mary. I have one last instruction for you."

Mary sat stiffly in one of the high back chairs that faced the desk. Rachel stayed firmly behind the desk using its size as a buffer. She spoke in an uncharacteristically soft voice. Mary's antenna went up. She focused sharply on Rachel's voice, knowing that Rachel was going to tell her something difficult. "Mary, you understand the importance of what we are doing here more than almost anyone." Rachel paused and Mary nodded.

"We are talking about the future of this country and 330 million people.[30] If we don't win this struggle quickly, I believe that we are headed for a bloody civil war. Some of the ghettos are aggressively arming as we speak. It would not take that much to light the tinderbox. Do you agree?" Rachel waited.

---

[30] The census at this time was linked directly to citizen identification cards. The estimate of 330 million people is substantially higher than the published estimates from the government as those estimates do not count noncitizen immigrants (whether legal or not), any inmates in prison, or anyone the government had identified on its "Subversive List" such as artists, musicians (other than country music performers), and organic farmers. At this time (early 2041), the Subversive List was quite long. There was a small town in southern California that had 2,540 inhabitants. The census listed only fifty residents as everyone else in the town was on the Subversive List. The town actually voted to change its name to Subversive City, a name that it still proudly bears today.

"Yes."

"This is why I believe the flash drive is of such great importance. If it is something of real value, we can use it as leverage to speed up change, and even more importantly, if it falls into the wrong hands, they can use it to spark the tinderbox. I fear that once that fire is started, there will be no recovery except a long violent fight. Still, I feel an unreasonable optimism that all that can be avoided. Some influential people in the current regime feel that we need to restore balance in our society. Maybe not for the same reasons as you and I do, but that is not so important right now. The most important thing is that we share the same goal." Rachel noticed Mary becoming impatient. Mary had heard all this before. Her eyes shifted to the time projected on the wall. Her body leaned forward ready to get to her feet.

Rachel continued. "And you are one of the most important assets we have in this fight. Your skills at intelligence and knowledge of this organization are essential for us." Rachel paused for a second before she pushed forward. She knew this would be hard for Mary to hear, especially about David. "You are more valuable than Jack, Tom, and David. You can't sacrifice yourself for them. If you have to make the choice, you can't be captured or worse. Do you understand?"

Mary didn't hesitate. "You want me to sacrifice Jack, Tom, or David for my freedom if I have to."

"Yes, exactly, and if need be, all three." Intuition was one thing, but Rachel could not bear to lose Mary.

Tom and David burst through the employee exit, leaving the main clubhouse and the Dungeon behind. Heavy moist air greeted them as the sun hid low in the sky behind menacing dark clouds. The ground was wet from the recent rainfall, and the light faded as the day turned from late afternoon to early evening. Tom's heart raced. Each heartbeat thundered loudly in his head. He expected armed guards around every corner, but so far, their luck held.

The tennis facility was on the west side of the club's grounds a half mile from the main clubhouse. The most direct route was along Washington Way, but that was a wide-open internal street. Tom hesitated for a moment, deciding if it would be safe to make the dash in the open, but then he heard distant gunfire. He hastily checked for bullet holes expecting to find some, but relief flooded through him as he found himself whole. The gunfire reverberated like a rapid series of firecrackers followed by shouting, car horns honking, and what sounded like a large commotion. David shrugged. He pointed toward the front of the clubhouse. "It sounds like it's coming from the entrance. We'd better get a move on." Tom saw one of Bob's men running toward the front of the club, shouting as he went. [31]

---

[31]   The incident being referred to is most certainly an altercation between the two rival CEOs (Craig Kingleston and Colby Mayfar) of the remaining mobile communication companies in the US at

"We can't take the street. It's too open. Let's circle the facility through the woods." Tom took off at a run toward the trees that boarded the club's property. It felt good to churn his legs and concentrate on the short run. The tree line stretched almost the entire way to the tennis facility, dominated by large leafy oak and maple trees. Tom calculated how long it should take to reach the tennis facility by estimating the distance and their pace—seventeen minutes and twenty seconds. As they reached the cover of

---

the time. The Freedom to Compete act of 2022 did away with most anticompetition legislation. The prevailing argument was rooted on constitutional grounds. Mainly, that the commerce clause was overused and the sacred document did not give the federal government explicit authority to prohibit monopolies. The legislation started a very costly and damaging wave of consolidations.

The CEOs of the two competitors were fierce rivals, whose rivalry peaked with vicious advertising campaigns where both companies used doctored video of their competitor CEO doing outrageous activities. The ads always contained the legend "Not Meant as Factual," absolving the company from any liability. The CEOs were both members of the club. Apparently, Mayfar used the long entranceway to the club as a means to slow Kingleston's progress by slowly swerving his car from side to side. Kingleston flew into a rage for fear he might lose his tee time. After repeated attempts to swerve around Mayfar, he crashed into the back of his rival's automobile.

Both men jumped out of the car and started shooting. Each man emptied his entire ten-bullet clip at each other. Even though they were no more than fifteen feet apart, neither managed to hit each other or their vehicles. The golden rooster on top of the dome was not as lucky. Even today, you can see the dent above one of its eyes. No charges were ever filed against either man. They were both permitted to carry the concealed weapons as they were upstanding members of their private gun clubs, satisfying the requirements of the Responsible Use of Firearms Act. Once the ammunition was spent, the two men hurled insults at each other from fifteen feet apart until the club's security easily separated them. Kingleston lost his tee time and had to start his round forty-five minutes late. He was unable to finish because of darkness.

the trees, David grabbed his arm, grasping for breath. "Hey, let's slow down. Running isn't my thing." He sputtered the words in between gasps for air.

Tom slowed to a fast-paced walk, allowing David time to catch his breath, hopelessly throwing off his calculations. "You've got to start working out. You only live once." Tom recalculated the time it should take to reach the facility and frowned as his estimate more than doubled.

"Been meaning to get started, bro, but life keeps getting in the way." David grinned, still out of breath. By life, Tom assumed he meant women. David's success with the ladies was notorious.

They crept inside the tree line in the small wooded area, weaving their way through trees, low brush, and ferns. Most of the earlier rain had evaporated in the day's heat, but Tom's sneakers sunk into a few muddy areas. At one point, they startled a small doe that bounded away in the opposite direction. The tennis facility wasn't far ahead. Although the club was primarily known for its golf course, it also had an extensive tennis facility that featured ten hard courts enclosed in a large bubble-looking building, eight outdoor clay courts, and one outdoor grass court. Adjacent to the bubble was the tennis building, which housed the small pro shop, the porch café, the locker rooms, and the small tennis instructor's office. Each summer, the club hosted the Westchester Amateur tournament. The tournament lasted a week and usually attracted a few hundred spectators.

The bright white tennis building was two stories tall. Four small columns at the front supported a half circle portico that covered the entrance. The tennis building was more casually decorated than the main clubhouse. A distinctive, spongy, bright green carpet covered the entire first floor and most of the second. It was one of the ugliest things that Tom had ever seen. Some unknown designer decades earlier wanted to simulate grass. It was so hideous it became unique, and even though every year some members groused about it, no one had the heart to change it. The second floor of the building was mostly the café, which opened out onto a large porch that overlooked the outdoor courts toward the back of the facility. No guards covered the entrance to the facility.

Tom and David stood on the edge of the tree line. No cars were in sight. They heard a siren in the distance, coming from the main entrance to the clubhouse. Tom hoped they hadn't found the security guys in the Dungeon yet. As he hesitated, he looked for signs of danger when David slapped him on the back. "Let's go, Tommy. Everything looks clear."

The duo jogged to the facility and quickly walked through the front door of the tennis building. They needed to find John. Nothing seemed out of the ordinary. The small pro shop was still open. They had the usual merchandise of tennis shirts, hats, shorts, skirts for the fashionable tennis player, tubes filled with tennis balls, and a number of the other latest tennis accessories neatly lined up on display.

To the left of the pro shop was a large sweeping staircase that curved its way to the right and spiraled toward the café on the second floor. Doors to the two locker rooms flanked the staircase, the male locker room to the right and the female locker room directly opposite on the left. John's office was on the second floor next to the café.

Tom whispered, "Let's go straight to John's office. It's getting late for lessons." They quickly skipped up the sweeping staircase to the second floor. Tom heard the faint sounds of tennis balls being struck somewhere on one of the outdoor courts.

An attractive hostess leaned against a podium, waiting to greet guests at the cafe. She was unusually tall, had long bleached blond hair streaked with pink and purple, had an athletic build, freckles, and impossibly white teeth. Tom knew that the different colors in her hair was code. One combination meant that she was available while a different grouping meant that she was in a committed relationship. There were numerous other possible variations on that theme, but the meanings kept changing and he was never interested enough to keep up with it. Smiling seductively at David, she said, sweetly, "Have you come to see me? It's been awhile."

David flashed a bright smile and lingered for a moment. "Nicky, I've been so pressed for time lately. I've been meaning to call you. Nice tan." Nicky's face beamed at the compliment. Tom shoved David in the back to move him along. Looking over his shoulder, David called out. "I'll call you tomorrow."

"You do that," she answered as Tom and David hustled past the café toward John's office. They were in luck. John sat behind his desk, stared at a computer screen, a perplexed expression on his face.

Tom led the way. He rapped on the glass door, and John motioned for them both to come in. John's small office had a full-sized glass wall overlooking the tennis courts, a desk, one leather chair that he sat in, and two small metal chairs facing the desk. The top of his desk was made of heavy glass. The room had a small corner closet and a lockable filing cabinet that ran the length of the interior sidewall, which rose about three feet in height. A shelf full of trophies hung on the wall behind him. John won most of the trophies when he was a teenager, but Tom noticed one or two small ones that belonged to Jack.

John was a tennis phenom in his teenage years. He was completely ambidextrous, swinging the racquet with equal effectiveness with either arm. The unusual skill gave him a distinct competitive advantage. When John was fifteen, he reached the finals in a state amateur tournament. His opponent was the governor's son. Before the competition, the governor ordered John to throw the match. Despite John's intention to obey the governor, he found himself ahead with match point. Still, he intended to lose when his opponent charged the net, giving John an easy opportunity. Instead of dumping the ball into the net, John ripped a forehand. He rifled the ball directly at the governor's son, hitting him squarely in the groin. The boy went down in a heap, and never played tennis again as he developed an unreasonable fear of getting struck by the ball. John's competitive tennis days were ruined. The next day, his corporate sponsorship was withdrawn, and in John's next competitive match, the linesmen were so biased that John left the match after the third game, never to compete again.

John was in his late forties, tall and thin but strong. His jet-black hair was drawn back in a short ponytail; he had a thin, oval face, and a light complexion. John preached to anyone and everyone about the benefits of sunblock and sunglasses. He was usually mild-mannered, but today, his face told a different story. He looked angry.

"So where's Jack? I've had to cover for him all day long. Lucky that Mrs. Johnson canceled her two o'clock, or I wouldn't have had enough people." John spoke fast and hot.

Tom said, "We don't know."

John hesitated, and for the first time, he recognized the look of concern on Tom and David's faces. He rubbed his face with his hands and leaned back in his chair. "Sorry about jumping on you, Tom. It's been a tough day without Jack. I hope he hasn't gotten himself in some type of mess."

David grinned. "Well, we think he's gotten himself neck-deep. Do you have any idea where he may have hidden something special?"

"Something small or large?"

"Small, but important," Tom answered, careful not to give too much away.

"Did you check the Dungeon?" John asked.

"Yes, but no luck. We thought he might have some locker space here since he spends so much of his time at the tennis facility." Tom filled with disappointment as he quickly glanced around the office. He was not sure what he expected, but he did not see it here.

John swiveled in his chair and pointed to the first set of file cabinets. "They're not locked. Jack keeps his racquets in there. Maybe he put something in one of the covers? He doesn't have any space in the locker room. We try never to go in there. We meet the clients by the courts." Tom and David opened the file cabinet to check out the racquets.

The phone rang, and John answered it. "Yes, Bob, what can I do for you?"

Bob responded slowly. His voice sounded tired. "We are looking for Jack's brother Tom. If he shows up, I need you to call me. Don't try to apprehend him, he is probably armed and dangerous."

"Seriously, Bob, do you really think Tom's dangerous? What has he done?" John spoke purposefully loud enough for Tom and David to hear.

"Listen, John, I don't have any idea what the kid is supposed to have done, but this comes from pretty high up. Just let me know if he shows up." Bob disconnected the phone.

Tom and David finished checking Jack's three racquets without any luck. Tom glanced at John. "We didn't do anything, John. We're just looking for Jack."

"You had better be careful. Bob sounded serious. What's Jack got himself into?" John asked.

David and Tom looked at each other, and then David made the decision. "It's best that you don't know that much. The people after us are way more dangerous than Bob. He's a pussycat in comparison."

"Jack mentioned that he left me something where home is. Do you have any idea what that might mean?" Tom asked.

John leaned back in his chair. A few seconds passed. Tom noticed the stress in John's face. Lines appeared in the corner of his eyes; sweat fell on his cheeks. John nervously drummed his fingers against the glass desk. Finally, he said, "Have you checked Jack's duffel bag? Sometimes he refers to that as his home away from home. He carries it everywhere."

David smiled. The idea seemed like a good one to him. "Not yet, John, but that might work. You wouldn't happen to know where the duffel is?"

John was lost in thought. He ignored David's question and started talking. "We have a bit of a problem. People have seen you come in here, and they'll eventually find out that you saw me." John wasn't looking at Tom and David. He seemed lost in his own thoughts as if he was watching a video play out in his mind and did not like the ending.

"You guys need to hide out until it gets dark at least." Glancing out the window, John said, "Looks like you need an hour or two. I'll send George out with a golf cart and have him park it near the golf shop. I'll give you fifteen minutes and then call Bob. I'll tell him that you came to look at Jack's stuff and just left in a cart. I'll give him the number of the cart. They'll track it to the golf shop. You guys should hide out in the old curling area on the other end of the club's property. No one uses that, and few people even know about it."

"The curling area? Where's that?" Tom said slightly confused.

"Don't worry. David knows where to go. You can go through the woods."

David smiled. "Of course, we've been known to party there once in a while. No one goes there."

John stood. "Listen, Tom, Jack is more than an employee to me. Against my better judgment, I'm fond of the boy. If there is anything you guys need, call me on this number." John wrote a cell phone number on a scrap of paper and handed it to Tom with a shaky hand.

Tom took the paper and thanked him. "We better get going."

"Good luck, guys. Bring Jack back safely." John turned to look out the window. Tom thought he saw his eyes mist over.

Tom and David left John's office, and as they were leaving the tennis building, Tom tossed the scrap of paper in the trashcan. Tom looked at David. "He's done enough for us."

30

Robinson woke from his nap with a start. The remnants of a very vivid and disturbing dream that ended with Warren Scott laughing maniacally as he dug what appeared to be someone's grave lingered in his consciousness. Dirt splashed across Warren's shirt as his piercing black eyes appeared to be on fire. Robinson had the distinct impression that the grave was meant for him. He involuntarily shook his large frame and felt the sweat on his back as he chased away the last images from his nightmare. The trays of chocolates were still on the table next to him. A few remained, but Robinson was so agitated by the dream that they didn't tempt him.

What to do about Warren? He hadn't called in yet, and it had been a few hours since Steven passed on his message. This wouldn't be the first time Warren went dark, but in the past, Robinson had always known what he was working on. This time, it felt different, and Robinson wanted to know what was going on.

Robinson first met Warren shortly after Warren graduated from college. Robinson bought Warren's family business from him, but during the process, he got to know and respect the intense young man. Robinson prided himself on his ability to judge a person's character, and in Warren, he found someone who was clearly a man of action. He was bright and intense, but there was something else—something more valuable. Warren was ruthless. The usual norms about right and wrong had little impact on him. It also didn't hurt that he enjoyed his old man's political connections.

At first, Robinson hired Warren on a hunch, as a lobbyist in Washington, to do his bidding. With the business-friendly Originalists in power, new legislation was drafted continuously, and Robinson wanted more than his share of the action. Warren was exceptional. He combined a naïve belief in the Originalists' small government philosophy with a killer's instinct to get things done. He could also be charming when it suited him.

Warren was so successful that he became Robinson's lead lobbyist while still in his early twenties. The relationship then branched out into private business negotiations. Eventually, Robinson thought of Warren as his "persuasion" man, someone who pressed the necessary buttons when logic failed. Warren kept his methods secret, which was exactly how Robinson wanted it, but there were always rumors. Robinson dismissed most of them as exaggerations, but in the end, he didn't really care. So long as Warren got results, and there was a discrete distance between the two that permitted Robinson to argue plausible deniability, he was happy.

Things, however, started to change over the last year. There wasn't much business left in Washington as free market capitalists had extorted most of what they wanted from government. Warren's emphasis was increasingly on private matters, and he was slipping—two major failures in the last six months alone. Both times, Warren's involvement actually cost Robinson money.[32]

---

[32] Once such situation involved Andrew Templeton. Templeton was an avid fisherman and the sole owner of Templeton's Collectables. Templeton's Collectables was a global institution with a stellar reputation for buying and selling sports memorabilia. Robinson dispatched Warren who hatched a familiar plan. He set up a "fishing" trip with Templeton for a little rest and relaxation, which would devolve into an all-weekend drug and orgy fest. Everything was going according to plan when, during the first night, Warren paraded out a wide vari-

Robinson wondered whether it was time to find a new "persuasion man" and put this one out to pasture. Chills ran down his large body at the thought of "retiring" Warren. It wasn't because he felt some type of warmth or affection for the man; it was because he feared that it couldn't be done. Warren would never leave the action peacefully, and if Robinson was honest with himself, Warren scared him. Over the past six months, he was becoming more volatile, and something was wrong with him physically. He had lost too much weight, and even Robinson could see the dark circles and tired look on his face. The charm that Warren used so often in his early years was almost completely gone. It was replaced with something else. Something sinister that bordered upon desperation.

When Robinson made that final decision to be done with Warren it would have to be forever. Warren knew too much and was too dangerous a creature to leave untended. Robinson knew whom to call when the time came. Steven wasn't right for this job. He needed an outsider—a very good outsider. It would cost plenty, but sometimes those types of expenses were worth it.

---

ety of prostitutes. Warren believed in being prepared, so he left no stone unturned. The variety was truly dazzling, but Templeton flew into a rage at the lurid suggestions and demanded to be returned to shore. Warren was unaware that Templeton had incurred a debilitating boating accident years earlier that made sexual encounters, impossible.

Robinson ended up buying the business at twice the cost that Templeton originally offered to sell. The deal was still profitable for the Phoenix Group as Robinson produced fake sports memorabilia and sold them as the genuine article. This practice continued for years (greatly increasing the company's value) until a manufacturing error produced "original" autographed Mickey Mantel Red Sox uniforms. The ensuing scandal destroyed the two-hundred-year-old company. Some of these "original" jerseys can still be seen in sports bars around the world.

Robinson shook his head, trying to clear it from these long-term concerns. He had to focus on the immediate. There was time to worry about Warren's future later. He wondered what information had Sheppard so rattled. Sheppard had a number of contracts with the government. Most of them were military in nature. *Did Sheppard sell arms to the wrong people?* The thought made him smile, but the grin did not last long. He had to find out whether Warren was involved in this Sheppard mess. There was only one way to be sure.

Robinson left his study and waddled his way to his office. He needed to talk to Warren. His knees ached under the strain of his great weight. Robinson's apartment had two floors. He was on the top floor, which was reserved for Robinson alone. Here he had his private office, study, media center, and a bedroom that he used for special occasions. The first floor was reserved for Robinson's family and entertaining business acquaintances.

Robinson's large office had three giant-sized reclining chairs with small tables situated next to them. Two distinct arms swung out in front of each chair. One was used for writing, and the other had a keyboard that operated the computers. The floor was lushly carpeted with a deep red shag. Robinson liked the feel of the carpet against his toes. Rich mahogany bookshelves covered three of the four walls in the office. The shelves were filled with hardcover history books, covering different time frames in history. One entire wall was dedicated to Ancient Greece and Rome.[33] Other

---

[33] Robinson promoted himself as a renowned historian. He actually appeared on a number of panels and documentaries as a historical expert despite having no academic experience in historical studies except *Introduction to History: The Impact of Fast Food Restaurants* in college where he received a C+. No one seemed to notice the earbud that he wore on these occasions or the pensive delay he normally had before answering questions. After Robinson's death, when his collection of antique history books were being prepared for auction, it was discovered that the books were fakes, and

bookshelves were dedicated to more contemporary topics. All the major American wars were represented one way or another.

A large touch-screen monitor made up the entire fourth wall. Robinson used it to project computer images and access information from the Internet. The room had no windows. The cityscape easily distracted him and he wanted one room where he had no choice but to focus on the job at hand. The air-conditioning blew loudly from floor vents injecting a chill in the air.

Robinson settled himself in one of the recliners and pulled a keyboard within typing range. He powered up the computer and dialed Warren's cell phone.

Warren answered the call on the second ring. His face projected on the wall monitor, and appeared larger-than-life. He was driving his Italian-made sports car. The car phone also functioned as a videophone. Robinson liked to see the person he spoke with, but he usually blocked his image, not returning the favor.

Warren's larger-than-life face startled Robinson as it came into focus. If it wasn't for the eyes, Robinson would have had a hard time recognizing him. Robinson started the conversation testily. "What happened to your hair?"

Warren grinned as he stroked his newly shaven head. "I thought it was time for a change. I like it."

"Well, I don't. Looks like you got a nasty cut on your forehead."

"That's nothing. Probably looks worse on the video. It was just a shaving accident. What can I do for you?" Warren drummed on the steering wheel. It didn't seem as if the car was moving.

Robinson was already getting annoyed at the whole conversation, his anxiety rising. "What are you up to? Steven says you have him and his guys busy all over Westchester."

---

inside the hardcover shells were really an immense collection of comic books. To his credit, Robinson favored classic comics such as Superman, Batman, etc. The auctioneer (who was working on commission) was quite relieved at the discovery as the comic book collection was much more valuable than antique history books.

Warren smiled broadly. There was still some twinkle left in his eyes and a flash of his old self. "I'm procuring some valuable information for you. You are going to love it, but I just need a day or so to give you the details."

Robinson zoomed in on Warren's face, using the controls on the keyboard. It looked as if Warren's left eye twitched. He wasn't getting a good feeling. "Have you stolen anything from Charles Sheppard?"

Warren hesitated for a fraction of a second, but Robinson didn't notice. "Sheppard, no, not him. Don't worry, you are going to be pleasantly surprised." The missing flash drive presented Warren with a real problem. If its contents got into the wrong hands, it could cause major trouble. Trouble that would be traced to him and would finish him. He couldn't tell Robinson that he had stolen it until he had the drive secured. Besides, he didn't take it directly from Sheppard. He took it from Mr. X.

Robinson stared closely at Warren's face but couldn't read the dishonesty. He failed to see the knuckles on Warren's hands turning white as he strangled the steering wheel. "Okay, Warren, but you know I only like pleasant surprises. Don't disappoint me *again*. I need Steven to focus on an important assignment for me. You are going to have to make do without him."

"No problem, Carl. I've got everything under control."

Robinson hated when Warren called him Carl.

Warren squeezed the leather steering wheel hard. His hands ached from the effort. *Robinson could be a pain in the ass. His jealousy was becoming a problem.*

Warren pressed a button on the dashboard, and Steven's even flat voice responded. "Yes, Warren."

"Did your men finish the search of Jack's apartment?"

"They tore it apart, but they didn't find any flash drives. Look, Warren, I need to make some arrangements for Robinson. He wants me to drop everything else. I have two of my men at the club with Bob. They had a lead on Tom, but I haven't heard back yet. I tried them, but they're not answering. I am sure Bob has some additional resources you can tap into for the time being." Steven wanted to hang up and never speak to Warren again. His finger lingered over the disconnect button, but that was just not the order of things.

"I spoke with Carl earlier today. He told me all about your secret mission. Good luck. I'm sure you can afford to leave the man stationed at my house with Heather." Warren disconnected the call. *Whatever Robinson wanted Steven to do could not be that important. Robinson would never do anything really big without consulting with me first,* he thought. *Robinson depended upon me to solve all his big problems.*

Warren stared out of the windshield, his eyes squinted angrily. He was on the long entrance to the club, stuck in traffic. The cars weren't moving, and he heard a siren up ahead. *Some idiot must have gotten into an accident.* Warren's blood pressure rose. He opened the glove compartment and saw his small black leather travel case. It was just large enough to hold four treatments and clean syringes. Warren carried it with him just in case. It might be a long night, and the sight of the black leather case reassured him.

Warren glanced at his reflection in the rearview mirror. The blood vessel in his left eye must have burst as it had an angry red hue about it. *Damn allergies,* he thought. Still, it added a little menace to his good looks, giving him a fiery look. Not too bad if he looked at it the right way.

The woman in the Mercedes in front of him shut off the engine. *What in the world was going on?* Warren had had enough. He turned the wheel and slammed on the gas. Burning rubber, he skidded off the pavement and screeched onto the grass. Accelerating, he jammed the car into second gear. The tires spun, and the engine squealed. The sports car was finely tuned for balance but helpless on the wet grass. The car fishtailed, swinging wildly away from the road. One of the tires caught, and the car careened sharply left through some tall grass and onto the golf course. The car ripped up the fairway until the wheels spun helplessly in the mud as Warren frantically worked the gears.

After a few minutes of spinning and digging, it was clear that he was stuck on the seventh fairway, a short distance from the entrance road. Warren angrily turned off the engine, grabbed his black case, and flung the keys on the passenger seat. The club was only half a mile ahead. *Someone else could park the bloody car.*

As Warren slammed the car door shut and turned for the entrance to the club, he froze as he heard the sound of shattering glass. He turned slowly, and his blood started to boil. A golfer on the tee box waved his driver in the air and angrily shouted at him. Warren's hand instinctively reached for his holster and the handgun concealed at the small of his back. He caught himself before his fingers grasped the gun. With a forced smile on his face, he looked back at his car.

Miraculously, the golf ball crashed through the passenger side window and back out the driver's side window. A shiny, new white Titlist Pro VXXL golf ball sat on the fairway a foot from his car. Warren casually turned back to the car, slowly unzipped his pants, arched his back, and urinated on the golf ball. This was the best he felt all day. After he was finished, he waved back at the irate golfer and headed onward to the club.

CHAPTER

32

Bob sat anxiously behind his desk in his small, cramped office. His attention nervously flickered between a series of video feeds on his large flat-screen computer monitor. Each feed projected a different image from one of the club's security cameras. Nothing looked out of the ordinary. Well, that is if you consider a shootout between two members at the entrance to the club as normal, and of course, Bob was still trying to erase the image of Warren urinating on the golf ball from his mind. What bothered him most wasn't what Warren did to the ball, but the look of pure joy on his face while he did it. He feared that it would take a long night with a bottle of Tequila to cleanse his mind of that disturbing image.

At the touch of a button, a different video feed projected on to the wall opposite his desk. He was running a version of facial recognition software using the photograph from Tom's employee identification card. So far, he had no hits. Tom was here somewhere. Steven's men had seen him, but the club's security system was mostly focused on the entrances to the club and its perimeter. The members wanted to keep undesirables out of the property. They were not concerned with monitoring internal areas, leaving many blind spots for Tom to navigate through.[34]

---

[34]   Not only was the club's security system geared to prevent unwanted intruders, it was also intentionally set up not to survey most of the club's internal grounds. Five years earlier, one of the new members was unfortunately killed when he was run over by a golf cart on the

Although he wouldn't admit it publicly, Bob liked Jack and Tom. Jack, in particular, had a way of making him laugh. Unlike most troublemakers, the brothers understood their place at the club. Bob knew that Jack, in particular, occasionally broke the rules, excessive drinking, light drug use, gambling, and perhaps the rare theft, but he never confronted Bob or the other security guards, and never made a fuss when Bob caught him. Bob hoped to find Tom before Warren arrived, but time had run out. Even for Bob, Warren was scary and unpredictable. He hadn't always been this bad, but he had gotten progressively worse over the years. If Bob held Tom in his custody before Warren arrived, he might be able to shield the boy and limit the damage somehow. Now that Warren stalked toward the clubhouse, it would be too late for that. Whatever the fuss, he hoped there was a way to solve it. He didn't relish the idea of Warren taking out his frustrations on the brothers. People had gone missing before.

Technically, Bob worked for the club. He was officially their head of security and had a small staff at his command. That was *technically*, but in reality, Bob made substantially more money providing muscle to club members. They paid well when they

---

ninth fairway. The driver of the cart was heavily stoned and intoxicated at the time. He apparently careened through a wooded area and tried to launch the cart over a sand trap. He was in a rush to get to the bar at the halfway house as his thermos of mojitos had been exhausted. The cart didn't clear the trap and, instead, landed on the new member who held a sand wedge in his hands. The driver of the cart was the club president. A video camera at the halfway house filmed the incident. The new member's family was somehow able to retrieve the video before it was erased. No criminal charges were filed against the president of the club, but he was required to pay a substantial settlement to the dead man's family. After that incident, the club pulled all the internal security cameras. The club president went on to serve three more terms, and upon his retirement, the club renamed its mojito drink the Barney Blast after the popular president.

needed a little help, and Warren Scott always paid the most. Bob didn't mind the work. He reasoned that most of the time, people deserved what they got. They should understand their place in the world. Sometimes they just needed a little reminder. He provided the reminding.

From a very young age, Bob secretly desired to become a pastry chef, a passion that was inspired by his grandfather. On Sunday mornings, Bob's grandfather baked. He had no official training, but Bob figured that he was as close to a magician in the kitchen that he would ever find. The smells and tastes that came out of the oven on Sundays (always from a haphazard array of ingredients) amazed and delighted a young Bob. Those Sunday mornings were Bob's most treasured childhood memories—Bob's grandfather in a full apron wearing his white chef's hat and a broad smile. He looked ridiculous, but no one had the courage to mention it. At first, Bob was the official tester, and later he gradually worked his way up to assistant chef, but all the magic came from his grandfather. When Bob turned thirteen, his grandfather gave him his own chef's hat, something he still owned, cherished, and used when he baked.

Bob's grandfather was a mason by trade. He had massive legs, extraordinarily large shoulders, and forearms that would make Popeye jealous. He was loud, gregarious, and generally well liked by almost everyone. Bob's father was quite the opposite. He had a thin build, kept mostly to himself, and had a hard time making friends. Bob's father worked the heavy machines at construction sites, something Bob's grandfather joked was *woman's* work. While the two men were opposites in most things, they shared a love of the drink (as Bob's grandfather called it). But the drink had very different effects on the two. When drunk, Bob's father got mean and abusive while his grandfather's otherwise large, friendly personality, just grew even larger and friendlier. On Sunday mornings, Bob's grandfather recovered quickly from Saturday night's excesses, channeling his energy into baking, while Bob's father brooded in the darkness of his room, seldom emerging until midday.

There were only the three of them. Bob never knew his mother. She skipped out on them sometime within Bob's first year. Bob's father never talked about her, but his grandfather spilled out a few unkind words from time to time. Bob inherited his grandfather's body type—wide, thick, and strong. After Bob's ninth birthday, Bob's grandfather (when schooling permitted) brought Bob on construction sites and taught him the trade and art of masonry. Bob didn't mind the work. He appreciated the rhythm of a construction site; everyone had a proper place and a clearly defined role. The summer before Bob went to college, Bob's grandfather died in a tragic workplace accident. One of the crane operators was out of place and accidentally knocked into the scaffolding where Bob's grandfather worked. He was twenty stories up and never had a chance. Bob's father turned further to the drink and lost himself in one of the ghettos. Bob couldn't even find him now if he wanted to, but in reality, the thought never even crossed his mind.

Besides Bob's pastry ambitions, he was also an accomplished high school wrestler. He obtained a scholarship from a big college in the Midwest and became an all-American wrestler during his sophomore year. He didn't enjoy academics much, but he liked wrestling all right and was good at it. While attending college, Bob enrolled in as many baking classes as possible and did surprisingly well. He had a real talent for combining flavors and exhibited patience in the kitchen. Still, no one took his dream seriously. Even the teachers at the school, who should have known better, assumed that Bob was just another jock looking for an easy credit. Quite frankly, his size and dominating performances in the wrestling ring scared them.

During the fall wrestling season in Bob's junior year, he suffered a serious knee injury, cutting short his college wrestling career. After the injury, the school had little use for Bob, thus ending Bob's secret ambitions of becoming a pastry chef. The scholarship disappeared, and so did Bob's invitation to attend the school. With college finished and Bob's dreams of creating desserts dashed, Bob's wrestling coach connected him with a private security training school and helped facilitate his entrance into the booming and lucrative world of private security. With a loan from his coach, Bob started his security career. It took a few years to pay back the coach, but Bob was currently debt-free, and he saved a good portion of the extra money he pulled doing odd jobs for club members. [35]

Things were good for Bob, but he couldn't shake the feeling that his life was a bit shallow. Unable to find a spouse, he had no one to share his life with. Bob just couldn't connect with people on that level, a personality trait that he inherited from his father. He enjoyed his own space. It was always the same. The closer he got to someone, the more claustrophobic he felt. He ended every relationship before he suffocated. It didn't mean that he couldn't like people. He did like people, not a lot of people, but he liked a handful at least. He just needed his space. Bob stopped trying to find someone special years ago, deciding that it just wasn't in his nature to be that intimate with another human being.

Bob glanced up as Warren limped into his office. Forewarned by the video cameras, Bob made a discernable effort not to react to Warren's appearance, but it was disconcerting nonetheless. Warren looked as if he had just survived a serious car crash, but even in this condition, Warren was still impeccably dressed as always. He wore a light blue silk golf shirt, tan slacks, black belt and fine Italian-made black shoes, but Bob noticed mud splat-

---

[35]   Bob still held on to his dream of becoming a pastry chef. He anonymously started a popular Web site known as *Baking with Betty*. The site's cult following enjoyed the creative mixture of flavors, and the hulking woman known as Betty who demonstrated different recipes from time to time.

tered on the shoes and the left cuff of his pants, stains that the usually impeccably dressed man would never allow.

Warren wasn't smiling, his face contorting into an angry scowl, his red eyes blazing with a fiery intensity. "What's the latest with Steven's guys? Did they apprehend Tom?" Warren stood stiffly at the doorway to Bob's office, staying in the hallway and wrinkling his face as if he had just smelled something unpleasant.

Bob stood. He had no desire for Warren to enter his office and thought it best to meet him at the door. "We just retrieved them from the Dungeon. They got a tip that Tom was in the Dungeon—ah, the employee locker room. Apparently they saw Tom and the bartender, David, both down there. After that, the story gets jumbled. Somehow, Tom got the jump on them, and David and Tom were able to take them out. One of the guys was shot in the arm and both have concussions. We found them locked in a broom closet. I've got the club's doctor bandaging the gunshot wound. They're in the holding room next door." Bob thought it best not to mention Johnny's role in the failed mission. Nothing good would come of involving the diminutive informant.

"Incompetent fools! A sixteen-year-old kid and an untrained bartender got the jump on them?" Bob saw the veins on Warren's newly shaven head pulse with anger. "Any sign of Tom since then?"

"I just got a call from John, the head pro at the tennis facility. Tom was there fifteen minutes ago. He left in a golf cart. We tracked the cart to the golf pro shop. I sent two guys to check it out. They might not be as trained as Steven's guys, but they should be able to handle one kid." Bob finished with a thin, confident smile on his face.

"I can't believe this," said Warren. "Get the word out. I'll pay triple the usual amount for anyone who helps us capture Tom."

Bob was stunned. "That's a lot of money. At that level, we'll have a full-scale witch hunt for him. Things could get messy."

"I don't care. I want him captured now." Warren glanced around Bob's neat, small office with an expression of distaste.

"Let's debrief Steven's guys." Warren shuffled out of the doorway with Bob following closely behind.

The interrogation room was next to Bob's office. The door was unlocked. Warren entered first, followed by Bob. Steven's men were seated on two metal chairs, their shoulders slumped low, their eyes glazed over and unfocused. The doctor had just finished bandaging the shorter man's arm; blood had already soaked through the white gauze wrapping. The doctor's medical kit was open. Bob noticed a thin stainless steel needle with the remnants of black dissolvable thread clinging precariously to it.

Both men clumsily stood at attention as Warren entered the room. The taller man knocked over his chair in the process, which made a metallic clanging sound as it bounced off the hard tile floor. Both men had large bruises on their faces. The taller man had a painful looking red welt on his temple while the shorter bearded man had a nasty, bluish green, bruise on his forehead, shaped in the outline of the butt of an assault rifle. Both men looked groggy, but they knew enough to stand at attention when Warren entered the room.

Upon seeing Warren, the doctor nervously packed up his black bag and quickly left the room. He bumped into Bob on the way out, trying to give Warren as wide a berth as possible. He muttered an apology as he quietly shut the door behind him.

Warren smiled coolly at the men and asked for an explanation, his left eye twitching uncontrollably. The taller man spoke, giving a succinct summary of events in a military-style staccato. His voice stammered at points as Warren's piercing gaze unnerved him. His story was short and to the point, but he ended with a rambling apology. Still smiling, Warren wandered to the corner of the room toward the assault rifles. They were still wet; a small puddle had formed underneath them. Warren grabbed the nearest one, examining it. He seemed particularly interested in the cracked butt.

Warren, still holding the rifle, turned back toward the taller man. "These things happen. You didn't know that Tom was going to get help from the meddling bartender. What do you think they were doing in the locker room?" Warren sounded friendly, but his smile was cold. He raised the assault rifle close to his eyes, studying the stock. It appeared like the first time he had ever seen a gun like that, but Bob knew better.

"It looked as if they were going through the locker, sir. There were piles of stuff on the floor. I don't think they found anything of value." The man reported to Warren, looking more at ease than when Warren entered the room. He even managed a thin smile and a shrug of his shoulders.

Warren gestured for the men to sit as he slowly walked up to them. Glancing at Bob, he said, "You went through that locker earlier in the day, correct?"

Bob looked at Warren apprehensively. He didn't like seeing Warren handle the assault rifle, even if he had already taken out the ammo clip when he retrieved the weapons. "Absolutely. There was no flash drive in the locker. We went through it closely." Bob supervised the search himself. He made sure his guys didn't take anything and that they replaced Jack's stuff neatly.

Without warning, Warren swung the rifle like a baseball bat, hitting the taller man flush in the face. The blow made a sick thudding sound as the heavy metal violently smashed into the man's head, knocking him from his chair. Blood poured out of his head as the rifle ripped open a nasty wound on his forehead. The man moaned as he clutched his head, his hand becoming slick with blood. Warren's face contorted in fury as he reared back and kicked the man with his fine Italian black shoes in the stomach. "Shut up, you pathetic loser!" Blood mingled with the mud on Warren's loafers.

Warren turned to the shorter, bearded man. The security officer's eyes were wide with terror. He was unsure what to do. It was not in his nature to let Warren hurt him, but Warren Scott was an important man. "Do you have anything to add to his report?"

The shorter man looked into Warren's eyes defiantly, his broken nose bandaged with white tape. He made his choice. He spoke loudly and confidently and leaned forward ready to defend himself, "No, sir."

Warren held the blood-splattered gun away from his chest, careful not to get blood on his fine silk shirt. The injured man curled on the floor at his feet in a fetal position. Warren hesitated and then smiled at the bearded man. "You, I like. You are not a scared little boy like this man. This is a business for men, not boys." Warren tossed him the rifle and said, "Don't ever be careless again," and stalked out of the room. Bob exhaled for the first time in what seemed like ages and followed Warren out of the interrogation room.

Warren spoke as he walked. "What I don't understand is why Tom would go to the golf course. What connection did Jack have with golf? He was a tennis instructor. It doesn't make any sense. I understand the tennis facility, but the golf course doesn't sound right to me."

CHAPTER

33

Charles Sheppard watched the sunset from his balcony, contemplating the task ahead while holding a glass of Pinot Noir lightly in his right hand. The day's clouds had broken just enough for him to glimpse the sun's last orange rays melt away into the horizon. The vastness of the horizon had a soothing effect on Charles, giving him a sense of proportion, helping slow his active mind, and calming his nerves.

Everything was progressing very rapidly now. All the chess pieces were moving into place. Charles just needed to organize his thoughts for tomorrow's meeting. It was probably the most important sales pitch he was going to make in his lifetime. If he was successful, there was a chance—maybe not even a good chance at this point, but still a chance—to avoid a bloody revolution and restore the country to greatness. If he failed, the country would turn down a different path—one that was dark and violent, and where it would lead, Charles could not predict.

Charles knew all five of the business leaders he invited to tomorrow's meeting personally, four men and one woman. They were all powerful, smart, visionary, and pragmatic. They were not slaves to any one ideology. They used the tools at hand to better their positions, and if the tools were not available, they typically made them. Charles needed to focus on the economics of action. If he sunk into an amorphous moral debate, the meeting would quickly break down in failure. Everyone had a different definition of "fairness" and a different moral code, rendering those terms useless. These were businesspeople, and he had to make a business case, which he was confident he could do since he was a businessperson, a very good businessperson.

Charles knew his case was strong. America had undergone a long period of decline. Over the past decade, notwithstanding the government's statistics, the country's GDP declined each consecutive year. The wealthiest 1 percent increased their share of the economy, but it was a shrinking pie. It was clear to anyone paying attention that everyone's standard of living was sinking. If American economics was a game of *Chutes and Ladders*, the country was falling down a long chute with no bottom in sight.

The current difficulties traced its origin to the year 2000 but really accelerated after the 2018 election when the Originalists' influence and power leaped forward. They rode a wave of discontent, promising tax cuts, deregulation, and enhanced personal liberty. Their *constitutional*-based policies founded on a near unfettered belief in "free market" capitalism accelerated the country's decline. Massive governmental spending cuts shrank demand for goods and services at a time of high unemployment and weak private demand. The policies tossed the country into an even deeper recession, which was met with even more austerity budgets. It worsened a storm that had still not quite ended.

Tax cuts and loopholes that benefited the wealthiest helped create vast deficits the Originalists used to justify violent slashes to programs that helped the poor and supported the country's long-term future (i.e., education, infrastructure, healthcare, research).[36] The flat tax was established, which created the same

---

[36]   Even as of April 2041, Originalist politicians repeated the mantra that tax cuts paid for themselves. It became an article of faith for like-minded politicians in the early twenty-first century despite a mountain of evidence to the contrary. The internationally acclaimed documentary by Michael Plenty, *Liar, Liar, Pants on Fire*, effectively ended the debate as to whether Originalists and their ideological predecessors believed in the fallacy that tax cuts for the wealthiest

tax rate for every citizen without regard to his or her level of income. The tax rate for capital gains and dividends was reduced to zero, thus creating the only regressive income tax system in the developed world. The VAT was established, applying a consumption tax on all goods without exception for food or basic necessities, which also contributed to the regressive nature of America's tax code. Business deregulation created environments where large businesses squashed competition and dominated labor relations. Trust in the nation's basic institutions (finance, food, medical, etc.) eroded quickly as these companies were left to their own devices to regulate themselves. The food supply suffered frequent contamination, and environmental disasters became commonplace. Banks took incredibly risky positions that failed and were then bailed out by taxpayers. Medicines became unreliable. Crime skyrocketed.

America's once vibrant middle class became a shell of its previous self. The country led the world in concentrated wealth with the gulf between the rich and everyone else as wide as the Grand Canyon. The diminished domestic demand for goods and services crippled all but the largest multinational businesses. Healthcare was apportioned on a basis of wealth. Emergency rooms turned away patients that did not have the means to pay. Most families drained their entire savings to pay for healthcare services for sick, particularly elderly, relations. Economic mobility was essentially gone.

Charles was confident he would win the economic argument. Everyone, including the wealthiest, would benefit from a

---

actually increased tax revenues or whether the argument was a simple ruse to fool an uninformed electorate. The documentary uncovered written evidence and even video recordings of major Originalist economists and think tank organizations who clearly indicated that they were aware of the silliness of this particular claim, but that did not prevent them from repeating the concept over and over again until many Americans believed there had to be some truth in it.

more equitable society. The American worker needed hope and a chance to better his or her life. Xavier had all the data, but no one would even ask for it. The real question was whether he could inspire action.

Action involved risk, but to convince these people to take that risk, he needed to persuade them on an intellectual *and* an emotional basis. Charles smiled. In the end, every good sales pitch came down to the same thing—personal advantage. He had to make it personal: how everyone's life in that room would be made better by action and if they failed to act, how they would be left behind at a great disadvantage. Every good salesman knew the secret to a good sales pitch, and Charles was the best.

The view from the balcony was spectacular. The darkness quickly enveloped the city and contrasted beautifully with the twinkling of the man-made lights. Charles stretched his legs as he leaned against the balcony's railing. He felt like doing a late run, and considered taking a jog now instead of tomorrow morning. He checked his antique Rolex and discovered that the Knicks-Heat game would soon start. Time had slipped by faster than he had realized. Charles was a minority owner of the Knicks and had his usual bet on the outcome with the Heat's owner— one million dollars per game. Both sides had been known to influence the outcome of a particular game by creative measures, which included, among other things, food poisoning, late-night prostitution, and parties where a variety of hangover-inducing drugs were made available. Basically, almost anything was permitted except direct bribes to the players or the officials.

Anyway, Charles ran better in the morning. The new media center beckoned him. He wanted to try out the cutting-edge fourth-dimensional system. Not only did the three dimensional viewing feel as if he was on the court with the players, the fourth dimension was also supposed to add in the appropriate aromas and motion at the correct time, further enhancing the experience. Charles had a little trepidation as to how that would work for a basketball game, but he was impressed with the demonstration in the shop. Who was he to stand in the way of progress? Besides, if the meeting went poorly, tonight might be his last.

CHAPTER

34

Bob and Warren pulled up to the tennis facility in Bob's specially designed electric golf cart. The cart, unlike the carts used by members, ran unrestricted, could easily reach 45 mph, had a small siren, and a blue neon flashing light. The extra wide tires gave the cart substantially more traction than its normal brothers and the back seat had a security bar that Bob could secure one or two people to. Night had just fallen. A few well-placed spotlights lit the tennis building, making the tennis bubble look like an alien spaceship in the distance. Bob's men found no trace of Tom at the golf course. Warren wanted to talk to John in person. He was sure something was amiss.

Bob blended into the night with his all-black attire, an assault rifle slung over his left shoulder. The weapon was loaded, its familiar weight reassuring the security chief. He had never needed it in the past. Just the sight of the large, well-muscled security guard wielding the deadly weapon was enough to subdue even the most hardened criminal. Bob was sure that Tom would be no problem. Still, it was nice to have.

Bob leapt from the cart while Warren slowly ambled out, grimacing, his limp even more pronounced than when he shuffled into Bob's office. As the two entered the white building, Warren muttered, "I hate tennis, stupid European sport.[37] I used to play. Even now I could beat most of these dopes."

This time of night was usually slow at the tennis facility. Things generally picked up again after dinner as play continued well into the night on the lit courts. As the two passed the tennis pro shop, Bob glanced at Warren's knee and asked him, "Do you want to take the elevator?"

Warren scowled. "What are you talking about? The stairs are much faster." Warren hobbled up the stairs two at a time. He paid no attention to the hostess as he limped toward John's office. John would be waiting for them.

Warren reached John's office and flung the door open without knocking. John looked nervous. Warren could see it on him like a cloak. His white tennis shirt had sweat marks rippling from under his arms. His hands trembled slightly as he abruptly stood up, knocking some papers onto the floor in the process. Bob followed Warren into the office, closing the door behind him, his mood subdued.

---

[37]   Warren's attitude toward tennis was probably influenced by the long drought experienced by American male tennis players. At this point in time, no American male tennis player had won a grand slam event for twenty years. Only five years earlier, a large athletic equipment manufacturer tried to pass off a French-born tennis player as Nick Johnson from Southern California in an effort to recharge American enthusiasm for tennis and boost sales of racquets and equipment. The hoax was initially successful until the night before the French Open Finals when the pressure overcame "Nick Johnson." He was seen streaking down the Champs Élysées wearing nothing besides a beret, screaming "Vive le France" and carrying a bottle of Beaujolais nouveau. Upon winning the tennis tournament the next day, Nick Johnson told the world that he was really Philippe LeBlanc from Dijon, France. Still, the athletic equipment manufacturer tried to cover it up, but the French wine company ran full-page ads featuring a picture of the naked man thanking him for showing his true colors and his support for their wine. Sales of the wine skyrocketed throughout Europe.

Warren glanced around the small office in silence, his face twisted into a disagreeable scowl. John stammered, "Please have a seat." This was the first time he had met Warren, but he had heard his name mentioned, and Bob had warned him not to play any games. Warren was a serious man.

Warren soaked in John's fear as a runner might use a protein bar while in the middle of a long run. He drew strength from it. He ignored John's invitation and slowly stalked toward him, his attention caught by the trophies on the shelf behind John. Picking up the largest trophy, Warren read, "Division A Championship, Ages 13 to 15." Warren swung it roughly on John's desk, making a startling clanking sound against the glass desktop. John flinched at the noise. "Very impressive. It looks like you had quite a promising career."

John looked toward Bob, who stood rigidly at the doorway with his arms crossed. His body looked tightly wound, like a spring ready to uncoil, but his facial expression was emotionless. "I was pretty good when I was a kid, but that was long ago." John answered.

Warren spun abruptly, his face only a few inches from John's. Warren stared aggressively at John, his glare ripping into him with a cold, hard malice. "What happened?" Warren asked, amused.

John looked away, uncomfortable with Warren's close proximity and the smell of his cologne. "I thought teaching was a better career." There was no conviction in John's voice.

"Of course you did." Warren flashed a broad smile and walked toward the other side of John's desk. "Please sit down. Tell us about your visit from Tom. Was he alone?"

John cautiously sat in his chair, hoping that Warren would follow his example, but Warren stayed standing. John sounded more high-pitched than usual. "David the bartender was with him, but I don't think he was that interested in what was going on. Tom wanted to check Jack's equipment to see if he left him anything. I pointed out where Jack leaves his racquets." John pointed to the file cabinet. Bob moved slowly. He opened the cabinet and, with a nod from Warren, examined Jack's three racquets.

John continued, his voice gaining strength as it droned on. "I don't think he found anything. When he was finished I watched them leave, and they both went into the golf cart . . ."

Warren stopped listening. He knew John was lying. A sharp pain suddenly stabbed through his head. Warren's vision blurred. He grabbed the edge of one of the chairs to steady himself. A quick wave of nausea went through him, and then the world refocused again. With the pain in his head throbbing, Warren walked out of the office without a word to John or Bob.

Still unsteady on his feet, Warren staggered to the men's restroom. It was empty, and he locked the door behind him. On random occasions, migraines plagued Warren. Usually there would be some type of warning that enabled him to take medication, but this time, it just appeared suddenly. Warren ran the cold water from one of the four sinks, his hand slipping against the brass faucet. He splashed water on his face. Warren didn't have his pills with him. He had a box of them in his locker, but that was all the way back in the member's locker room at the main clubhouse.

Fortunately, Warren did have his travel case of treatments with him. His hands shook as he removed the black case from his deep front pocket. Warren had never used the treatments to alleviate a migraine before, but he was confident it would work. As far as he could tell, it was close to a miracle product.

Warren hastily pulled on the Velcro tab and opened the case. His vision was blurred around the edges, and his legs felt weak. He unbuckled his belt and let his trousers drop to the floor. After drawing a full dose, Warren injected the fluid into a vein behind his left knee. He didn't notice how puffy his knee had become with repeated injections. Usually he switched to the other knee after a few days, but he had forgotten how many injections he had given himself in his left knee.

Warren felt instantly better. Strength returned to his legs and his vision cleared. Warren tossed more cold water on his face. Feeling relief and a surge of energy, he started laughing and flung water at his reflection in the mirror. Still laughing, he saw his fractioned image through the water drops on the mirror. He could have sworn he saw his father's eyes stare back at him from some of the faces.

Collecting himself, Warren returned to John's office where he found Bob sitting in one of the empty chairs, silently facing John. Bob immediately noticed the dilated pupils, the exaggerated limp, and the wild look on Warren's face. His anxiety reached a new level, knowing that anything could happen from here.

Warren snarled at John. "I will give you one last chance to tell me the truth. Tell me everything you know, and stop with the lies. *Understand?*" He slowly slunk toward John, the threat increasing with each inch.

John's mind told him to do as he was told, warned him that he had no other choice. But it was the tennis match with the governor's kid all over again. Intellectually, he knew what he should do, but his body refused to behave. He would not rat out Tom and David. He could not. John stammered, "I told you everything I know. It's all true." He averted his eyes, avoiding Warren's fiery red glare.

Bob's head sunk noticeably lower. He shook it from side to side in disappointment. Warren glanced at the big security guard and nodded. Bob talked into his phone in a soft voice. Warren smiled happily as two of Bob's men entered the room holding a third person. It was George, his dark skin turning a shade or two lighter than usual. He had a cut on his right arm, and the beginning of a welt under his left eye. Both of his arms were cuffed behind him with plastic restraints. He was obviously terrified, his eyes wide, his jaw clenched.

Bob stood up and directed his men to drop George into the empty chair. George stared at John silently pleading for help.

John's mind whirled. It was one thing to sacrifice himself, but he couldn't abandon George—reliable, dependable George with a song never far from his lips. George was married with two beautiful girls. John had known him for a decade. John settled further into his chair, closed his eyes and hung his head, defeated. It was match point and Warren had just aced him.

"Oddly enough, John, witnesses tell us that this guy was the one that got out of cart number 22." Warren clearly enjoyed himself as he waved at George. Smiling, he said, "Personally, I don't see the resemblance to Tom. It would be hard for you to confuse the two."

Warren hesitated for a moment, soaking in John's reaction. He slowly glided beside John who sat still, his head still hung low, his eyes focused on the desktop. Warren ordered the guard closest to George. "I want you to shoot him in the head when I get to three. If you hesitate to shoot, I will kill you. *Understand?*" The guard nodded his head and drew his handgun from his holster. He held it to George's head, his hand firm and his eyes hard.

Turning to John, Warren said, "You have until three to tell me everything." Warren smiled broadly, "One... Two..."

John shouted as if awakened from a trance. The words came quickly. "Wait a second. Tom didn't go to the golf shop. I sent him to the abandoned curling area on the other side of the property. I asked George to drive the cart to the golf area to confuse you. He doesn't know anything. He was just doing me a favor. Tom's just a boy!" John held his head in both of his hands, eyes still averted, unable to look at George or Warren.

Warren swiftly pulled a six-inch straight blade from a secret hiding place under his pants by his ankle. He violently grabbed John's ponytail and snapped John's head back, placing the knife at his throat. "Was that so difficult? Why didn't you just tell me the truth from the start?" Tears rolled down John's eyes, but his expression was hard and defiant and he stayed mute. He never begged the governor when he was a kid and he would not beg now.

Warren continued. He spoke just barely above a whisper, his lips almost brushing against John's ear. "I can end your life right now. One flick of my wrist and everything you are would end in a bloody heap. No one would really care. I would enjoy it." Warren pressed the point of his blade against John's exposed throat. A small trickle of blood ran down his neck onto the collar of his white shirt.

Warren whispered even lower, just loud enough for John to hear. "If you are lying to me, I will kill everyone you care about. *Understand?*"

John said, "Yes."

Warren yanked John's ponytail harder and violently slashed across his hair. The ponytail came loose, and John's head snapped forward. "I don't like ponytails." It sounded more like a snarl from an animal than human speech.

Looking over at the security guard, Warren said, "Three."

The guard hesitated. He wasn't prepared for that. He glanced at Bob for direction. Incensed, Warren threw the knife at the security guard with a quick flip of his wrist. Bob lunged for his guy, pushing him hard out of the way. He got there a moment late as the knife lodged in the guard's right shoulder. The pain forced the security guard to drop the gun as he toppled to the floor. Warren moved surprisingly fast. He lunged at the fallen man, grabbed the handle of the blade, and twisted it. The security guard groaned loudly. Warren growled. "Next time you hesitate, I will kill you. Good thing for you that Bob is more generous than I am." Warren pulled out the blade from the security guard's shoulder and wiped the blood on the fallen man's shirt. He limped out of the office without uttering another word.[38]

---

[38] George's full name was George Windhiem. George, who was not a religious man, interpreted this episode as a sign from God. He resigned from the club and moved his family out West. Settling in Jerome, Arizona, George came into contact with the cult leader Sammy Soundstem. Sammy's cult believed that God could be

Bob met Warren outside the tennis facility. Bob was furious, but he carefully controlled his emotions. Bob's men were not toys for Warren's amusement. Warren stepped over a line, and Bob would get him back—maybe not now, but there would come a time. Warren spoke to the hulking man. "You have got to upgrade your guys. I'm headed back to the club. I'll be in Room 9. Make sure you take Tom alive. I don't care about the bartender." Warren hopped in a random golf cart and motored toward the main clubhouse, leaving Bob behind, seething.

---

understood under the influence of Peyote (and various other halluci-
nogens) while singing pop music from the eighties. Upon Sammy's
death, George took over the cult and wrote a number of successful
Broadway musicals.

CHAPTER

35

The curling area was located off the internal road, Franklin Freeway. It wasn't really a freeway. It was a two-lane road, but the club like the way the name sounded and that was good enough for them. There was a small parking area and a white wooden sign with gold lettering that pointed toward a trail that headed into the woods. The trail mostly consisted of white gravel with unevenly placed steppingstones. It led a quarter mile into the heavily wooded area on the west end of the property where it unceremoniously ended at the base of a small white building known by members and employees of the club as the Curling Shack or simply the "Shack."

The Shack was the least ambitious building on the club's grounds. It was a simple, white, one-story wood structure. When it was operational, it had bathrooms for both genders, one tiny co-ed locker room, and a small sparsely decorated lobby with a tiled floor, a few round metal tables and chairs, and a fully stocked bar.[39] Tucked behind the Shack was the curling area with two lanes that were only operated when temperatures fell below freezing.

---

[39]   Few members every actually went down to the Shack; however, its rare use and remote location made it a very good place for secret liaisons. On more than one occasion, the coed locker room was used for activities other than its stated purpose, giving it the unofficial nickname "The Love Shack."

Since the curling area had closed five years ago, the windows were boarded up with plywood, the curling lanes themselves were covered with plastic tarps, the white paint bubbled from the wood siding, and the forest had begun taking back its ground. Weeds and long grass encroached on the gravel pathway and brushed against the sides of the building. The main entrance door was locked with a simple metal latch and combination lock. David and Tom easily forced it open, using a sturdy branch for leverage and ambled inside the building to avoid the rain that sputtered down from time to time in spurts.

Tom paced back and forth while David sat with his back up against one of the walls. It was dark except for a small battery-operated lantern that club management had left behind. It flickered to life, casting off a white hazy light that barely lit up half of the room.

The inside of the Shack was in disrepair. The water was turned off. All the fixtures and furniture were removed. Dirt, leaves, and branches littered the floor; and Tom noticed a few empty wine bottles. The place smelled musty and felt damp. The walls were marked with graffiti, standard messages usually exhorting love for one person or another. Tom smiled as he noticed a large scrawled message that said "*Wendy is Hot.*" He immediately recognized his brother's neat handwriting. As Tom glanced around, he also noticed another message that said "*Fourteenth Colony Rules*" written in red spray paint. Tom pointed to the message, and David shrugged his shoulders and beamed one of his bright smiles.

Tom's pacing started unnerving David. "Listen, Tommy, stop all the pacing and sit down. Eat this." David tossed Tom one of the protein bars he had taken from Jack's locker.

Tom caught the bar and sat next to David. "You know nobody calls me Tommy."

David smiled. "I do. You've got to relax for a moment. It will be fully dark soon, and we'll be on our way."

Tom studied the ingredients on the wrapper of the bar in the dim lantern light. "You know there are thirteen carcinogens in this thing. If you eat enough of it over time, it'll kill you."

"Seriously, I don't think that's my biggest problem. I'll take my chances."

Tom had to admit that he had more pressing concerns than dying from cancer and ripped opened the protein bar. He hadn't eaten anything all day and hadn't noticed how hungry he was. "So tell me about the Fourteenth Colony. How did you get involved?" Tom mumbled his words as he munched on the cancer causing snack bar.

"It's the real deal, Tommy. I met Rachel when I was really young. She didn't tell me about the movement until I was sixteen. Someone has to step up and make things right. Things can't keep going the way they are now, and Rachel knows everything. Man, I don't know how she does it, but she seems to be connected to everywhere and to everyone. She wants to change things without violence, which is good for me because you know I am more of a lover than a fighter. I hope she gets the chance." David grinned and shrugged his shoulders, but he didn't look confident. There was something in the way his head hung low and how he averted his eyes that gave Tom a bad feeling.

"But you don't think she'll get the chance?"

"It's hard to say. Things are beginning to move. There are rumors that the ghettos are getting organized. Once violence starts, it will be hard to stop." David shrugged his shoulders. "I'd hate to see it get like that."

"What do you think Jack found on that flash drive?" Tom asked.

"That's the big question, Tommy. If it came from Heather then it probably has something to do with media. There've been rumors for years that they try to brainwash us through television. I've heard they use subliminal messaging on the *Rags to Riches* show. Perhaps he has proof. That would create a stir."

Tom was unconvinced, but he lacked any better ideas. He let silence fill the room for a moment and then asked the question that was most on his mind. "What's the deal with Mary? Is she one of your girlfriends?" He desperately tried to hide the anxiety in his voice, aiming for detached nonchalance, but he sorely missed the target, sounding anxious instead.

David's face turned serious. His usual grin vanished, his eyes pinched together, and his brow creased. "Mary is a very special girl, Tommy. I'd rather we not talk about her."

Tom fell silent. He did not have enough data to know what to make of David's response. After a few seconds of running through all the possibilities, his head started hurting, and he gave up. "Thanks for helping me try to get Jack back."

David's face lightened up once again. "No need to thank me, Tommy, Jack is like a brother to me. I couldn't bail on him. Everything is stacked up against us. You know what I mean—school, jobs, everything. Sometimes I feel like we live on the edge of a razor, one misstep and we fall off, but we can still watch each other's back. I know he would do the same for me." David slapped Tom on the shoulder. "Don't worry so much, we're going to get him back."

Tom shook his head. "I wish I was so confident. We still have to find the flash drive and trade it for him."

"Seriously, dude, we are on the right track. John was brilliant. The flash drive is in Jack's duffel. He didn't take it to Julian's last night. I remember making a joke about it. The duffel is not in the Dungeon and not at the tennis facility. That leaves two places." David held out two fingers for emphasis, "One, he left it in room 9"—he ticked one finger—"or two, he left it in the kitchen last night." He ticked down the other finger. "We practically have it already." David grinned confidently. It was easy to see why everyone liked him.

Tom smirked. "I really don't know how you do it."

"I would say good looks and a sparkling personality, but I don't have any idea what you're talking about." David laughed lightly.

"You never seem to worry about anything. Everything is easy for you. Sometimes I can't get out of my own way. I get lost in all the data and possibilities."

A mouse scurried across the floor. He ran up to the discarded wrapper from Tom's protein bar, sniffed it curiously, found nothing of interest, and ran on. David's eyes focused on the mouse for a moment and then swung around toward Tom.

"I'll tell you a secret, Tommy, something that I've never even told your brother. When we get him back, you've got to promise not to mention it to him or anyone else. I'm serious. I'll kick your karate butt if you spill it." Tom nodded. He thought about reminding David that he knew jujitsu, not karate, but he thought better of it.

"My mom died when she was thirty. I was seven at the time. It turns out that she had a very rare disease. It weakens the arteries that go to your brain, and then one day, you just die. There is no treatment for it and no symptoms. My dad couldn't deal with us by himself so he split. My aunt took us in. She's friendly with Rachel who took a liking to us. Rachel kind of looked after us. Not like a parent, but more like a godmother, making sure we were doing okay."

David paused for a second before he continued. "It turns out that this particular disease is genetic. You inherit it from your mother. One in four people come down with it."

"Sorry about your mom, but if only 25 percent get the disease, then 75 percent never come down with it. Can they test for it?"

David grinned. "There is no test, Tommy. The life expectancy is thirty years. I know I have it. I just know it, so the way I see it, I have to pack in a lot of living before I get to thirty. There is only so much bad luck a person can get. I figure that I've used mine up."

Tom wasn't sure what to say. He wanted to ask questions, but there seemed like no point in it. He made a mental note to check into it after they retrieve Jack. Tom heard a scraping sound outside the Shack. "Did you hear that?"

David bounced up to his feet. "Probably just a squirrel or some other critter. Let's get a move on. It's got to be dark by now."

CHAPTER

36

A very long day was becoming an even longer night for Xavier. He last slept over forty hours ago. He sat as still as a statue behind the antique desk in his home office. The door was locked, and the lights were dim. You had to look very closely to see his chest moving as he breathed slowly and rhythmically. In times of crises, Xavier preferred to shut down every distraction and let his mind spin uninhibited by his surroundings. He usually carried a blindfold with him so he could avoid outside stimulus when his office wasn't available. He liked to be prepared.

He had been sitting like this for the past two hours. Saturday night was usually family night in his home but not tonight. He explained to a disappointed wife and son that he had work to do. His son Bobby was only eleven years old. He was actually one of two children that Xavier had fathered. His older son was off to college with a scholarship from Charles Sheppard. Bobby was quite an accident. Xavier and his wife got caught up in a moment and assumed pregnancy was something in their past. Nine months later, Bobby entered their lives. Even now, Xavier could hear him in the game room playing the virtual sports edition of the latest gaming experience. *Probably soccer*, thought Xavier with a smile. As unplanned as he may have been, Xavier couldn't imagine life without Bobby. He needed to make sure Bobby had a future.

The smile stirred Xavier from his trancelike state. He rubbed his hands across the antique desk's old wood. The president of Roosevelt Bank had once used this desk in the 1930s as he safely guided the bank through the Great Depression. It was sturdy, dark, and impressive. Over the years, it had collected a number of small dents and scratches. He rubbed his hands over these defects affectionately, almost like a caress he might give his wife. Xavier loved the desk even more because of these "faults." He thought of each one as a battle scar. When he closed his eyes, he imagined the old CEO of the bank wrestling with life and death decisions for his company with thousands of jobs and his customers' life savings at stake. Against the odds, he made it through the depression with, Xavier imagined, some help from the old desk. Usually Xavier could draw strength from the old warhorse, hoping that some magic was still left in the wood but not today. Today, the desk was just made of ordinary oak, and he just felt old and drained.

Slowly, Xavier reached for his personal mobile phone. It was the latest design that ensured secrecy. It was impossible to trace the location of the call or the number, at least not until next month when some hacker figured out how to beat its unbeatable defenses. Xavier unfolded a scrap of paper that he had carefully taken from his front right pant's pocket, and placed in on the desk. The neatly folded paper had a telephone number written on it. Thumb shaking slightly, he dialed the number.

On the third ring, a groggy voice answered. "Who is this?"

Xavier breathed deeply, gathered himself, and began. "Hello, Mr. Robinson. You don't know me, but I am a close associate of Charles Sheppard, and there is something we need to discuss."

The voice on the other end of the phone changed from groggy to angry. "Charles Sheppard, how did you get this number? This is my private line."

Xavier concentrated hard on projecting confidence. He forced his voice to be strong and clear. "That is not important, Mr. Robinson. I think it indicates that I am a serious person."

There was a short silence on the other end of the line. Xavier could hear Robinson breathing heavily as if he the large man was pacing back and forth. "Okay, how close are you to Sheppard? When was the last time you saw him?"

Xavier said, "I met with him earlier today."

"Good, then tell me what he was wearing."

Xavier closed his eyes and summoned up a mental picture of Charles from their meeting earlier in the day. "Charles was wearing a white shirt, blue slacks, blue sport jacket, and his antique gold Rolex watch."

Robinson laughed. "You forgot to mention the usual, arrogant, smug look on his face. What's your name and what do you want?"

Xavier had replayed this conversation in his mind for the last two hours, making a continuous mental loop. He followed his predetermined script. "My name is not important. What is important is that I want to end my association with Charles Sheppard. I think he has changed. He has become dangerous." Xavier paused, letting silence fill the line.

"Dangerous. The man is a menace and has been one for years! If you want a job interview, you should call my assistant tomorrow. I will have someone meet with you."

Xavier spoke quickly before Robinson could hang up. "This is not about a job, Mr. Robinson. I have in my possession some very damaging documents that could ruin Sheppard if they got into the wrong hands."

Robinson was indeed pacing back and forth in his media room. He was watching the Knicks-Heat game, hoping that the Heat would rally and beat the Knicks with a big fourth quarter. "Well, you certainly piqued my interest. Why don't you e-mail me those documents at my Phoenix Group e-mail address, and I'll get back to you?"

Xavier looked at the framed picture of his wife and two boys on his desk. It was taken last winter at their country house in Duchess County. There was snow on the ground, smiles all around, and a well-constructed snowman in the distance. It was the only decoration he had in his office. He sighed into the phone. "I thought you were a serious man, Mr. Robinson. I must be mistaken."

"Maybe that was a hasty suggestion. What do you have in mind?" Xavier could hear the eagerness in his voice.

"I will e-mail the documents to your personal server at your penthouse, only. You will have five minutes to review them. You will not be able to copy them or print them during that time. They are saved in a special format. If you attempt to copy or print them, they will immediately erase and I will know and we will have no deal. If you want the originals and the ability to ruin your friend, Charles Sheppard, they will cost you fifty million dollars. I will call you tomorrow to get your decision."

Robinson whistled into the phone. "That is a lot of money. These documents had better be good." Xavier knew Robinson would be reluctant to divulge his private server. He could almost hear the internal debate in Robinson's mind. Finally, Robinson said, "Okay, you have a deal. Send the documents to this address . . ."

37

Bob pulled his golf cart off Franklin Freeway and onto the parking area by the old curling turnoff. His two guys, Larry and Joe, pulled into the parking spot next to him a few moments later. The parking area hadn't been repaired in years. Weeds popped through the cracked pavement, creating an uneven green mosaic. There was an old streetlight, but it was not lit. Why waste electricity on the abandoned parking area?

Bob had patched up Larry's shoulder at the tennis facility with liquid skin sealer that closed the wound and stopped the bleeding. The knife went in deep, and there was a good deal of blood, but it didn't hit any arteries. Larry would have a scar, but Bob doubted that the large dope would mind. He would probably think it was cool and would take off his shirt at happy hour trying to impress girls. Larry wasn't one of Bob's smarter guys, but he was a lot quicker than Joe. Bob was convinced Joe was borderline retarded.

Bob slowly ambled out of his cart. The day's events weighed heavily upon him. He hated unpredictability and chaos. He liked being in control, and nothing about this situation made him feel comfortable. The parking area was mostly dark. The only light came from the golf carts and a small trace of moonlight that offered little help as the moon hid behind a smattering of swirling clouds.

Joe said, "I hate this place. The whole curling area reminds me of those zombie movies where people come back from the dead to eat everyone." To further make his point, Joe did his best zombie impression, walking stiffly, and moaning quietly.

Bob was in a surly mood, and Joe only made it worse. He stared hard at him. "Who cares what you think? Keep it up and you'll have a lot more to worry about than zombies. I promise you that. It's just an old shack in the woods. Break out your flashlights."

All three took out their sturdy yellow flashlights. Bob carried his assault rifle while Joe and Larry both held automatic pistols—more than enough stopping power for anything they would find out here. Bob pointed his light at the sign indicating the trail to the Shack. "There is only one path out to the Shack. Keep alert. I don't want to be surprised by Tom and David coming at us."

Joe flipped off the safety on his gun and swung it out in front of him in a shooter's stance, obviously enjoying himself. Bob shot him a look. He spoke sharply. "Listen, both of you. I don't want any shooting unless they are armed and they threaten you. Joe, if you start shooting at these kids for no reason, I am going to rip your head off." For emphasis, Bob raised himself up on his feet and expanded his chest, making him quite a bit larger than Joe who was no small man himself.

Joe dropped the gun to his side. "I got it, boss. No shooting unless we got to." Bob gave him one last menacing look for good measure.

The three headed down the gravel trail to the Shack. The trail was just wide enough for two people walking side by side, but in this case, they walked single file with Bob in the lead and Joe bringing up the rear. The ground was wet from a recent bit of rain. The men ducked around the moist overgrown tree branches that swung onto the path as they marched in silence. Bob gave up any hope at stealth as their boots stomped heavily on the gravel path. They arrived at the clearing for the Shack in a few minutes without any surprises.

Bob started to feel a wave of relief. So far, there was no sign of Tom and David. He hoped that they were long gone. If at all possible, Bob hoped they were off property and out of Warren Scott's reach. Bob regarded the Shack closely as he slowly swung the assault rifle from side to side, silently instructing Joe and Larry to flank him as they approached the white dilapidated building. As he got within a few feet of the door to the Shack, Bob's heart sank. The door had been forced open. From the looks of the metal latch, the split in the wood was fresh. Bob hadn't realized just how much he was hoping that Tom and David had gotten away.

Bob gathered Joe and Larry toward him. The boarded-up windows prevented him from looking inside the Shack. Bob whispered, "There are three doors going in the Shack. I'll take this one, Larry goes around toward the west, and Joe goes around the east." Looking at his wristwatch, he said, "In sixty seconds, we all go in. Kick open the door and go in loud. Remember, absolutely no shooting unless they are armed and threaten you." Joe nodded his agreement, eager not to anger his boss.

The three men broke up, and each went to his assigned door. Bob's heart started racing. He wasn't worried about his own safety. He wore an armored vest and couldn't imagine Tom or David shooting at him. He just hoped that they didn't do anything stupid. He stared intently at his watch, the second hand moved extraordinarily slow. A cool breeze blew a few raindrops off a nearby tree that landed on his cheek. He reached for the doorknob. Still twenty seconds left, and then he heard the side door crash in. Joe jumped early. Bob lunged through the front door, shouldering his way into the Shack, assault rifle sweeping back and forth.

Three shots rang out. They echoed loudly in the small confines of the Shack. And then two additional shoots followed the first three. Bob swung the flashlight across the room. He couldn't find Tom or David. He only saw Larry and Joe. Larry held his right arm, grimacing in pain. His gun had fallen on the floor.

"Where are they?" Bob shouted. Joe stayed silent while Larry moaned, sinking to the floor. Tom and David were not in the Shack. Joe jumped the time and started shooting like the idiot he was. Larry grunted. "That idiot shot me in the arm."

"You shot at me also. You almost took my head off!" retorted Joe.

"I wish I did," muttered Larry.

Bob hastily checked Larry's arm. The bullet went straight through. He would be able to patch him up well enough with the first aid kit in the golf cart until they saw the doctor at the clubhouse.

Bob turned toward Joe. His blood boiled, adrenaline racing in his veins. Bob had his father's fiery temper. He usually tried to control it by thinking about baking recipes or, sometimes, combinations of flavors that might be interesting. He tried to force the thought of spiced whipped cream and pomegranate arils whipped into a crisp light meringue in his mind, but all he could picture was his hands wrapped around Joe's neck.

"Why did you break in early?" Bob simmered with anger as he crept toward Joe.

Joe shrugged his shoulders. "My watch is busted, so I counted the sixty seconds off in my head. I thought I was right."

Bob paused. It took every ounce of restraint not to rush Joe and pummel him. "Why did you start shooting? I told you no shooting!"

"I thought I saw something moving, and it looked shiny like a gun." Joe pointed toward the discarded protein bar wrapper on the floor, which a small brown mouse was inspecting closely.

"You thought the mouse had a gun trained on you?" Bob couldn't control himself any longer. He launched himself at Joe, grabbed him around the waist, lifted him cleanly, and power drove the big man into the ground. Joe went down in a heap. He rolled on his side moaning. Bob sprung to his feet, and as he was about to bring his boot down on the idiot's big ugly face, the thought of a blueberry rum crème brulee topped with Appleton-spiced Jamaican rum popped into his head. He hesitated with his foot raised menacingly and stopped himself.[40]

---

[40] Immediately after this incident, Bob transferred Joe Jensen to the landscaping staff where he worked for the next five years until his true talents were discovered. One day, while watching a Yankees game, Joe started blurting out statistical information concerning the NY players and their opponents like a machine gun spitting bullets. He was practically a fountain of information that just couldn't stop. The numbers and statistics just flowed out of him. The amazing display quickly became legendary around the club, not just because of the talent, but also because of the fact that Joe, who most people thought was more than a little dimwitted, actually displayed such skill with numbers. Joe's story piqued the interest of a minority owner of the Yankees who was also a member of the club. The club member was so impressed that he offered Joe a job as the team statistician. Joe took the job. He lived at Yankee stadium behind the manual scoreboard, which he also operated during games. He lived rent-free and earned a small living stipend. He retained the job until he died an old man of ninety-five. Joe was famous for creating a new series of statistics for avid baseball fans. His most famous being the highly predictive Moon Shot Stat based upon a complicated formula involving batting average, on-base percentage, slugging percentage, batting average with runners in scoring position, runs batted in, home runs, the remaining term on the relevant player's contract, and the phase of the moon. After Joe's death, he became indoctrinated into the Yankee Hall of Fame next to Derek Jeter.

CHAPTER

38

The clubhouse's distinctive dome shone brightly in the distance as the giant spotlights did their work. The golden rooster looked confident on top of his perch, but Tom had his doubts. The sight of the stately clubhouse lit at night had always impressed Tom in the past, but tonight, he felt differently. Tonight, he got the feeling that the place was stale and rotting from the inside. All the bright white paint and golden roosters in the world wouldn't change that.

Tom and David cleared the woods fifty yards from one of the two side entrances to the clubhouse. The darkness engulfed them in shadows. The pathways immediately surrounding the clubhouse was well lit by antique-looking black metal lampposts that appeared to belong on the streets of London centuries earlier. The side entrance closest to David and Tom was quiet. During the day, members commonly used the door after returning golf carts, but it was late and too dark for that now.

David said, "Man, I hate when my socks get wet. My feet just kinda stick to them." He shook his feet as he walked as if he could wring out the wetness by shaking them furiously.

"I wouldn't go to the Dungeon for a clean pair. We have to be quick. They—whoever they are—will be looking for us."

"No problem, Tommy. I'll go to room number 9. I have the key Jack returned to me yesterday. You check out the kitchen. Don't stop for dinner unless you get some for me!" David grinned, "And we'll meet back up at the employee parking lot on the opposite end of where I parked my car, just in case they're watching it." They agreed on the plan during their hike from the Shack to the clubhouse, reaching the clubhouse by way of a small deer trail that cut through the woods.

The club was usually busy on Saturday nights. The main dining room would be jumping with members and their guests by now. The club always featured live music on Saturdays. Tonight, Mary was performing.

The side entrance was quiet. All the members and their guests were entering the clubhouse through the main entrance. Tom saw parking attendants busily parking cars in the members' lot and jogging back for the next guest. Being a valet was a relatively lucrative job at the club. The cash tips could be generous so long as they didn't scratch any of the cars. Tom scanned the familiar line of cars entering the club, feeling as if he was truly seeing them for the first time. He wasn't sure why, maybe it was his conversations with Rachel and David, but he saw things differently. In the past, the long line of new cars made him envious, the rich and powerful going out for the night. Tonight, he wondered. Perhaps they came to the club because it was the only place they felt safe? Maybe they felt trapped in their wealth and power, surrounded by the rest of America, the part that wasn't doing very well.

As Tom and David reached the clubhouse, they stopped just outside the door. David took in air in gasps from the short sprint. Tom opened the white wooden door, and they both quickly stepped into the hallway. The light was dim. The beige hallway walls were separated horizontally by a long, white chair rail. The top half of the wall was divided by white wooden framing, creating large rectangular boxes. Inside of each box was a picture or artifact relating to the founding fathers of the country, almost all of which were fakes or poorly made copies that were passed off as originals. A staircase leading to the second floor and the guestrooms was on their immediate left. David turned before he launched himself up the stairs. Looking back, he said, "Don't worry, Tommy. See you in a few." He winked and took the stairs two at time full of energy and optimism.

Tom turned down the hallway and headed for the kitchen. The hallway led passed a number of rooms available for members' use. The card table room was typically empty. Tom had never seen anyone in that room, but a few guests were drinking cocktails in the billiard room while two of the four tables were active with members wielding mahogany cue sticks. On his left was the Library, which only had two occupied tables. The diners were probably having a quick bite after playing a late round of golf and were casually dressed. No one seemed particularly happy. The room was quiet. One middle-aged woman sat by herself finishing a salad while she read from an electronic reader. The other table had what looked like a married couple eating dessert. They weren't talking.

Tom hustled along. He reached the side entrance to the kitchen and pushed his way through. *So far so good*, he thought. He didn't see any of Bob's men. The kitchen was busy. The sound of the metal clanking of pots and pans filled the large room with its own particular music, as did the rhythmic sound of cutting and slicing. Tom quickly scanned the kitchen, looking in desperation for Jack's duffel. He spotted the head chef. Antonio was a world-renowned talent from Italy that the club's website boasted about. He had a very keen eye. Nothing went on in his kitchen that he didn't notice.

Tom had met Antonio on a number of occasions when he waited tables. Jack first introduced him two years ago. Tom was more than a little nervous when he first met the tall, thin Italian chef, but he took an instant liking to the gregarious and friendly man. He spoke with an accent, and his eyes always seemed to twinkle with the satisfaction of someone that did what they loved. At least to Tom it felt that way. He was sure that some of the assistant chefs might have a very different assessment.

Tom skirted the salad preparation area and made his way toward Antonio who oversaw the preparation work for tonight's entrees. As Tom approached, he caught Antonio's eye. Antonio smiled broadly, waving both hands in front of him. "Thomas, what are you doing in my kitchen? Have you decided to stop all that silliness they teach you in da school and come work for me?"

"Maybe some day, but not right now. I need a favor."

Antonio waved a thin hand. "Hold on a second, Thomas." He turned to one of the assistant chefs working on a nearby table. "What are you doing to that chicken? You've gotta pound it thin, not play patty cake with it. Put some muscle in it, you, or I pound you. I told you the same ding yesterday."

Turning back to Tom, Antonio smiled. "This is a busy time. What can I do for you?"

Tom's face was tight. He hoped Antonio could help. "Jack worked the event last night. Did he happen to leave his duffel bag in the kitchen?"

Antonio's face turned solemn. Something in Tom's eyes alerted him to the seriousness of the situation. "Let me see. Jack, your brother, came in late. I remember. He usually comes in late, but yesterday, he was very late. I pointed at him. He grinned. He always seems to be happy and hustled da door."

"Did you see what he did with the duffel?"

Antonio hesitated for a second as he recalled a mental picture. "He took it with him. He held it over his shoulder. He no changed into his uniform yet. I no see it this morning." Antonio shrugged.

Tom's face went white, and his legs felt weak. Disappointment leeched most of the energy from his body. Antonio said, "Is everything all right? I like Jack. He's always late, but he makes me laugh, and he loves my lasagna."

Tom's voice was tight. "It'll be fine. Jack just left something in his bag that I need. No problem, Antonio. Looks like you have things cooking around here."

Antonio's face brightened. "You come back later. Tonight's special is glorious. You going to love it. I'll save you a plate. You look hungry." Antonio patted Tom on the stomach.

"Thanks." Tom turned and left the kitchen by the same door he came in, hoping that David was having better luck.

39

Tom charged down the hallway, using long quick strides, hustling toward the exit. Nothing good would be accomplished by lingering in the hallway. As he reached the door, he heard the announcement. The club rarely used the public announcement system, so it immediately registered with him. His blood turned ice cold. The hair on the back of his neck stood on end. "Tom, there is a pickup for you in Room 9." A silky smooth female voice repeated the message three times and then fell silent.

Tom froze, his body as rigid as if it was carved from stone. The message was obviously for him, and it didn't sound like good news. If David found anything worthwhile, he would meet Tom at the parking lot. Something must have gone wrong. David was in danger. The nameless, faceless maniacs must have been waiting for him in the guestroom. Tom should have anticipated it. He blamed himself. His stupidity was going to cost David dearly.

Tom could bolt. He could make a run for it, maybe reach David's car, but he couldn't leave David in danger. Not after he risked his neck to help. David was his responsibility now. Besides, where would he go? He was no closer to finding Jack then he was earlier in the day. Tom took a deep breath and headed for the stairs, certain that he was walking into a trap. He had never been to the guestroom area, but David had described it well enough for him to find it.

Tom reached the second floor and slowly ambled toward the guestrooms. The closer he got to room number 9, the deeper the feeling of dread that overwhelmed him. First, he passed room number 1 and then each room in consecutive order, moving more slowly as he went. Finally, Tom stared into the shiny brass number 9 on the black wood door. His heart leaped forward, uncertain what was behind it. The blood rolling through his body sounded like thunder between his ears. He looked down and noticed small traces of mud at the base of the door that David must have left behind on the soft carpet. His hand slowly reached for the doorknob. The brass fixture felt cold in his grasp as he cautiously turned the knob.

The door wasn't locked; the doorknob turned, and Tom swung the door open. Everything moved as if in slow motion. Tom entered the small guestroom. A bald fiend held David securely around the neck with his left arm while his right hand pressed a handgun hard against his temple, the barrel of the gun indenting against the flesh on David's head. The garish white wristwatch on the man's arm was cracked down its middle, the time off by hours.

The chair near the desk was overturned, but otherwise, the room looked tidy. A fresh red bruise sprouted over David's left eye, the tissue already puffy and it promised to turn into a nasty bruise. David grinned sheepishly as Tom entered the room, trying to mask the fear that obviously gripped him.

Tom had never met Warren Scott before. Even if he had, he probably wouldn't have recognized the man. Warren wore a nasty scowl. The collar of his golf shirt was ripped slightly. Probably the most unsettling thing was the look in his eyes. Sure, they were fiery red and blazing hot with intensity, but there was another quality. There was something truly sinister and deadly inside, almost inhuman.

Warren grumbled. "Why don't you close the door behind you, Tom?"

Tom swung the door shut and stepped forward. Almost overcome with revulsion, Tom tasted bile in his throat. In front of him was an evil person. Not just a bad person or someone who did bad things, but an evil person with no moral compass. Tom had never met a man like this before. He wanted nothing more than to get his hands on him, but Warren held David tightly. Tom's mind spun. He calculated all the times, angles, and distances. There was no way for him to reach Warren or to grab his gun, which now felt heavy and useless in his pocket. Any sudden movement would mean the end for David.

Warren's face twisted into an evil grin. "I am happy you could join us. I want the flash drive that your meddling brother has stolen from me. Hand it over!"

Tom saw nothing in the room he could use to his advantage. "I don't have it yet," he said.

Warren laughed. It was high-pitched and menacing. David struggled against Warren's iron grip and sputtered, "I told you! He needs to go off property to get it." Warren tightened his grip around David's throat. David started to turn red. Tom readied to jump. Even if his chance of success was low, he wasn't going to watch while David was choked to death.

Warren nodded at an open computer tablet that was on the bed. "Take a look at the screen, Tom." Warren loosened up the pressure around David's neck slightly. David took in air in short gasps.

Tom walked carefully to the tablet, wary of taking his eyes off Warren. He looked at the screen and saw a live video feed. It was a hospital room. Tom reached down, grabbed the screen, and brought it close to his eyes for a better view. Jack was in a hospital bed. A private security guard sat next to him. Numerous tubes came out of him, and oxygen flowed through a mask, but Tom was sure it was Jack.

Tom's eyes hardened as he glared back at Warren. All he wanted was to kill him. He would have gladly risked his life for the chance to end Warren's life, but he had David and Jack to worry about. Tom had never felt this way before, but he practically shook with rage, his jaw clinched shut, and his chest tightened.

"Don't even think about making a move, Tom. If I don't call that guard every hour, he will end your brother's little life. He simply shuts off the machine and leaves the room."

"What did you do to him?"

Warren laughed again, spit flying from his mouth. David tried to pull his head away, but Warren's grip was firm as he yanked David back into position. "Me, nothing. He just fell down some stairs. Clumsy boy. What's important is what you will do. Will you save them both?"

"What do you want from me?"

"It's simple, Tom, I need that flash drive, and you are the only one who can get it for me. Bring me the flash drive, and I will swap it for this worthless *bartender* and your brother. You have my word on it, and I never lie." Sweat glistened on Warren's bald head. "If you don't, you will never see them alive again."

Tom picked up on David's lead. "It will take me a little time to get it. It's off property."

Warren curled his lips upward in what was supposed to be a smile, but looked more like an ugly snarl. Tom fought back the impulse to throw up. "I'm a reasonable man, Tom. I'll give you all night. Call me at nine, one, nine, five, five, five, seven, seven, seven, seven by nine tomorrow morning. We'll arrange for the swap then. If I don't hear from you, I'll assume the drive is lost, and I will enjoy myself with these two. It won't be quick, Tom. *Do you understand?*"

David mouthed the words "Find Mary" to Tom. Tom nodded. Head still spinning, Tom backed away toward the door, and Warren gave him his final instructions. "Don't try to open the drive, Tom. I will know if you open it or copy it, and then everyone dies." For emphasis, Warren reached down and clamped his teeth on the top of David's ear and ripped. David shrieked in pain as blood spurted from the open wound. Warren spit out a small chunk of David's ear. Blood smeared on his lips and chin. "Get going, Tom. You don't have much time."

Tom shot Warren a hard, steely look and left the room. In the hallway, he breathed in deeply, his body shaking in anger. He pounded his fists into the wall next to the door in frustration.

CHAPTER

40

Tom entered the main dining room looking for help, looking for Mary. He was out of ideas and low on hope. Dinner was in full swing, and the dining room buzzed with the soft sounds of conversation and the sporadic clinking of silverware tapping against good china dishes.

Two musicians checked their instruments on the raised platform at one end of the room. Mary was not in sight. A small room for visiting band members was located directly behind the raised stage where they could change their clothes and store their stuff.

Tom slid along the edge of the dining room. He noticed a few members spot him with raised eyebrows. No doubt that the club's general manager would receive some complaints about the appearance of the untidy employee out of uniform. Tom could not care less, but he could not afford to make a scene. With a sigh of relief, he made it to the dressing room and pushed his way through the swinging door.

Tom had never been in the dressing room before. Two long brown couches were situated one on each side of the room. They looked old and beat up. Two small metal desks with chairs faced each other toward the back of the room. Each desk was accompanied by a high-powered white light and large round mirror. Miscellaneous musical equipment was set off to the right side of the room near one of the couches.

As Tom entered the room, the conversation ended and was replaced by a forced silence. Everyone swung their faces toward him, the intruder in the midst of a close-knit group of people—six musicians, five men, and one woman. Mary was nowhere in sight. An older man stepped forward. He had dark skin, close-cut curly white hair with small islands of black peppered throughout, and a neat gray goatee. He was shorter than Tom and held a saxophone affectionately in both hands. The instrument looked more like an extension of his body than something manmade. In a surprisingly strong, baritone voice full of authority, he questioned Tom. "Can I help you, friend?"

A large man holding drumsticks rose from one of the couches and walked toward Tom. His gait reflected an aggressive physical swagger. Tom looked directly at the saxophonist, avoiding the drummer's glare. "I need to see Mary for a moment. Do you know where she is?"

The older man shot Tom an appraising look, his eyes slowly rumbling over Tom's body. Tom wasn't sure what he was looking for. Maybe he was deciding if there was any music in him. The drummer stood next to the saxophonist with his beefy arms crossed over his chest, his body language daring Tom to start something. The drummer was only four feet away from Tom. Tom calculated the distance to land a short right kick to his stomach. He would have to follow that up with a left knee to his head to do any real damage, but the other musicians were crowded nearby. Things would get messy after that.

Reluctantly, the saxophonist said, "Wait here a moment." He turned and knocked on a small door in the back of the room that Tom had not originally noticed. Tom heard a soft response from inside, and the saxophonist stepped into the room, closing the door behind him. It didn't take long for him to return, his expression grim. Waving for Tom to step forward, he spoke to him in a low protective voice. "They call me Ray. Mary will see you. We will be just outside this door. We are all family here, my friend." There was more than a little hint of a threat in his voice.

Tom shot Ray his best, sincere, nonthreatening look; said thanks; and stepped into the small room, which felt more like a large closet than a room. Mary leaned against a tiny metal desk. There wasn't much space for the two of them.

Tom stood frozen, momentarily forgetting to breathe. His mind, which was whirling around at hyper speed a moment ago, stopped in mid-thought. Mary looked dazzling in the green dress and had just finished applying her makeup for the performance. Tom had never seen a more beautiful woman. He didn't even think it was possible.

A shudder involuntarily rippled through Tom and somehow, he remembered why he was there in the first place. He desperately needed Mary's help. His jaw ached from being clinched tight, and he was unconsciously squeezing his right hand into a fist.

Mary asked, "Where's David?"

"They've got him" were the only words that escaped Tom's lips. For a moment, Mary's face lost a little of its color, and then she surprised him. She stepped forward, took his right hand into hers, and separated the fingers. An electric shock jolted Tom back to his senses. She spoke in a sweet voice. "Tell me everything. Don't leave out any details." For a moment, Tom was intoxicated by the sweet scent of her perfume.

Tom regained his senses and paced the small room, three strides each way. He started the story from the moment he entered the Dungeon, and tried to include as many details as possible. The entire process proved cathartic. He felt a heavy weight lift from his shoulders as he progressed through the day's events. He hesitated when he got to the part where Warren held David in his grasp but pressed forward with the rest of the story. He did leave out the ear incident but stressed how evil the bald assailant seemed to be. Mary, for her part, wanted to interrupt Tom dozens of times with questions, but she restrained herself, knowing that it was important for Tom to recite events in his own way. Being a good analyst, she didn't want to taint Tom's version of the facts and fought back her own concern and worry about David's safety.

When Tom finished, Mary excused herself from the room, shutting the door behind her. Left alone, Tom felt hot in the small confines of the room. The day's events took their toll on him as he rebuked himself for his utter failure. Thoughts flashed into his mind in staccato fashion, each one grim. He must look like a complete idiot to Mary. Nothing that he had done had worked out. They were no closer to finding the flash drive or getting Jack back, and now David was in serious danger. He wanted to get his hands on the bald-headed maniac. Maybe he could ring the truth out of him? How bad was Jack hurt? He couldn't just stay here. He needed to do something, something worthwhile, but what? Where was the flash drive? What was on it? What would he tell his Mom if he didn't find it? For a fleeting moment, he thought that maybe Mary would leave him behind, thinking he was more of a liability than an asset. Just when his imagination started to spin completely out of control, Mary returned. She smiled lightly at Tom, but her eyes were all business. "Wait for me outside. I need to change, and then we have got to find this flash drive."

Tom's heart jumped. He was not sure why, but he felt a spark of hope. He stepped out of the small chamber and back into the dressing room. The room was empty except for Ray. He was talking on the phone in his baritone voice, asking a replacement singer named Sweet Suzanne to take Mary's place.

He put down the phone and warily looked at Tom. "I don't want to know what you've got Mary into, friend. You look like trouble to me. You keep that girl safe." He stared hard into Tom's eyes. Tom nodded in response. Ray turned and left the room, closing the door quietly behind him.

Mary emerged from the small room wearing a plain black shirt and a black pair of pants. Most of her makeup was scrubbed off, leaving her face slightly pink from the friction. She looked as if she could have been an employee at the club. She had a small red knapsack slung over her shoulder. With a curt smile, she said, "If Jack had the duffel when he entered the kitchen and didn't take it with him when he left the club, the bag has to be somewhere around here. I think we should try the kitchen again. Maybe he left it there on his way out and Antonio didn't notice."

The plan sounded as good as any to Tom. He nodded, and the two left the dressing room. The band had already started performing.

Tom and Mary left the dining room the way Tom came in, around the edges. As they entered the hallway and headed toward the kitchen, Tom heard a familiar voice call out his name. The voice sounded like glass shattering and he stopped cold in his tracks, probably out of habit. He knew the voice belonged to Wendy. He was supposed to be working dinner tonight. He spun slowly on his heels to face the head food coordinator.

Tom expected a scowl and a dressing down from the severe-looking woman. Instead, her usually sharp face was softened with a look of concern. She approached quickly, her eyes scanning the hallway looking for trouble and spoke in a low, hushed voice. "I spoke to Rachel earlier. Is there anything I can do to help?"

Tom was shocked. He didn't expect Wendy to be on his side. Before he could think of what to say, Mary chimed in. "We are looking for a duffel bag that Jack had with him last night. Do you have any idea where it might be?"

Wendy didn't hesitate. "Sure, I remember watching Jack go into the employee bathroom next to the kitchen carrying the bag. I was looking for him because he was so late. When he came out, he didn't have it anymore. He probably left it in the bathroom."

Tom's face broke out in a wide beaming smile. He felt an urge to kiss Wendy in gratitude, something that would have seemed absurd only this morning, but he didn't want to push his luck. "Thanks, Wendy, sorry about tonight."

A pinkish hue tinged Wendy's face. "Be safe. Both of you."

Tom nodded and hustled toward the employee bathroom with Mary at his side, feeling exhilarated, feeling that he had turned a sharp corner. For the first time that day, he felt like he had a chance to get his brother back.

CHAPTER
41

The Knicks beat the Heat convincingly. For some reason, the star point guard for the Heat looked lethargic. Sheppard smiled. Apparently, the young man has a particular weakness for chicken wings, tequila, and classic episodes of the cartoon *Tom and Jerry*. Sheppard arranged for an all-night marathon on the local Miami television station and a visit from some female companions complete with buckets of super hot chicken wings, bottles of top-shelf tequila, boxes of lime, and shakers full of salt. The party lasted until well after the sun came up.

The hour was getting late. Tomorrow was a big day for Charles. He was a fervent believer in sleep. While the rest of his college class pulled all-nighters preparing for final exams, Charles made sure his head hit the pillow at his usual time, believing that he learned while he slept. Sleep permitted his brain freedom to think things through and to remember the details, and the details were the key to Charles's success. But he still had a few phone calls to make before he could consider going to sleep for the night.

Sheppard sat in his office. He used the latest version of video conversation technology. After punching in a few numbers, he saw Clint's large face staring back at him in three-dimensional form. Clint was working at his desk in his home office. Sheppard could make out a half dozen computer screens, most of them ran different programs with streams of data flowing across them like tides across oceans.

Clint looked tired and stressed. Sheppard noticed dark circles under his eyes and Clint's usually perfectly maintained hair was disheveled as if he had been running his hands through it trying to solve a particularly nasty problem. Sheppard started the conversation. "How is it going, Clint?"

Clint grinned. "It's kind of like building a ship in a bottle. Slow and steady as she goes. If you get a little too jumpy, the whole bottle falls and crashes."

"Do you think we will be ready for tomorrow's meeting?" Sheppard peered closely into the monitor. He knew Clint well and wanted to read the man's response.

Clint frowned. "How did I know that you were going to ask me that question? We are going to bump up against it. I'll do my best. I need some help from Xavier, but I've been waiting for him to call me back for an hour." Clint shifted in his seat, which made the three-dimensional image fuzz in and out for a moment.

Sheppard smiled at his friend. No one would try harder. "Well, I can't think of anyone else that I trust more than you two. If there's a way, I am sure you two will get it done. Xavier is under considerable pressure. I am sure he will call you back shortly. Thanks."

"No problem. There is plenty of time for sleeping after the good lord calls you home. Anyway, this type of stuff keeps me young. Now let me get back at it." Sheppard smiled and disconnected the call.

Charles leaned back in his chair and thought of his parents. There was virtually no one left that knew the truth behind Charles's lineage. Charles was not born the biological son of Susan Sheppard and Richard Sheppard. The Sheppards adopted him when Charles's true biological mother and father died in a tragic train accident.

Charles's biological parents worked in the Sheppard garment factory in upstate Pennsylvania. They were in their early twenties when Charles was born. Being young and poor when they married, they were unable to have a proper honeymoon. Six months after Charles was born, they had saved up enough money for a long weekend trip to Philadelphia. It was the honeymoon they had always wanted, complete with a stay at a hotel that provided their own sheets. They spent the weekend carrying little Charles all over the big city and, exhausted, took the train home, hoping for a relaxing return to Watertown, their hometown. Unfortunately, two towns outside of Watertown, the train derailed. The tracks were not properly maintained, the rails slipped, and the train flipped violently on its side. Both parents died instantly, but little Charles, who was strapped into his car seat, miraculously survived the horrendous accident without injury. He was briefly known as the "Miracle of the Pennsylvania Pomegranate." (The Pomegranate was the unfortunate name of the train.)

Neither one of Charles's biological parents had any living relatives that they were aware of or would publicly admit to. An hour before they took the train to Philadelphia, Charles's mother forced her husband to write out a simple will. In the will, they granted custody of Charles to the Sheppards if anything were to unexpectedly happen to them. They had met Richard a month earlier at the company Christmas party. It was a badly kept secret that he and Mrs. Sheppard wanted children and were having a hard time conceiving. Charles's biological parents must have put two-and-two together and, on a lark, thought that the Sheppards would make loving parents for their son.

Susan Sheppard was a religious woman who believed the tragic incident was part of God's unknowable plan. Somehow, Charles's parents were meant to die so they could raise the son that they had always wanted. The adoption was a simple-enough matter to arrange, and Charles Charney (otherwise known as the Miracle of the Pennsylvania Pomegranate) became Charles Sheppard, heir to the Sheppard Companies. He was the only child that the Sheppards would have, and he could not have been more loved if he had been their own biological child.

Richard Sheppard started his career in the garment industry but eventually made most of his money in defense contracts. His first factory was located in Watertown, PA. As he expanded to military equipment, the garment portion of his business became much less important to his overall holdings.[41] Over time, the factory in Watertown began losing business to factories overseas, but he always kept the factory open even though it just barely broke even under the most optimistic accounting system. The more expensive workers in Watertown were extraordinarily loyal and productive. The increased productivity almost made up for the added expense. Almost, but it never mattered to Richard. He loved visiting the factory and never considered shutting it down. He frequently took Charles with him and talked extensively with the people on the line. He infused into Charles the belief that every person was unique and valuable. The size of their net worth, or lack thereof, was not the determining factor of their value. Richard established a generous scholarship fund that he used to send children of long-time employees to college. Many ended up as members of the Sheppard Group as the company expanded. Xavier was the product of one of those scholarships.

Charles never forgot his roots. As he took over the company from his parents, he kept the factory in Watertown open. Even as other factories in the United States lowered their wages to compete against their counterparts overseas, Charles never lowered the wages at Watertown. The factory still breaks even, and Charles always attends the factory Christmas party.

---

[41]   The Sheppard Group's small garment line is most famous for the Sheppard swimsuit collection. In 2035, the company in a joint venture with a military subsidiary developed the technology for spray-on Lycra bathing suits. The technology was surprisingly easy to use, but the swimsuits were extremely revealing, which did not sit well with the religiously conservative, largely overweight country. They did not sell well in America but were very popular on European and South American beaches for decades.

Charles wondered if his parents (particularly his mother) would be disappointed in him. He had expanded the Sheppard Group tenfold from the middle-sized company that he had inherited, but did he do enough for the people of Watertown and others just like them? He certainly made money as the political winds blew the Originalists into office. Charles's mother had always fervently believed that Charles was given to them for a higher purpose, that some divine will was in play that mere mortals were unable to comprehend. Maybe this was his last chance to make things right, to restore just a little bit of balance and give people like his biological parents and the others in Watertown a chance at a better life. He wouldn't mention anything about Watertown in tomorrow's meeting. Tomorrow was all about the bottom line and personal gain, and that was all he thought he needed to win the day.

Tom and Mary reached the employee bathroom in no time. Nervous energy ricocheted through Tom's body as he felt close to the flash drive for the first time all day. This had to be right. Glancing at Mary, he said, "Give me a moment. Let me know if anyone comes." Tom ducked into the shabby bathroom.

His eyes quickly scanned the dirty tiled floor, not seeing anything promising at first. He heard someone in the stall at the far end of the bathroom, humming quietly to himself. Then he crouched down on all fours and noticed a blue denim duffel bag crammed under the sink. Tom smiled as he crawled under the sink to grab the familiar-looking bag. The bag had "Jack's Home" neatly written in Jack's handwriting in all capital letters in bright red marker. Tom reached the bag, yanked the thing loose from under the sink, and smartly bumped his head against the white porcelain sink as it came free. Head stinging, Tom rubbed his hand over his mop of curly brown hair.

Mary burst into the room, startling Tom. He reflexively bobbed his head backward, bumping it into the sink again. "Damn," he said quietly.

Mary looked charged, her eyes wide, and her posture jumpy with anxiety. "I saw Bob coming down the hallway, and he looked angry."

Tom jumped to his feet, slung the bag over his left shoulder, and scanned the bathroom, eager for some type of inspiration. He felt trapped in the small restroom. They needed to find a way out and hopefully avoid the hulking security chief in the process. He had finally found the duffel bag, and he wasn't about to lose it to Bob just yet. It felt heavy on his shoulder, as if Jack and David's life were somehow stuffed into the duffel itself. *Either that or Jack had taken up bowling*, he thought.

Mary said, "There" and pointed to a window at the end of the bathroom on the exterior wall. The toilet flushed, and the stall door opened. One of the junior chefs walked out, wearing his all-white cooking uniform. With a sly smile, he nodded at Mary, winked at Tom, and headed for the sinks. Mary's eyes narrowed and her face turned red.

Tom hustled to the now vacated stall with Mary right beside him. He pushed in the metal door. The window was six feet up and shut tight. It was only half a window, but Tom calculated that it was large enough for him to squeeze through. He heard running water as the junior chef washed his hands while whistling something cheery and romantic. Tom reached up, grabbed the edge of the window, and heaved. The window was stuck. There was a good chance that it hadn't been opened in years.

Tom's heart started pounding. He stood on top of the toilet, straddling the white porcelain bowl with his feet, trying not to notice what he actually stepped on. From this vantage point, he gained slightly more leverage that he applied against the window. Grunting, he heaved upward with all his strength. The window creaked under the strain but wouldn't open. The whistling stopped; the water from the faucet shut off. They were quickly running out of time.

Tom had to break the glass. He grabbed the gun from his pocket. Mary tossed Tom a sweatshirt to wrap the gun into. The bathroom door swung open. Tom broke the glass, shattering the window into hundreds of shards. Even with the muted effects of the sweatshirt, the glass still sounded like an explosion. He was sure Bob had heard it.

Tom swept the glass away from the sill and laid the sweat-shirt carefully on top of the ledge, covering the remaining broken shards, and threw the duffel bag out of the window. Tom hoisted Mary up smoothly in his hands. She felt light in his grasp as adrenaline took over, and he gently guided her out of the window. Tom heard voices outside the bathroom door. Bob was question-ing the junior chef. There was no time. Tom grabbed hold of the bottom of the windowsill and kicked off the toilet. He pulled as his shoulders strained with his entire weight. Mary grabbed and heaved. The bathroom door opened. Tom heard Bob's low rum-bling voice shout like thunder as he wiggled his way through the window and into the April night.

The cool air stung Tom's face as he hurriedly grabbed the sweatshirt and gun and sprinted after Mary. She raced forward, carrying her red bag slung over her right shoulder and the duffel in her left hand. Tom fought the desire to look back at the bath-room window. He heard Bob curse. He didn't think Bob could fit through the window, but the last thing he wanted to see was Bob pointing a gun at them. Tom called out between gasps for air, "Let's go to the parking lot. We can take David's car and get out of here."

Mary veered left toward the employee parking lot without breaking stride. The grass felt wet and spongy under Tom's sneak-ers. He had an almost irresistible urge to check the duffel for the flash drive, but he knew that it could wait. Mary slowed as they reached the edge of the parking lot. Breathing heavily, she asked, "Where's the car?" Her lips and face were flushed with pink from the exertion. Tom tore his eyes away from her with a surpris-ing reserve of willpower. He scanned the lot. "We parked on the south end." He pointed to David's car at the end of the lot. The lot was three quarters full and lit by a half dozen working lamp-posts. Only two cars were parked anywhere near David's car. They were both newer than most of the other cars in the lot. One was a black pick-up truck.

Tom started at a fast-paced walk, zigging through the parked cars. The parking lot asphalt was uneven and cracked beneath his feet. His left leg brushed up against a small hatch back, soaking his pant leg. As they cleared the majority of the cars and reached a gap between themselves and David's car, Tom noticed Julian walking toward them. Mary hesitated, but Tom pushed forward. He cried out, "Hey, Julian, how's it going tonight?"

Julian nervously shifted his eyes around the parking lot. "Tom, I'm surprised to see you." His voice was loud, too loud, and sounded strained.

Tom and Mary continued toward David's car. Julian moved between them and the car. "Why is that?" Tom asked as he slowed to a halt when it was obvious that Julian blocked their path. Tom sensed something was wrong. Julian was one of Jack's good friends and was always quick to greet him with a good-natured smile or a dirty joke. Julian was uncharacteristically tense, and Tom didn't like the way his eyes skittered around the lot.

"They are after you, Tom. They're offering a lot of money for you." Julian pulled his hand from behind his back. He held a knife. Tom instinctively shifted between Julian and Mary, protecting her.

"Come on, Julian, you're Jack's friend. This is all about Jack and getting him back safely. He's been taken and he's hurt." Tom and Mary inched forward.

"Jack's a big boy, and we're talking about a lot of money. I have a lot of debts, Tom. Just come with me quietly, and no one will get hurt." Tom sized up Julian. He was shorter and lighter than Tom, but the knife looked long and sharp. Tom thought he could take him. Unfortunately, another person stepped from behind the pick-up truck, and he cast a big shadow. Tom hadn't met him before. He was built wide like a power lifter and looked strong. He sounded like his mouth was full of rocks and a menacing scowl was written across his face. "Enough money for the two of us to share," he said. Tom noticed that he also held a knife in his right hand. Not quite as long as Julian's knife, but it looked like it had a sharp edge and was well used. The parking lot lights were just strong enough for Tom to notice a thin scar across his right cheek.

Julian shrugged. "Benny is right. There is enough money for us to share. Don't be a hero, Tom, just come with us. Benny will hurt you, if you try to fight."

Benny glided toward Tom. There was no mistaking the sneer across his face. Julian might be reluctant to attack, but Benny was confident and itching for a fight. "They will pay the same if he is bloodied up a bit." Benny lunged forward, slashing the knife at Tom's face. Tom dodged backward and swung a right hand to Benny's solar plexus. Benny blocked the punch with his elbow and thrust the knife at Tom's chest. Tom skipped to the side and landed a right hand to Benny's stomach. His hand hit all muscle. Benny grunted slightly and stepped back. His eyes bore into Tom as if he assessed him for the first time. A thin smile slowly crept across his lips. "This is gonna be fun," he grumbled.

Benny started circling Tom. Tom tried to keep an eye on Mary and Julian, but the hulking man in front of him demanded his full attention. Benny darted forward and swiped the blade at Tom's side. Tom stepped forward, caught Benny's right arm with his left, and brought his elbow across Benny's head like a hammer, but Benny barely flinched. Benny grabbed Tom around the waist and pushed his weight against him. They both went down hard with Tom underneath the hulking brute. Tom got a whiff of the big man and almost gagged. *Not much for hygiene*, Tom thought as he swung his weight around and twisted on top of Benny. Jujitsu was all angles and leverage. Tom brought his head down hard, connecting with a vicious head butt. He landed it flat on Benny's nose and burst it open. Blood spurted everywhere, but Benny still held on strong to the knife. Tom brought his right fist back to hammer Benny when Benny kneed him hard in the groin.

Tom doubled over and rolled off the large man, all of the air knocked out of him, stars materializing in the air in front of his eyes. Benny pounced on Tom, pinning his arms against the pavement and brought his knife up to Tom's face. A victorious smile plastered across his face, his gravely voice loud, "Now let's see if we can make you look pretty like me." Tom was in trouble, and then he heard the gunshot. Benny froze, wondering if he had been hit. All eyes turned toward Mary as Julian screeched in pain. Mary had shot him in the leg. Julian crumpled to the ground. He dropped the knife and both his hands clutched his leg. Blood spattered the asphalt.

Mary trained the small pistol on Benny. Tom shook off the brute and got up. Benny slowly got to his feet. "We were just messing around. No need to shoot anybody." He wiped his bloody face against his shirt. Julian groaned in the background.

Tom sprung forward and shot a left foot to Benny's stomach, bending him over. He then landed a roundhouse right foot to Benny's head. The force of the blow knocked the big man to his knees. He shook his head, dazed, and spat blood.

Tom laughed lightly. "Just messing around, Benny. Try taking a shower." [42]

Tom turned toward Mary. Her right hand shook slightly as she still trained the gun on Benny. Tom said, "Let's go." Pulling gently against Mary's shirt until she lowered the gun and stumbled toward David's car. Tom froze. He said, "Shoot, I don't have the keys. I'm going to have to hot wire it."

Mary reached into her pocket and with shaky hands took out a set of keys to David's car. Tom grabbed them, saying, "I'd better drive." Tom felt a pang of jealousy. With everything that was

---

[42]　"Benny the Knife" had a long-storied criminal career until he was finally apprehended in his late fifties. He was famous for cutting his victims on the face and for his terrible odor.

going on, he still felt jealous that Mary had David's keys. He sighed. *They must be very close.*

Mary got into the car, her face even whiter than her usual fair complexion. Tom, trying to reassure her, smiled broadly, saying thanks. As he started the car, Mary opened the passenger door and threw up.

43

Tom drove the car while dazed; he had no plan and no idea where he was going. He also didn't have a license, but that was the least of his concerns. He knew how cars worked and had all the inputs he needed to safely operate one. The guards at the checkpoints only stopped cars heading into the affluent areas. They hardly glanced at Tom as he drove the other way. He turned the car seemingly at random while his mind raced in all directions, not settling on any one thing. His usually orderly thought process resembled a ball in a Klinko game, capable of bouncing in any direction at any time. He glanced at Mary. She was quiet, but it looked like the color had started to return to her face. Abruptly, he swung the car to the side of the road, pulled to a stop, and shut off the engine. They faced the mighty Hudson River. Tom smelled the smoke coming from the battery-making factory down river just slightly south from Tarrytown. Tom was back in his old neighborhood. He was not sure why, but he parked outside his old house. He shut off the car and stared at the river in silence. The size and motion of the wide river settled his mind, just as it did when he was a child.

"It's been a while since I've been back here," he said as he stared out the window.

"Where exactly are we?" Mary responded, her voice shaky.

"We're outside my old house. We lived here before my father died. After he died, we just couldn't afford it anymore and had to move. The car just seemed to go here on its own." Tom turned from the river and looked at the front lawn of his old house. He shook his head slightly. His mom had loved that garden. Every year she battled a war against weeds and deer, planting different varieties of flowers that she swapped with neighbors. Now, like most of the houses in this neighborhood, the management team pulled up everything and replaced it all with green colored gravel. Tom hoped his mom would never come back and see it this way.

Turning toward Mary, Tom spoke softly. "There is a small nature preserve just around the corner. It used to be a brick-making factory over a hundred and fifty years ago and is now just forest. I used to spend time with Jack there when we were kids. No one goes there. We should be safe for the moment. Let's go, and we can check out the duffel when we get there. We need a plan."

Mary nodded curtly, and they both left the car. Mary carried her red bag, and Tom held Jack's duffel securely slung over his shoulder. They quietly walked to the river, both lost in their own thoughts. No one was out in this quiet suburban neighborhood. Tom noticed a few lights on in some of the houses, but he didn't see any faces. No one watched them as they walked. They arrived at the nature area, and Tom led them onto a small path into the woods.

The preserve seemed exactly the same as Tom remembered it six years ago. He took the small deer path that led to the brick-making factory. The only sign that the factory had ever existed was the outline of the foundation where it once stood. This was where he and Jack had spent most of their time together when they were kids. They fought epic battles of good versus evil usually well into the night. Now it was quiet—very quiet. Tom could just make out the mating call of frogs in the distance.

Trees and vegetation ran wild in the nature area: mostly oaks, maples, and evergreens with grass, weeds, and a few well-armed shrubs with sharp and angry thorns covering the ground. The old deer path that they took still looked active. It was dark, but the clouds had scattered and the moon was almost full, casting off enough light that they found their way. It didn't take long before they made it up a small hill and to the clearing where the remnants of the old factory's cement foundation still stood. From here, the Hudson River was just barely visible above the tops of the leafy trees, but what they could see, sparkled peacefully in the moonlight.

Tom awoke from his trance and sprung forward. He removed a sweatshirt from Jack's bag and placed it on the ground. Smiling, he announced, "Deluxe accommodations, complete with a river view." He waved his arms and bent at the waist in a low exaggerated bow, feeling awkward in Mary's presence.

Mary smiled despite herself and said, "You really know how to treat a girl" and gracefully sat on the sweatshirt. Tom followed by sitting close to her, but not too close. He placed the duffel on the ground between them. He stared at it for a long stretch of time in silence. Suddenly he was reticent about checking it. The almost irresistible urge to rip through it and find the flash drive that gripped him at the club faded with a wave of anxiety and doubt. If that flash drive wasn't in the bag, everything was lost. They would have nothing to trade. He had no doubt that the bald-headed maniac holding Jack and David would kill them both without hesitation.

For a moment, Tom hoped that the flash drive would just pop out of the bag like toast from an old-fashioned toaster. Tom spoke first. "I guess we had better check it." He reached into the bag with trembling hands. The duffel was packed with Jack's stuff. He had some clothes in there, from the smell, not all clean, a few things to eat, and miscellaneous junk. Jack pulled out the clothes first. He carefully dropped them in a pile making sure he didn't dislodge any flash drives by mistake.

Once the clothes were out, Tom shrugged at Mary and vigorously rummaged through the rest of the bag, looking for something that felt hard and small like a flash drive. The light wasn't good, but eventually, his hand closed around something that fit the description, and he pulled. Slowly, he opened his hand and smiled when he saw a small black flash drive. He couldn't help but laugh nervously as he handed the device to Mary. "Well, at least we found the thing," Tom said, relieved.

"Now that we have it, the question is, what do we do with it," Mary's voice was tight with anxiety. "We need a plan," she added.

Tom started pacing, his mind quickly sorting through the possibilities. "We could contact Rachel and ask her for help?" He pulled the old bulky mobile phone from his pocket.

Mary shook her head. "I love Rachel and respect her very much, but this flash drive represents more to her than getting David and Jack back. If we contact her, she will be torn by her desire to save David and Jack and the value it has to push the movement forward. I don't know which one she would choose." Mary thought about her last conversation with Rachel. She was convinced that Rachel would side in favor of the movement, and she was even more convinced that she would take her out of play. That just couldn't happen. Mary needed to see this through to the end. Even though David was older than her, she felt responsible for him. She had to be the one to get him out of this mess, and there was Tom and Jack to think about. She couldn't desert them now, not now. Tom needed her. Besides, she never actually told Rachel that she would sacrifice the others for herself.

Tom tossed the phone at the duffel and continued pacing. "Okay, we are on our own then. I don't see as we have a choice. We need to call the kidnapper and try and exchange this flash drive for David and Jack. Once he has what he wants, I don't see any reason why he would care about David and Jack." Tom looked at Mary for confirmation.

She nodded solemnly but not convincingly. "I don't think we have a choice either."

Tom continued, "Okay, we agree on that. The question is where and when to make the switch." He stopped pacing and looked around the clearing for a moment. A broad smile lit up his face. "I think we make the switch right here. I know the place well. This place is as good as any."

Mary scanned the clearing, her keen eyes straining in the darkness. "I don't know, Tom, maybe a public place would be best."

Tom pointed to an oak tree on one side of the clearing. "Jack and I built a small tree house in that tree. It is perfectly hidden. I can make the exchange, and you can hold up in the tree house. We tell him that we only make the exchange if he comes alone. If we see other people, we call it off. I know the area well enough to make a run for it if they bring lots of people. There is no way to approach without making a lot of noise. If things get out of hand, you can cover us from up there. We'd have the element of surprise."

Mary's face turned a slight shade of green. She did not relish the idea of using a gun again anytime soon, but maybe the surprise would work in their favor. "I'll need to reprogram your gun. I only have two rounds left in mine."

"Done." Tom removed the gun from his pocket and handed it to Mary. He almost forgot he had it. "I wish we had a copy of this drive so we would have another bargaining chip."

Mary smiled. "I can do that. I brought some equipment with me that can copy the flash drive without opening it. They would know right away if it was opened and when it was opened. I can only make one copy. After that we risk the integrity of what is on the drive."

Tom smiled; he felt exhilarated. His spirit soared as hope infused his body. It didn't hurt that Mary was smiling at him, and she was close enough that he got a strong whiff of her perfume. "Will they know that we copied the drive? He was clear that we couldn't copy it."

Mary shrugged. "This is the latest technology from India. I don't think he will know if it was copied unless they really investigate the drive with military level equipment, and even then, it would take a week. I'm sure they wouldn't expect us to have this technology."

"Okay, let's do it." Tom settled down next to Mary while Mary took a small black plastic box out of her red bag. "What do you think is on the flash drive? What is worth all this fuss?"

Mary shrugged. "Rachel thinks the government is about to crack down hard on the ghettos. Maybe there are military plans on the drive?" While Mary made a duplicate of the flash drive, Tom searched Jack's bag, looking for sustenance. He pulled out one protein bar, a bag of potato chips, and two packaged beef jerky sticks. For some reason, Jack loved the dried, salted pieces of meat. Tom explained to Jack all the chemicals and preservatives that were used to make the things, but Jack just smiled and kept eating them anyway. Tom choked back his desire to read the ingredients on the labels. Sometimes, it was best not knowing. Not much for dinner, but Tom added a small bottle of vodka that he found in the bottom of the bag.

When Mary finished copying the contents of the flash drive, she handed the original back to Tom. She smiled at the pitiful display of food. "Now that is the worst-looking picnic I have ever seen." She grabbed two green apples from her bag, adding it to the small assortment of food and shrugged. "Not much better, but that's all I have."

The two split the food and started talking while they ate. Tom asked, "How long have you known Rachel?" He really wanted to ask about David, but he thought it was safe to start with Rachel.

Mary thought for a second. "Basically my entire life. My parents died young and she sort of looked after me. I've been part of the Fourteenth Colony for three years now. She really wants to change things without violence. I totally respect that. It has to change, Tom. We can't have the whole country be owned by a few people and everyone else fighting for scraps. I know the ghettos are turning violent. Either change happens soon, or things will get very dangerous for everyone."

"I just don't understand why nobody told me about the Fourteenth Colony until now." Tom clenched his right hand into a fist. "Why couldn't they trust me? Jack should have confided in me. Then maybe I could have helped—-maybe I could have helped Jack before all of this happened." Tom punched his leg in frustration. "I feel like I don't even know them at all."

Mary's face reddened slightly. She knew more than she could tell Tom. She knew that his family was more involved in the Fourteenth Colony than he suspected, but that was Rachel's job to tell him the whole truth. All she managed to say was, "I'm sure they trust you. Rachel wouldn't have brought you in if she didn't trust you. They wanted you to join the movement because you wanted to, not just because they were part of it. You have other options and choices."

Tom's face brightened. "When we get Jack back, we are going to have one long family discussion."

Mary smiled and changed the subject. Tom watched her closely. He studied the details of her face and the cute way her eyebrow raised when she was adamant about making a point. If there were a form to sign to join the Fourteenth Colony, he would have signed it right there and then. He believed in what she was saying, but she could have been speaking gibberish. He was lost and would follow her anywhere. All thoughts of his contract with ICS were driven from his mind. If someone asked him, he wouldn't be able to remember what the initials stood for.

"So, was that the first time you shot somebody?"

"What gave me away? The throwing up?" Mary smiled, and Tom felt another jolt of energy. They talked for the rest of the night—not really about any one thing but whatever flowed into their minds. They shared a lot in common. Tom was passionate about the sciences. There were definite rules of action and reaction even if they were not completely known yet. Every experiment was repeatable, and Mary was passionate about computers and hacking. To her, it was a game with winners and losers, but all the data and methods were systematic. The two were not exactly the same, but they were similar. Some of the conversation was driven by their nervousness about tomorrow while the rest was driven by something else—something Tom couldn't name, but he was happy it was there.

Late into the night, long after the stars had already come out, Tom winced as he twisted his back. Concerned, Mary asked, "What's wrong with your back?" Tom thought back to the staircase in the cemetery from earlier in the day when he hurt his back protecting Mary from his clumsiness. It felt like a lifetime ago. "I must have banged it when that smelly oaf fell on me," he lied, not wanting to remind Mary of the accident.

Finally, feeling a little sheepish about his lie, Tom asked, "Speaking of oafs, did you call me a clumsy oaf when we were in the tunnel earlier today?"

Mary chuckled. "Could you blame me? That was oaf-like behavior."

Tom never asked Mary about her relationship with David. He was close a few times, but the words always seemed to fight their way back into his mouth before he could utter them.

They drank sparingly from the vodka and finally got sleepy. As the conversation died down, Tom felt a sharp edge poke him from one of his pockets. He reached in and took out the photograph of his family that he had taken from Jack's locker earlier in the day. The picture had been taken at just about this spot. He flipped over the back of the picture and saw Jack's neat handwriting. He wrote one simple word on the back. "Home." Tom thought it might be important, but he was tired, and it would be daylight soon. He closed his eyes and fell asleep to the rhythmic sounds of the frogs in the distance.

CHAPTER

44

Mozart filled the house as the sun's early morning light softly beamed through the windows. Warren was already awake and in his bathroom. He didn't get much sleep last night. When he closed his eyes and his mind eventually settled into an uneasy slumber, he kept having dreams about his father, Franklin. And they weren't the nice type of dreams that he tried to think about from time to time about the last time he saw his father—the vivid memory of his hands around his father's bloated throat watching the light go out of his eyes—but the bad kind, the kind where his father looked at him with those disapproving eyes, always telling Warren how useless he was, how Warren wouldn't amount to anything, and how he had wished he was never born.

Warren had already taken a double dose of his treatments. Usually, they filled him with energy and power, but this morning, he felt a little hollow and sluggish. He stood in front of his bathroom sink, frozen by an unreasonable fear. He grasped the edge of the sink with both hands as he felt an icy chill flow through his body. He was afraid to look in the mirror. He desperately wanted to do anything but look at his reflection. Still, he feared that he had no choice. Summoning up his courage, he stared hard into the monitor. He didn't see himself looking back, but he saw his father staring back at him with those wide black eyes filled with hatred. He yelled, "Damn it, I killed you!" and punched the monitor with his left hand, shattering the glass and cutting his knuckles. The illusion broken, he now saw fragments of his own reflection staring back at him, crooked and misshapen.

Blood dripped from his hand, but he paid little attention to it. After wiping it with a hand towel, he left the bathroom and made his way through the coat closet and downstairs to visit his guests. One of Steven's men had stayed overnight to guard Heather and David. *Bob should be here in a few minutes*, he thought. As he walked down the stairs, he wasn't concerned that he hadn't heard from Tom yet. There was still plenty of time. The boy would call him. He was convinced of it.

Once this mess was finished, Warren had some choices to make. Yes, he could offer this information to the fat man. He would love it. It would give him a way to end Sheppard's career and drive his rival into ruin. Yes, the fat man would reward him greatly for this information, but Warren was growing tired of his relationship with Robinson. Perhaps he could sell the information back to Sheppard. He would pay dearly for it. But why limit himself? There were other fish in the ocean. Perhaps it was time to ally himself with a new group and use this information to forge a new bond? There were all sorts of very powerful people that would love to have a relationship with him. *Yes*, he thought, *I need to make a list.*

Suddenly, Warren had a bounce in his step as he approached the guard who groggily sat on the stool outside of the two interrogation rooms in a dazed, sleep-deprived stupor. Warren ignored him and walked into the room where Heather was being held. She was asleep in her chair with her head slumped over on the table in front of her.

Warren slammed the door behind him loudly, waking Heather with a start. "Hello, princess," Warren said. "I hope you had a restful night."

Heather's head shot up with her eyes wide open with terror. She shook her head slowly, tears rolling down her cheeks. The harsh white light in the interrogation room did not flatter her. A red bruise marred her left cheek, and her eyes were puffy from many hours of crying. A cut high on her left shoulder was smeared with dried blood, and her hair was stringy with dirt and sweat. Her skin had lost that healthy brown glow that she had earlier in the evening and was now a pasty white. Warren had spent some time with Heather last night, draining the spirit out of her. He knew that she didn't have any useful information to give him, but he enjoyed playing with her, sure that she enjoyed it also, even if she would not admit it.

"Where did we leave off last night?" Warren asked, taunting the young woman.

Heather responded, "Please, I don't know what you want. I can't tell you anything else."

Heather slumped her head on the table, lifting both arms protectively over it as Warren loomed over her. The cuts on his left knuckles had stopped bleeding. The blood was now just dried, dark-red crusts. As Warren reached out to touch Heather, his earpiece rang. Warren backed up and answered the phone. "Yes?"

Tom's voice answered him. "I have what you want. I am ready to make the switch for Jack and David. What assurances can you give me that they are still okay?"

Warren smiled. He heard the weakness in Tom's voice. "Assurances, my dear boy. I don't need to give you any assurances. Their lives are in my hands."

Tom paused for a moment. Warren left him in silence, enjoying the moment. Finally, Tom spoke, "Bring David with you and the video feed of Jack. I will give you the flash drive when you give me David and let me know where to get Jack. I want you to come alone to the nature area in Hudson Hollow behind the baseball field near the river. Do you know where that is?"

Warren laughed. "The nature area in Hudson Hollow behind the baseball field? I know exactly where that is, but I won't be coming alone. I'm going to bring Bob with me. I imagine that is acceptable to you. I will be there in two hours. You haven't been a curious little boy and opened the drive, have you?"

"No."

"Good, don't disappoint me. At the first sign of trouble everyone dies. *Understand?*" Warren disconnected the line, happy with himself. Things were looking up as he looked down his pointy nose at Heather who still kept her head down, covered by her arms. "I am very sorry, princess, but I don't have time to play with you right now. Maybe later." Warren turned and stalked out of the room, locking the door behind him.

The guard stood at attention. Warren said, "Cuff the bartender. I am going to take him on a trip with me shortly." Warren hobbled up the stairs, looking forward to his meeting with Tom. *Did the boy really expect me to let them all live?* As Warren reached the top of the steps, his surveillance system kicked on with a warning tone. He saw Bob's extra large head staring into the screen. Warren shuffled to a keypad and pressed a series of numbers that opened the front door and let Bob in.

Bob wasn't as enthusiastic about helping Warren on this assignment as Warren would have guessed. He assumed that Bob was worried about performing up to Warren's standards. Warren agreed to pay him a bundle of money for his efforts, and Bob reluctantly accepted. *He certainly isn't Steven, but he has proven himself handy more than a few times,* thought Warren. Warren couldn't imagine that Tom was much of a threat—nothing more than a boy in the woods.

Warren was lost in thought when he heard Bob clear his throat. "Looks like you cut your hand, Mr. Scott. Do you want to bandage it?" Bob nodded toward Warren's left hand.

Warren looked at the injury and shook his head. "Nothing but a small accident. It doesn't bother me."

Bob scanned the open layout of the house. This was the first time he was in Warren's home, and a cold chill went through his body. "Do we have a plan?"

Warren smiled. "Yes, we most certainly do. I just spoke to Tom. We are going to meet him in a nature area in Hudson Hollow that I am familiar with.[43] We meet them in two hours. It's a small place, but it's private enough. We'll bring David and a tablet. I trade them David and Jack for the flash drive. You should be back at the club for lunch."

Bob thought for a moment, unconsciously swinging his assault rifle in his hands. He wore all black with a black Kevlar vest. It was better to be prepared than be caught off guard. "Sounds easy enough. Do you want me to call in some of my other guys?"

Warren shook his head, his expression turning tart. "We don't need anyone else. I hope you haven't gone soft on me. We're just talking about a boy in the woods."

Bob grunted. "We make the switch after you check the flash drive, right?"

As Warren limped toward the kitchen, he waved his right hand, which was already bandaged from yesterday. "Of course. It should be easy enough. I don't need the boys once we have the flash drive."

Bob watched Warren limp away. The man was spiraling downward very quickly: the dark circles under his eyes, the veins popping on his bald head, the cuts on his hands and his head, the ugly welt on his arm, and the limp that got worse by the hour. Still, Bob had little choice. He could not refuse Warren Scott and the money was good, actually very good, but he had a bad feeling about this.

---

[43]   Warren was indeed familiar with this particular nature preserve. He tried to purchase it and some additional land on behalf of the Phoenix Group four years earlier but was overwhelmed in a maze of legal paperwork that he could not extract himself from. Robinson titled his proposed project for this sleepy suburban neighborhood as "Sweet and Sexy." His plan combined an adult entertainment center complete with strip club, casino, and a dog track plus a state-of-the-art chocolate factory for his candy-making company. He ended up building his Sweet and Sexy Center in New Jersey just outside of Summit.

CHAPTER

45

The morning light was bright and welcoming. Charles Sheppard breathed in deeply as he left his apartment building. He had a restful night's sleep and was eager to start his usual Sunday morning jog. Scotty, his longtime bodyguard, accompanied him. Scotty was long and thin and one heck of a runner. He ran last year's New York City marathon in well under three hours.

Sheppard wore a blue pair of running shorts, a white shirt with the latest whisking technology, a runner's watch with a white rubber band, and an orange New York Knicks hat to keep the sun off his face. Scotty wore gray sweatpants, and a gray sweatshirt with a dark blue V-shaped stripe. He would sweat a good deal in all that clothing, but it hid an arsenal of weapons that he carried with him just in case. The two were connected by earpieces that permitted them to talk to and hear each other relatively easily.

Sheppard stretched his calves and his back on the sidewalk in front of his apartment building. The street was mostly deserted at this time in the morning. He looked over at Scotty and said, "Looks like a nice day. Are you ready for a little run?"

"You know me, Mr. Sheppard. I would rather run than do anything else." Sheppard shook his head grinning. No matter how many times he told Scotty to call him Charles, he never did. It just wasn't his way.

Charles headed down the street toward the park at a slow paced walk. The condo was only two blocks south from an entrance. Seven thirty on Sunday was a premium time for Central

Pepsi Park. Only those that paid a substantial sum were allowed in the park this early in the morning on Sunday. Sheppard was, of course, a premium member. He smiled at the guard at the checkpoint and flashed him their identification badges. The guard scanned the badges, checked that the photographs matched the two men, and let them through the turnstile.

The sun was bright, and the day looked like it was going to be a warm one. Sheppard preferred to run along the paved path doing a small loop, running north up the west side, crossing over to the east side, and eventually crossing back to the west side where they started. The park looked empty. Premium membership was pricy. Sheppard heard Scotty's voice in his ear. "How long do you want to go today, Mr. Sheppard?"

Charles felt good, but he didn't want to be tired for his meeting later that morning. "Five miles today, Scotty. Later this afternoon, you can come back and run another twenty or so."

Scotty chuckled. "Not today, Mr. Sheppard. Five will do just fine." Charles knew that Scotty was lying. He would run later in the afternoon. He couldn't help himself.

Charles started running at a leisurely pace with Scotty ten feet behind him. The park was in bloom. The colors were vivid: sharp greens and bright flashes of yellow and orange flowers splashed the park with color. The air quality actually seemed better than usual, probably no need to take in fresh oxygen when he got back home, but he would take the precaution anyway. Charles liked to clean out his lungs after a run with special sanitized air. It was well worth the precaution; lung cancer was rampant.

Charles heard Scotty's voice in his ear. "Nice basketball game last night, Mr. Sheppard."

"I enjoyed it very much myself. I think we have a chance to make the finals this year. If we add just one more player, I think we'll have enough talent."

Scotty grew up in Los Angeles and was a lifelong Lakers fan, but he rooted for the Knicks when his loyalty to the Lakers wasn't in jeopardy. "It looked to me like the Heat point guard had a bad night, Mr. Sheppard."

Scotty didn't know anything particular about Sheppard's arrangements before the game, but Charles heard the questioning tone in his voice. "I hope you aren't accusing me of anything, Scotty." Charles chuckled.

"Not me, Mr. Sheppard. I know a lot better than that."

Charles pushed forward at a faster pace. The blood started pumping as Charles focused on his breathing. It felt good to work his muscles, churn his legs and arms. *Too much time indoors*, he thought, when he heard Scotty again.

"Mr. Sheppard, I don't like the looks of this runner approaching us from behind. He looks dangerous to me. Do you want me to stop him?" Scotty's normally cool voice was tinged with concern.

Charles looked into the side monitors of his cap. The cap had tiny cameras that were triggered by the direction of his eyes. Charles slowed slightly and said, "You're right. He's a very dangerous man, but don't stop him. Let him approach me."

Charles shut off his earpiece as Steven ran up beside him. Charles greeted the security man. "Good morning, Steven, how goes the fishing?"

"There is never enough time for fishing. I last went out a month ago for a midnight bluefish run. I got myself a few. Nice fish, they put up a decent fight."

Charles glanced at Steven. He wore a suit that was very similar to Scotty's. Charles had no doubt that he was also heavily armed. Charles was certain that he would already be dead if Steven's motivation was sinister. "I have never gotten the hang of fishing. Maybe some day you can show me the fine points."

"I would think you would be a natural," Steven responded.

Scotty closed the gap between the two. He ran awkwardly with one hand tucked under his sweatshirt. Sweat accumulated on his brow and soaked his sweatshirt as he looked for the first sign of trouble.

Charles kept running with Steven at his side, ignoring Scotty. "I imagine we have more to talk about than fishing. Have you grown tired of your association with Robinson yet?"

Steven edged closer to Sheppard, his blue eyes sparkling. "I am supposed to kill you. Right here during your run. I told you that you should change your routine, but you are almost as stubborn as he is."

Laughing, Charles pushed on. "Am I to assume that you have taken me up on my offer? Are you ready to switch teams?" Charles stopped running and looked Steven in the eyes, his feet still moving in place. Charles was breathing heavily and building up a good deal of sweat while Steven looked cool and dry.

"Yes, Mr. Sheppard, I would like to end my employment with Mr. Robinson and join the Sheppard Group. There is only so much a man can take." Charles detected nothing but sincerity from Steven.

"We have a deal then." Charles reached his hand out. Steven hesitated for a second and shook Charles's hand with an uncharacteristic smile on his lips.

Charles resumed his running. Steven matched his pace and stayed close to his side. "Robinson is not going to be happy when he finds out that his plan failed, and I am not riddled with bullet holes. Have you taken all the necessary precautions?"

"Yes, Mr. Sheppard. I've cut ties to everything that he knows about me. He won't find me until we want him to."

"Great, Steven. Join me for the rest of the run. We have a number of things to discuss, and call me Charles from now on."

"Yes, Mr. Sheppard."

CHAPTER

46

Mary was safely tucked into the old tree house high up in the oak tree. The makeshift ladder that Jack had built when they were kids was missing a few rungs, so Mary had to stand on Tom's shoulders to climb up, but he didn't mind; and from the clearing, it was impossible to see Mary even if you knew where to look. From that height, Mary had a reasonably good view of the nature area. If she saw trouble, she was supposed to throw a stone at Tom as a warning, giving him the opportunity to make a run for it.

Tom slowly paced along the crumbling cement foundation, his long legs taking looping strides. He tried to slow his racing heart, but so far, he had little success. He had no idea how this meeting would play out. There was a chance that the bald-headed fiend would release David and Jack. He certainly wouldn't need them anymore once he got the flash drive, but a lot could go wrong, and Tom had a hard time shaking the feeling that the kidnapper was evil. And evil people did bad things because they enjoyed them.

The sun was high, and the sky was blue. A few wispy, white clouds lingered in view. The nature area was relatively quiet; Tom heard a few rustling sounds from squirrels and birds flying in and out of trees. Tom swatted away a pesky bee that buzzed around his head, and then he heard the unmistakable sound of human beings trudging through the woods. Adrenaline kicked in as the sounds grew nearer. They were coming from the baseball field, the opposite direction than Tom had expected.

To Tom's overactive imagination, the noise sounded as if an army of black clad security officers approached. He glanced nervously toward Mary. No signal yet, and then Warren, Bob, and David poked through the woods and entered the clearing. The bald-headed man held David in front of him with a handgun pressed against the back of his head while Bob marched cautiously on his right side with an assault rifle pointed at Tom. Unknowingly, the bald-headed fiend held David directly between himself and Mary, providing effective cover.

Duct tape covered David's mouth, and his left ear was wrapped with a white cloth bandage. The bruise on his cheek had turned purple, but other than that, he didn't look particularly worse than he did when Tom last saw him. Upon seeing Tom, he shrugged his shoulders sheepishly.

The bald-headed man pushed David forward. He limped badly and had a crazy look in his eyes. His right hand was bandaged, the bruise on his right arm oozed puss, crusted blood stained his left hand, and the scar on his head was bright, red, and nasty. He looked tired as if he hadn't had much sleep, his face flushed with fever, his eyes having dark circles under them. Tom worried that the kidnapper had gone insane. Insanity wasn't a great thing under these circumstances. It certainly made the man unpredictable.

"Good morning, Tom. You can call me Mr. Scott. I hope you have lived up to your side of our bargain. I brought David, and I have the video feed of your brother in the hospital room." Warren pulled a tablet from behind his back and held it out to his side. "Come on, Tom. Come and take a look. I'm not going to bite." Warren chomped down with his jaw in an exaggerated bite motion and squealed a high-pitched cackle at his sick joke.

Tom nodded at Bob, who looked nervous as he watched Warren and David closely. Stepping to the side, Bob put a little distance between himself and everyone else. Tom cautiously stepped forward. He glanced at the monitor and saw Jack in the hospital bed. A security man sat ominously close to him. Tom felt angry. He drew upon the anger as a substitute for confidence and removed the flash drive from his pants pocket. "Tell me where to get Jack, let David go, and I will toss you the flash drive."

Warren cackled again. He dropped the tablet. It landed softly on a small clump of crabgrass. This time, he cuffed David on the head with his gun. The blow was sharp but not meant to cause any real injury. David grimaced and lurched to his side, but Warren kept his left hand on him. "It doesn't work like that, Tom. Just toss me the flash drive, and I will confirm that you haven't opened it. After I confirm that everything is in order, you can have David, and I'll let you know where to get Jack. *Understand?*" Warren's left eye started twitching; both eyes were bloodshot. Warren looked poised to strike David again. This time, Tom was sure he would do real damage.

Tom's vision clouded over angrily, but he had no choice. He tossed the flash drive to Warren. His eyes followed its looping path as if it floated in slow motion. It landed at Warren's feet. Warren's lips turned up into a sneer. "You see, Bob, I told you it would all work out easily enough." Warren picked up the drive and the tablet, and keeping one eye on Tom, plugged the drive into the tablet. Awkwardly, he punched in a few keystrokes and brought up the contents.

Tom's heart beat like a drum, each beat deafening. He stared intensely at Warren's face. Warren's eyes twitched faster. Sweat glistened on his forehead. The veins on his bald scalp came alive. Warren laughed. This time, it wasn't a menacing cackle but a loud high-pitched sinister laugh. Something was wrong.

Warren pointed his gun at David's head, anger flowing from him in waves. "You play games? I asked for the flash drive from the other night, and you give me names and pictures of past *Rags to Riches* contestants and their true identities and locations in

Europe. This is not want I want! This won't buy David and Jack's freedom. Everyone knows that show is a fake. I want the right flash drive! You have ten seconds to produce it, or everyone dies!"

Tom's mind whirled into hyper speed. He had the wrong flash drive. His chest tightened, and his stomach lurched. "*One!*" Warren started the countdown.

Tom had to think of something. He fought back the avalanche of panic that threatened to overcome him and let his thoughts roam. "*Two!*" The photo that he took from Jack's locker flashed into his mind. What did the writing on the back say again? *Home.* "*Three!*" Jack's clue on where to find the flash drive was "where home is." The two things couldn't be a coincidence. "*Four!*" Warren was enjoying himself.

Where exactly was the photo taken? He summoned up the image in his mind. "*Five!*" They were on the corner of the foundation, just a couple of steps from this spot. "*Six!*" Tom shuffled over a step or two and frantically looked on the ground. It must be here somewhere. "*Seven!* Time is running out, *Dad!*"

Tom kicked over some stones and saw an old brick from the brick-making factory. Written on the brick was one word in Jack's neat block letters: "Home." "*Eight!*" Tom bent down and turned over the block. Underneath it was the flash drive, identical to the one he had tossed to Warren. Tom thought he heard Warren's finger tighten against the trigger. "*Nine!*"

Tom grabbed the flash drive and yelled, "It's here! Don't shoot!" Warren stopped, his hand trembling, a satisfied smile across his face. The pressure on the trigger relented. "Toss me the drive, Tom, or everyone dies, and this time, there will be no countdown."

Tom tossed the drive to Warren. Bob had moved fifteen paces away from Warren and trained his assault rifle firmly on Tom, but his eyes were glued on Warren. Warren plugged the drive into the tablet, and almost immediately, a look of relief washed over him. His eyes stopped twitching. He pressed a few more keystrokes and smiled up at Tom. "Good boy, Tom. Was that so hard?"

Tom breathed heavily, his body still charged with adrenaline. "You have what you want. Now let David go!"

Warren dropped the tablet, but he kept hold of David. "I'm not letting anyone go. Bob, shoot him!"

Tom froze. He had no plan for this, and David was still in between Mary and Warren. Events slowed. Tom focused on Bob's face. He didn't respond right away. Warren bellowed, "*Bob!*" Bob's eyes hardened, and he swung his assault rifle at Warren. Bob rumbled like thunder. "No! They did what you asked. You told me you would let them go!"

The twitch returned to Warren's face, his smile replaced by a sneer. "Don't be a fool! You can't stand up to me!"

"Someone has to. They did what you asked. Let them go! *Understand?*" Bob's hand shook with anger as he aimed the assault rifle at Warren.

Warren laughed again. "What are you going to do? You are not that good a shot. You can't stop me!" Warren's lifted the gun to David's temple with a satisfied grin on his face.

Tom felt a sharp pain in his shoulder. *What the heck was that?* he thought as he tried desperately to come up with a plan.

Sheppard greeted his guests as they slowly arrived for his late-morning meeting in the basement of an exclusive wine shop that he owned on the upper west side. The retail space on the street level was expansive and richly appointed, the wines displayed in rows of dark, wooden wine racks. Featured wines were set apart in the middle of the store on wooden crates or empty casks. The back of the shop had a long, cherry wood bar where the store served wine during many of their special wine-tasting events. Rows of differently shaped, sparkling, crystal wine glasses hung from the ceiling behind the bar. All the Sheppard Wines were sold here along with a number of other premium wines both domestic and international. Straw covered the floor. The ambiance resembled a Tuscan wine shop from an earlier age. The store did a brisk business with a consistent flow of people, but it was closed to the public on Sundays.

A black, metallic, spiral staircase led to the basement. Sheppard often hosted intimate parties and gatherings in the basement of the store. The vaulted ceiling, the walls, and fixtures were all made of heavy dark wood that at one time had been used to make wine casks. The main room featured a large, round, wooden table made of distressed cherry wood. Six wooden armchairs were evenly set around the table. Off to one side was a plain oak serving table with assorted pastries, coffee, and tea arranged neatly on top of it. The main room was separated from the wine storage area by an antique bronze fence and gate. A few casks of Sheppard Wines were visible behind the gate, plus a number of crates of other wines that were sold in the store. Soft white light emanated from sconces that were attached to the walls and an adjustable chandelier that hung down in the center of the table. The lights could be adjusted to a flicker mode, giving the impression of candlelight, but that wasn't appropriate for this meeting.

Sheppard burned incense in the corners of the main room, providing a light smoky scent to the meeting. This meeting was for principals only. Bodyguards and anyone else brought to the meeting were required to stay upstairs in the wine shop. The only exception was Xavier, who stood nervously by the serving table tending to the desires of the guests.

Sheppard was dressed casually. He looked relaxed in a crisp yellow dress shirt, sharply creased blue slacks, a black leather belt and shoes, and his lucky antique Rolex wristwatch. He smiled at each guest, offered a few words in greeting, and directed them to Xavier for refreshments. All five guests were important, but one man stood out, Jacob Benjamin. Jacob was a short, thin man in his late seventies with thinning white hair, sharp features, including a small pointy nose, and bright blue eyes similar in color to Sheppard's that sparkled behind round wire metal frames. He was the majority owner of a conglomerate that owned large chunks of the American economy. He was normally very quiet and reclusive, but Sheppard had forged a friendship of sorts with him over the past few years. He proved to be an outstanding chess player, being every bit Sheppard's equal. Jacob was, by far, the wealthiest person in the room and had influence and contacts that surpassed everyone else, including Charles Sheppard. His support was critical to Sheppard's plans, and Sheppard had no idea what Jacob would do.

Sheppard welcomed the rush he felt before the meeting as if it was an old friend. His concentration narrowed, his mind sharpened, and his pulse quickened. As the last guest arrived, Sheppard nodded toward Xavier and addressed all five businesspeople. "Good morning, my friends. Thank you for taking the time to meet with me on such short notice. Please take a seat. I don't want to keep you any longer than I must."

Sheppard watched the four men and one woman settle into their seats carefully. They were wondering what all the secrecy was about. He felt a mix of anxiety and anticipation as he began his presentation. "We are at a tipping point in American history. We can not continue the way we are headed, and it is costing everyone in this room." That got their attention.

Sheppard launched into his talking points. "The middle class is shrinking so quickly that it will be completely gone within a decade. The 'American Dream' is practically dead. Americans have been turned from the most creative, innovative, productive people on the planet to little more than disinterested working drones. Without the realistic chance to move up the economic scale, Americans have lost the drive to compete and innovate. There is only so long, the government can keep the illusion of economic mobility alive. After decades of facing a stacked deck, the American worker is surrendering. Effectively, there is no one left to fight for them, and the worst part is that, they know it."

The chief of a large automotive company spoke first. She was in her late fifties. "My workers show up, but productivity is way down. It is hard to get them motivated. Some of my competitors have taken to adding drugs into the water at the worker camps to stem violence, but that reduces energy." She looked around the room knowingly and then continued, "The biggest complaint is about healthcare. Even though I have clinics for my employees at my factory sites, they complain that all their savings go for healthcare for an older member of their family. They can never get ahead, so they've given up."

A younger man in his late forties spoke next. He had bushy blonde hair and was in charge of a large technology firm. "I get the healthcare complaint all the time, but I have a real problem with the educated ones. These people are supposed to be the brightest of the bright, but after a few years of working, they figure out how hard it will be to pay back their corporate scholarships, and they completely lose their motivation and drive. I'm thinking about actually forgiving some of their education costs just so I have a chance to compete."

The mutual complaints continued for a while as Sheppard led the discussion about the many problems facing the country and the wealthy. He talked about the declining GDP, lack of domestic demand, food safety,[44] environmental concerns; and he even lingered on the National Parks.[45] The conversation was lively. All the guests shared their concerns except Jacob Benjamin who

---

[44]   Food safety was a very big problem in 2041. With the abolishment of food inspectors and regulators, the food industry was left to police their own activities. Not surprisingly, there were many dangerous outbreaks of food contamination diseases. To counteract uncertainties, many wealthy Americans purchased expensive food inspection equipment that needed a trained operator. Ordinary Americans were left with what was known as the Sniff Test.

[45]   The Protect American Treasures Act of 2029 was purportedly enacted to raise revenue, decrease spending on national parks, and protect access to the most valuable natural treasures. The act did little to raise revenue as the "bidding" process was a politically run affair used to reward supporters and cronies. The national parks were separated into two categories. The first category was open for sale with unrestricted use. Most of these properties were depleted of their natural resources (logging for timber, mining for minerals, or drilling for oil) and either developed for commercial uses or left abandoned or destroyed. The second category were designated "National Treasures." These properties were sold with the restriction that they be used only for tourist-related activities. Gambling Conglomerate Inc. purchased a number of these sites and honored the letter of these restrictions by constructing mega-sized casino resorts. The largest casino ever constructed was built spanning the Yosemite Falls. It wasn't until the Restore the National Parks Act of 2052 that the country purchased back many of these sites, restored them to their natural state, and reduced admission fees, enabling the vast majority of Americans to see them.

maintained a stony silence. Xavier handed out some data and analysis, but no one needed to see it. They knew what Sheppard knew—-that America was declining, and if something was not done to change the course quickly, the once great country was destined to drop out of the ranks of developed nations.

Sheppard felt good about his progress, but he needed more. It was not enough to know what was right or where one's own interests lie under the circumstances, but they needed a reason to act and take a risk because at the end of the day, he was asking them to take a risk. So, confident that he had won the intellectual argument, he started talking about violence. "Many of you are aware of the violence that took place in the Midwest ghetto uprising a few months ago, but I guarantee you that it was just the beginning. The ghettos are becoming better armed, more violent, and more organized. Unless we push the country to change, all they need is a spark to revolt. Just one spark and I think they now have it."

Charles paused and watched the reaction in the room carefully. The faces that had been nodding in agreement a moment earlier, looked shocked and frightened. The head of ICS spoke, "Charles, what are you getting at?"

This was the moment where Sheppard needed to hook them. He rubbed the face of his Rolex for luck. Everything was on the line. Just as Sheppard was deciding exactly which course to take, Clint stumbled into the room. The large man looked haggard, but he was smiling, telling Sheppard all he needed to know.

Sheppard spoke quietly, making sure he had everyone's full attention. "I know that each one of you is aware of the government's medical research into brain cancer. The government has developed a simple and easy vaccine. I am sure everyone in this room has taken that vaccine. I am also sure that you all are aware of the government's decision to only make the vaccine available to certain tax-paying members of our society." Sheppard knowingly glanced around the room; everyone leaned forward in their seats. "Well, you should also know that someone has documented proof of those decisions, including the government's decision to limit the access to the vaccine, and has already sent that information to a rebel group. If the poor and middle class believe that the government withheld access to the vaccine from them, the response will be severe. An armed revolt is certain to follow."

Sheppard heard a discernable gasp from one of his guests. "No, Charles, you must be joking. Who would do such a thing?" The ICS chief's voice was loud and questioning.

Sheppard paused for dramatic purposes and said, "Carl Robinson."

Two guests simultaneously said, "No, it can't be," and shook their heads.

"I know your personal feud with Robinson, Charles, but surely you must be mistaken. I have known him for years. He may be a snake, but he would never do anything like this," said the technology chief.

Sheppard smiled. "I know it is hard to believe, but I think he believes he has much to gain by aligning himself with the ghettos and underground. He is selling us all out to get ahead. I had a tip that he was up to something like this, and I've investigated him personally." Sheppard glanced at Clint. "Clint is my head of computer security. Clint, why don't you show us what you were able to find?"

Clint placed a round black box in the center of the table. Using a remote hand-held device, he activated it. Greenish holographic documents appeared in the air, floating above the device, rotating slowly. After a few moments, Sheppard nodded to him to speak. "Mr. Sheppard asked me to investigate his concerns a few weeks ago. I tried to access Robinson's private server and see if there was anything there, but it seemed like I had bitten off more than I could chew. His security is as tight as Fort Knox, and then I got lucky." Clint smiled, but the mood in the room was somber. Everyone studied the floating documents intently. Clint continued, "I got a sliver of daylight and pried open the security a little bit and found the documents that you have in front of you. These files were stored on his personal server account. The last file indicates that the documents have been e-mailed out." Clint finished.

The technology chief spoke, "Do we know who he sent the files to?"

Sheppard answered, "We are in a bit of luck on that one. He sent it to a group that calls themselves the Fourteenth Colony. They are highly connected to the ghettos, but to date, they have taken a nonviolent approach to their business."

"I've heard of them. They are very elusive, but everything I've read says they are nonviolent," explained the automotive chief.

The ICS chief spoke up. "I see the files, but I don't believe it. I don't mean to cast any accusations at you, Charles, but Robinson wouldn't do this. I am sure there is some mistake or some other explanation." Charles saw two other heads nod in agreement with the ICS chief. Jacob Benjamin maintained a neutral expression, his arms crossed against his chest.

Sheppard was failing. He needed everyone to leave this room committed to action, or nothing would be accomplished. Even worse, Robinson would have the proof that Sheppard was the one behind the leak to the Fourteenth Colony all along. He would fail under that type of scrutiny, and it wouldn't take long.

Charles was seldom short of words. He rubbed the face of his watch and tried to think of an argument that would work, when his thoughts were interrupted by the familiar voice of his personal assistant coming from his earpiece. "I am sorry for interrupting you, sir, but Carl Robinson is on the line, and he says it is urgent that he speaks to you. He is very persistent."

Charles smiled. Maybe this was divine providence? Perhaps his mother was right, and God had an important purpose for him after all. It was time to go all in. Charles activated his microphone and spoke to his assistant, "Put him on hold for a minute."

Charles rose and all the eyes in the room turned toward him. "Well, I have just received a phone call from Robinson himself. Let's put him on the video monitor and see what he has to say."

Xavier's face turned white as Charles pressed a button and a concealed video screen fell from the ceiling.

CHAPTER

48

A stabbing pain ripped through Warren's head; the pain was more excruciating than any previous migraine. He heard noises and voices. He couldn't identify them specifically, but he was sure he heard his father and his mother and maybe a few others. If all the noise would just die down for a moment, he would be able to think. There was precious little room left for his thoughts. *What in the world was wrong with Bob? Did he want more money?*

Sweat dripped into his eyes, stinging him, blurring his vision. He felt all the effects of a full-blown migraine. His eyes blinked against the light. Shapes became fuzzy. He held onto David tightly as if he was his last anchor to reality. *Everything is going to work out well,* he told himself over and over again. He just needed to make a list.

What to do? The passion gripped him hard. He not only wanted to kill everyone, but he *needed* to kill them all just to quiet the voices. He glanced over at Tom. All he saw was his outline frozen in space. *Maybe he should start with him?* The voices rose louder. They liked the idea also. One killing and the pressure might ease up, and he could deal with the rest, but the noises kept getting louder like an oncoming freight train. Bob was saying something, but it was hard to hear him through all the chatter.

Suddenly, three other black shapes joined them in the clearing. Maybe Steven came to set things straight? Warren cried out, straining his eyes for some clarity. "Steven, is that you?" *What in Jefferson*[46] *was going on here?*

Briefly, his vision cleared. Standing in the clearing were three armed men that Warren had never seen before. The leader had an assault rifle much like Bob's. All three had their weapons drawn, covering everyone in the small area. The leader spoke to Bob. "What's going on, Bob?"

Bob glanced at him but still kept his gun trained on Warren. "Hey, Ted. I want to shoot him dead like a dog, but I'm not that good a shot. I don't want to hit the man he's holding."

Ted laughed. "You're right. You are not that good a shot, but I am." Bob lowered his rifle.

Ted shouted, "No, we are not with Steven. We work for Mr. Benson. Do you remember him?"

The noise rose again. His father's voice shouted at him. "Don't be a loser. Shoot everyone!" He thought he heard Michael's voice and others that he had killed as well. Warren fought for control. *Benson, he owes me. I told him about the affair with his wife.* Warren found his voice. "Doug owes me. How did you find me?" *How mad could he be that I hadn't returned his calls? He worships me.*

"Mrs. Benson told us where to find you. I guess she overheard you talking on the phone."

Warren laughed uncontrollably. He lost all grip with reality. All the shapes morphed into that of his father. They laughed at him. They were staring at him with those wide, black, disappointed eyes. Warren muttered to himself, "I'm sorry, Father." Tears flowed down from his face.

---

[46]   During this time, many Originalists used Thomas Jefferson's name as a vile curse word as his view on government did not coincide with their own. The Jefferson memorial in Washington, DC, was replaced three years earlier in 2038 with the Reagan Memorial, complete with a life-sized statue of Ronald Reagan waving a cowboy hat in the air, and riding a horse.

"Mr. Benson wants to tell you that you should have learned your place in the world. Don't touch things that don't belong to you." Ted aimed his assault rifle, squeezed the trigger, and Warren's head exploded. The dead man lost his grip on David and fell backward with a thump. David remained standing, his body shaking uncontrollably.

"We had better be going, Bob. It wouldn't do to linger." Ted turned and led his two other men out of the clearing.

49

The shot sounded like thunder. Warren's head shattered in an eruption of crimson. David remained standing, blood and bits of Warren splattered on his shirt. Ted and his team left the way they came. Bob slowly shuffled toward David, his gun held low, pointed to the ground. Tom moved to join them. "Are you all right?" Tom asked David as he closed the gap.

David was a few shades paler than usual and slow to respond. "I think so." He started frantically brushing off bits of Warren from his shirt. "That guy was as ugly on the inside as he was on the outside."

Bob moved quietly. He grabbed the tablet and both flash drives and pocketed them. David said, "Thanks, Bob. I really owe you one."

Bob swung his head in a tight circle around the clearing for another moment and turned toward David. "You had better leave quickly. Someone is going to report that gunshot." Bob turned to leave, and Tom grabbed him by the arm.

"Do you know where we can find Jack?"

Bob thought for a second, his expression melancholy. "I have no idea. I haven't seen him. I hope you find him. I like Jack, but sometimes, these things just happen." Bob shook off Tom's hand and left the clearing the way he came in.[47]

Mary dropped from the tree and raced toward them. For a fleeting moment, Tom thought she might embrace him, but she ran toward David and gave him a firm hug, tears in the corners of her eyes. "You are just so damn lucky."

David shrugged. "How many times have I told you? I've got only good luck left."

Mary separated from David and punched him in the stomach. The shot had some force behind it, and David bent over. She looked at Tom and jumped into his arms, wrapping tightly around him. "You were awesome, Tom. I couldn't believe it when you found that flash drive. I was so worried."

Tom lost himself in the embrace for a moment, but only briefly. He pushed Mary away gently. His voice cracked with emotion. "Now I've lost the only lead we had to find Jack. We lost the flash drive. We have nothing to trade for Jack even if we find the right person to negotiate with." The weight of his failure drained all the energy from Tom. His shoulders sagged as exhaustion gripped him, and he dropped to the ground on his knees.

Mary spoke cautiously. "I think I know where they have Jack. Before I went to the club last night, I did some satellite surveillance on Warren Scott's home. An ambulance from Hoffman Westchester was at his house. They probably have him in the premium wing."

---

[47] Shortly after this incident, Bob retired as head security officer from the club. He apparently came into some money and started a bakery called Betty's Bakery where he met his wife and raised two children. The bakery was modestly successful. Bob worked the cash register and an elderly woman named "Betty" was visible as the baker behind the unusual desserts. Most of the regulars seemed to understand who was the talent behind the baking, and few batted an eye when "Betty" was replaced, from time to time, by a new, gray-haired lady.

Hope flooded over Tom. All was not lost. David said, "Let's get going. I've spent enough time with this maniac as it is."

Tom grabbed Mary's arm roughly. "Why didn't you tell me this last night? Is there anything else I should know?" His voice came out hot and angry.

Mary looked defensive. Red color rose in her cheeks. "I didn't know for sure that they had Jack, and besides, there was nothing we could do with the information anyway. We had to make the trade."

Tom was still angry. Glaring at Mary, his face pinched tight in anger, he said, "We have David back now. You don't need to help anymore. We can drop you off somewhere."

"It's not like that, Tom! Of course I am going to help find Jack!"

Tom turned his back on Mary and marched back toward Warren's body, some of the anger ebbing from him. "I think you're going the wrong way, Tommy," David asked, confused.

Tom ignored him and went through the pockets of the dead man. He found what he was looking for, Warren's citizen card and a fat roll of money.

Tom hustled back toward David and Mary. He looked only at David. He was still too angry to look at Mary. "We're going to need a way into the hospital. I'm sure this guy has the premium health insurance. We can use his card to get past the guards. The money might come in handy also."

"Brilliant," said David as they quickly trudged their way through the nature area. Tom and Mary both marched in silence, each one simmering.

50

Charles lowered the lights, and upon his suggestion, everyone moved toward one end of the room. They all had a view of the video screen, but from that angle, Robinson would be unable to see them. This was the biggest risk Charles had taken in his life. He forced his mind to focus and concentrate on the task at hand. He had to get Robinson to implicate himself but not mention how he got the documents. If Robinson mentioned that he bought the documents from someone that worked for Sheppard, then all blame would fall on Charles and everyone in that room would see through his plan. It was a crazy risk, but it was the only way Charles could win, and he could not lose.

Sheppard engaged the video screen and smiled at the larger-than-life–sized face of Carl Robinson staring angrily back at him. Sheppard knew what buttons to press. "Good morning, Carl. I am happy you called."

Robinson's large round face flared with anger. It twisted into a nasty scowl, blotched with red patches. "You are like some type of hideous cat, but you have lived your last life now. I don't care what type of deal you made with that traitor."

Sheppard cut Robinson off, careful not to let him rant in some direction he couldn't control. "I hear you have some damaging documents in your possession, Carl."

Robinson hated to be called Carl, and it especially infuriated him when Sheppard did it. Laughing, Robinson replied, "I most certainly do, Sheppard. I think explosive is a much better word, don't you?"

"Carl, I don't think you should disclose them to anyone. A lot of people could get hurt."

Robinson laughed angrily, the skin on his face and chins rolling with the laughter. "A lot of people are going to be hurt, Sheppard, particularly you and all your allies. My plans are already underway. You can't stop me."

Almost there, thought Sheppard. "You are not going to gain very much by distributing reports about the government's cancer research."

Robinson stopped laughing suddenly, his face turning fierce and ugly. "I have everything to gain, Sheppard, and you have everything to lose. The end won't be pretty for you."

Good enough, thought Charles. "We have nothing further to discuss. You are making a big mistake, Carl." Charles disconnected the call.

The room filled with a heavy silence as Charles regrouped his composure. He slowly turned to face his guests, his expression grim and confident.

The ICS chief spoke first. "I wouldn't have believed it without seeing it. He looks like he's gone mad."

The automotive executive added, "He's a very dangerous man. We need to stop him before he does any more harm."

All five faces nodded in agreement. They all looked scared and in need for some leadership.

Jacob Benjamin spoke for the first time that morning. Everyone turned toward him. He had a strong clear voice. "I will call Isaac. He will want to handle this personally." Isaac owned the majority of the Phoenix Group. Even though Robinson ran the holding company, he was only a small minority owner. Isaac spent most of his time out of the country.

Sheppard seized the moment. "The situation is already very serious. Robinson leaked those documents out to one organization already. We need to build an alliance with the Fourteenth Colony and start the country back on a path that will benefit all of us. I have a way of making contact with them, but it is time to know if we are all committed. We need to start here today. From here, we can expand the circle, but I need to know if we are a united group on this."

Starting with Jacob Benjamin, each person in the room agreed with Charles. They were committed to change. The right type of change, even if they wanted it for the wrong reasons.[48] Charles was spent. The meeting was over. As the guests made their way up the spiral staircase, Jacob Benjamin lingered behind. He held Charles's arm gently and whispered in his ear. "Quite a bluff you ran, Charles. I'll remember that the next time we play chess."

---

[48]   The secretive group took the name "The Wine Merchants." Each member of the group was given a different variety for a codename except for Charles Sheppard. He was known as Baucus.

Tom heard sirens in the distance as they cleared the nature preserve. The noise got louder as they reached David's car. David held out his hand for the keys, but Tom was still angry. "There is no way I'm going back in that trunk. I'm driving. We can all squeeze into the front seats." Tom swung open the driver side door without waiting for a response. David and Mary squeezed into the car next to him. Tom turned the key and drove down River Road away from the incoming police sirens.

"What do we know about this Warren guy?" asked Tom.

"You mean besides the fact that he was a homicidal maniac? I know that he was very connected. Not independently a real big shot, but someone a lot of people feared." David was still wiping off assorted bits of Warren's skull from his shirt with his face squeezed tight.

Mary added, frostily, "Warren Scott was the attack dog for the Phoenix Group. As you probably know, the Phoenix Group is one of the largest companies in America and into a lot of different businesses. His father was a congressman, and I am sure he has top access to medical facilities like the Hoffman Hospital chain."

Tom swung the car onto Route 9 and headed for the hospital. "He said yesterday that if he didn't call in every hour, the security guy would pull the plug on Jack. I don't know if that's true, but we definitely don't have much time. We're going to need a way into the hospital."

"I'll call the hospital as Warren's assistant and tell them to expect us—that they need to see us immediately and bill him for the visit." Mary pulled out her phone and dialed.

Tom smiled as he stopped at a red light. "That should work, but we need an emergency to get in." He reached over and ripped the bandage off of David's ear.

David squealed. "Come on, man, that hurt. Did you have to do that?" Blood squirted from David's ear. Things were getting messy.

"Now we have an emergency." Tom accelerated as the light turned green.

Mary finished the call, yanked a T-shirt from her bag, and handed the shirt to David for the blood. "What happened to your ear?"

"Tommy didn't tell you? That maniac back there chomped it."

Hoffman Westchester Hospital wasn't far from the nature preserve. The facility was a sprawling three-story brick hospital. A ten-foot high, metal, electrified fence topped with barbed wire enclosed the entire grounds. Two armed men manned the guard-house by the sole entrance to the hospital. A heavy metal barrier blocked their way; each guard held an assault rifle strapped over his shoulder. Once they got past the guardhouse, they would need to swipe Warren's card to get into the main entranced to the building and find their way onto the premium wing and Jack.

Tom pulled the car to the guardhouse and stopped at the metal barrier. Two armed guards warily left the air-conditioned guard-house to meet them. White lettering stretched across the front of their shirts stating "Hospital Security" on it. Tom lowered his window. "We need to get in, it's an emergency." He nodded his head toward David who moaned loudly for effect, pressing the blood-soaked shirt tightly against his ear.

The guard peered into the dumpy car carefully. "You can't get in unless you have an insurance card. You know that." He leveled his assault rifle, swinging the nozzle at the car. The second guard stood at a ready position with his weapon trained on the passenger door. They looked as if they meant business.

Tom handed the guard Warren's citizen card, which had Warren's insurance information on it. He also wrapped three one-hundred-dollar bills around the card. "I think Mr. Scott's office called ahead." Sweat rolled down Tom's face. He had no idea if the guard was going to let them in. If Warren's death was already reported, they could have updated his citizen's card, and they would be trapped. His vision kept being drawn to the assault rifles.

The guard cautiously took the card and the bills. He pocketed the bills and scanned the card on his hand-held reader. He apparently got the proper response as his demeanor visibly relaxed. He turned back toward Tom, handing him the citizen card. "This is highly unusual, but for a member of Mr. Scott's caliber, we will make the exception. Drive around to the right. You'll see the emergency entrance on your left." He waved off his partner who lowered his gun and stepped backward as the metal gate lifted.

Tom took the card back, breathed deeply, and accelerated past the gate. He drove around the right of the building past the emergency entrance and parked the car toward the back of the visitor's parking lot, feeling very out of place in David's beat-up compact among all the shiny new luxury cars. Mary had already bandaged David's ear, stopping the flow of blood. Tom grabbed a shirt from Jack's bag and tossed it to David.

David dropped his bloodied old shirt on the ground behind the car. "I never want that back."

"So far so good. Now we need to get through the main doors and into the premium wing. Warren's card should gain us access. We need to hurry."

Tom led the way with David and Mary trailing close behind. They passed by the huge, electric, flat-screen Hoffman Westchester sign with a picture of Bob Hoffman's smiling face on it. He looked better on the sign than in real life. A few people trickled in and out of the main doors. It was easy to tell the difference between the staff and the visitors. Tom hoped they would be mistaken for orderlies or nurses. He swiped Warren's card at the reader by the front door, and the two glass doors swung open with a hiss.

A receptionist with a pleasant, round face, sat behind a small wooden table in the lobby. A small waiting area was off to the left with personal viewing screens attached to the chairs. A gift shop was situated directly across from the receptionist with glass walls to highlight its wares. The ceiling was made of vaulted tinted glass, letting in filtered light without the heat of the afternoon sun.

The receptionist had three flat screens and two keyboards in front of her. She must have doubled as a telephone operator as she wore a headset and paid very little attention to the three as they entered. Tom spotted a directory right behind her. There were three main hallways to choose from, one directly behind the receptionist and two others going in opposite directions. Tom was lost as Mary pulled them to the hallway to the right. She nodded at a large sign written in gold cursive letters, spelling, "Premium Wing."

The three moved with purpose, hoping not to draw any attention to themselves. Tom spotted another gold sign placed outside of an elevator. Apparently, it only had one destination. A card swipe was affixed to the wall next to the elevator that was necessary to operate it. Tom swiped Warren's card, and the doors smoothly opened, revealing a large modern elevator with mirrored walls and marble floors. Once inside, there were no buttons to press. The doors swished closed, and the elevator silently made its way to the premium wing.

"When we get to the entrance, there will be at least one guard. We show him the card and tell him that Mr. Scott wants us to deliver a message to his guest." Tom quickly gave the details of his plan as the elevator stopped at its destination.

The premium wing looked like it belonged in a five-star hotel. Tom saw marble floors, dark wood paneling, and lit colored glass sconces by each door. Double doors made of thick cherry wood with small glass windows stood between the elevator and the patients, and sitting behind a simple wooden desk in front of those double doors was a guard wearing a black cap that said "Hospital Security" on it, with a handgun holstered at his side. There wasn't much activity on the wing, but Tom looked through the windows and saw a few doctors and nurses milling around. He didn't notice any visitors.

As Tom, David, and Mary got off the elevator, the guard stood with his arms crossed. He was taller than Tom with thick arms and a wide chest. His black hair was styled into a crew cut, and he had a close-cut black curly beard. He must have weighed two hundred seventy pounds. "Can I help you?" the guard said in a surprisingly quiet, high-pitched voice, his eyes darting and calculating.

Tom stepped forward, handing him Warren's citizen card. "We need to deliver a message for Mr. Scott. He has a guest staying in the wing." The guard took the card cautiously, carefully scrutinizing them. The big man swiped the card. Tom froze as the guard said, "Stand over to the side," the tone of his voice lowered by an octave, his eyes narrowed angrily. They must have updated Warren's status.

David stepped toward the big guard, his hands outstretched and a friendly smile on his face. "Is there a problem? We are in a bit of a rush."

Tom saw things move in slow motion. A small club magically appeared in the guard's left hand. He quickly swung it at David who didn't have time to do much but shift his head back. The club connected, but a lot of the sting was taken away as it glanced off David's head. Still, David went down. Tom saw an opening and lunged at the big man, taking him off balance. He drove the guard's back into the edge of the desk and brought his right elbow down across the man's head.

The guard fell to his side, dropping the club on the ground, and reached for his handgun with his right hand. As the guard pulled the gun out of his holster, Tom grabbed the big man's hand with both of his, and viciously smashed it on the marble floor, knocking the gun from the guard's grasp. It slid across the smooth floor, stopping ten feet away as the guard heaved Tom off of him with a mighty push with his left arm. Tom and the guard both sprung to their feet.

The guard grabbed the edge of his chair with both hands and lifted it menacingly toward Tom. Tom moved quickly, swung his leg, sweeping out the big man's legs, and toppling him with a thump. The chair clattered loudly to the floor. Tom reached for it, but the guard grabbed him by the ankles, tripped him up, and sent him stumbling headfirst. David whistled and tossed Tom the small club. He caught the club in one motion and brought it down on the back of the guard's head. The blow was quick and hard. The collision made a loud thumping sound. The guard's eyes roll in toward the back of his skull as he collapsed, unconscious. David grinned, fresh blood smeared across his forehead.

Mary said, "Tom, you better go find Jack quickly. I'll tie up the guard and disable the elevator. We won't have much time. There should be another elevator that we can take inside the wing that they use for patients."

David leaned heavily against the desk, looking queasy. Tom grabbed the "Hospital Security" hat from the fallen guard, saying "Good thing you're the lucky one" to David. David grinned and shrugged his shoulders. Tom turned and raced into the premium wing. He was close now. He could feel it.

Jack opened the doors and strode quickly into the wing. He resisted the urge to bolt down the hallway. He hoped the "Hospital Security" hat would be enough to avoid any questions as he put his best, nasty expression on his face and avoided eye contact with anyone. Each door actually led to a suite beyond. Most of the doors had no names on them. Tom's heart raced as he went further down the hall. His palms were sweating as he neared the end. Just two more doors left, and then he saw the name on the last door to his right "Jack Scott."

CHAPTER

52

This was it. Tom's body surged with another dose of adrenaline. He raced into the suite, calling out his brother's name. The room to his left was designed like a living room with couches, soft chairs, flat screens, and a soft shag rug. It was empty. The door to his right was open but led to an empty bathroom. Tom charged forward into the patient's room.

The hospital bed was empty. Tom saw a middle-aged, medium-sized man, armed with a holstered handgun, holding Jack's shirt and pants. The shirt was streaked with red. Tom couldn't hold it together anymore, his temper got the best of him. He charged forward at the man, shouting, "What did you do to my brother?"

Tom tried to tackle the security officer, but he was too fast and sidestepped the charge, shoving Tom in the back. Tom crashed heavily into the wall. Tom spun and attacked, throwing a volley of left and right punches, leg kicks, and one badly missing head butt. The man was lightning quick; he anticipated each attack before Tom made a move, easily blocking or avoiding each punch or kick. Finally, the rage fully took over, and Tom heaved a right hook with all his strength at the man's head. The security man swiftly stepped back and shot out his leg. Tom tripped over his foot as his momentum thrust him past the security guard. He fell hard to the floor, his head colliding against the marble tiles. He stayed on the ground for a moment, letting his head clear and the stars fade.

As he struggled to his feet, exhausted, he heard the security guard say, "Tom, I have been sent here to help you." The voice came out flat and emotionless. Tom heaved himself up on the edge of the bed and looked into Steven's face. "Who are you, and where is my brother?"

Steven still held Jack's clothes, and before he could respond, Mary and David entered the room. David had a new bandage on his head and right behind him followed Rachel and another man. He looked familiar, but Tom couldn't place him. He was thin, of medium height, had white hair, tanned skin, and was very well dressed. He had his arm around Rachel's waist, and Tom noticed an antique gold Rolex wristwatch.[49]

Tom shook his head. He didn't know what was going on. Charles Sheppard spoke to Steven. "They disarmed the hospital security guard at the double doors. Take care of him, and we will need a way out in five minutes." Steven tossed Jack's clothes on the bed and left the room.

Rachel stepped forward, her face full of concern. "Tom, we moved Jack for his safety. He is very seriously injured and in a coma. He's a strong kid, but the doctors don't know if he will come out of it or not. There is no way to tell."

Tom was exhausted. He leaned back against the bed, his legs buckling under him. He didn't know what to feel, but tears welled up in his eyes. "We did everything we could. We found the flash drive. Bob has it. We couldn't make a copy."

Rachel said, "Don't worry about any of that. Charles has given me the contents of the flash drive. We need to leave. Your mother is waiting for you."

Tom moved in a daze. He just couldn't think anymore. Mary held out her hand, and Tom gratefully took it. The temporary silence in the room was broken by a series of chimes and a vibra-

---

[49] Rachel was married to Charles Sheppard and had been ever since they graduated college.

tion from one of Tom's pockets. Tom reached down and took out the alarm/pillbox. He stared at the unusual looking thing in his hand and slowly remembered what it was.

Rachel spoke softly. "Tom, you have a choice. If you take the red pill, you will wake up in an hour or so, and you will have forgotten all this. We will tell you that Jack was involved in a serious crash with his bike, and you can go back to your life as it was. You can take the blue pill and move forward from here. The choice is yours."

Tom stared at the pills, his mind clearing for the moment.

CHAPTER

53

Robinson sat in his study frantically working a keyboard with his thick hands. He had the documents he purchased, but all the connecting e-mails and evidence that they actually came from Sheppard had vanished. Three empty trays were scattered to his left. The trays were filled with chocolates only recently, but Robinson was in such a state that he rifled through them, barely tasting the delicacies.

He ran the latest retrieval software, but so far, nothing worked. Nothing worked! He shoved aside the keyboard in frustration. *Sheppard will not escape this time.* Maybe he was able to buy off Steven, but it was only a matter of time before he retrieved all the damaging evidence. Robinson was confident that George would be able to solve the problem.

George had traced the original theft to Michael, which led to Warren Scott. When Doug Benson called, furious with Warren's treatment of his wife, Robinson was presented with an easy solution to his growing Warren issue. Doug wanted Warren killed and was more than happy to take care of it. Robinson consented, and at least one problem vanished.

The missing files connecting the documents to Sheppard were only a temporary nuisance. Robinson had already formulated a plan on the best way to disseminate the information. He would move quickly and decisively so Sheppard couldn't wiggle off the hook. For a fleeting moment, Robinson was happy that Sheppard was still alive. He fully anticipated the treat and the spectacle of seeing Sheppard burn in flames, disgraced, the arrogant smirk forever wiped off his face.

Robinson heard the smooth professional voice of his executive secretary in his ear. "A man is here to see you. He says Isaac sent him, and he is carrying the proper identification."

Robinson hesitated for a moment. He wasn't expecting a courier from Isaac today, but if the man had the proper identification, it would be a mistake to keep him waiting. "Send him up to the study. I'll receive him up here and make sure we are not disturbed." Robinson disconnected the call.

54

One week later, Tom sat stiffly in the chair next to Jack's hospital bed. All the equipment had been removed from Jack except for an IV that fed Jack fluids and nutrients while he battled his way out of the coma. The doctors had no idea if Jack would come around, but this week seemed important. The longer Jack stayed under, the lower his chances of regaining consciousness. If Jack woke, there was a good possibility he would have some type of brain damage, but the doctors could not be sure. The uncertainty was killing Tom.

Everyone agreed that stimulus was good for Jack. Hearing familiar voices in particular might help bring him out of the coma. Tom had many one-sided heart-to-heart conversations with Jack over the past week. At other times, Tom just read from one of his textbooks. He figured that Jack had unconsciously done more schoolwork over the past week than in his last year in high school.

Tom started in on another one-sided conversation. He apologized for being so busy all the time and not having enough time for him. He promised to make things right once he came around. Things would be different. Tom hung his head low. He couldn't lose his brother. It felt just like the time when his father died. He still carried around that hole in his heart, and he was sure his mother wasn't strong enough to bear the burden of losing Jack. She had gone to the cafeteria to bring back some food for Tom. Tom did not want to leave Jack alone. He couldn't leave his brother alone. He still blamed himself for being too late to protect him.

Tom lifted his textbook and was about to begin reading when he saw Jack's hand twitch. It was only for a second. He thought he had seen it before, but every other time, it had been a false alarm. Now he stared into his brother's face, tears welling up. "Come on, Jack, you have to get up. There is too much waiting for you here. Come on, Jack." Tom's voice pleaded.

Jack's eyelids fluttered. His head turned slightly.

"Come on, Jack, I need you!"

Jack blinked open his eyes. He turned his head. "Hey, Tom, am I late again?"

"No, Jack, you are right on time." Tom's face lit up, tears flowed freely down his cheeks, a great weight lifted from his heart.

Mary came out from the bathroom. She saw Tom's face. "Is everything all right, Tom?"

"Couldn't be better."

Mary noticed Jack's open eyes and rushed into Tom's arms. Tom held her tightly. Jack said, "No more chemistry."

Tom laughed and tossed his textbook on the bed. It wasn't chemistry. The title was *The Real American History* written by Rachel Sheppard. He had drawn a new symbol on the book's cover—thirteen small stars in a circle with a large fourteenth star in the center.

Shatter Point

BOOK 2

CHAPTER

1

April 22, 2041

Cliff stared at the lifeless body on the stainless steel autopsy table with a sorrowful frown etched on his face. "Damn it, Zeus, I thought you were going to make it." Cliff glanced up at the video projections of Zeus's brain development. The brain on the left screen was normally formed, but the right one was so over-developed it strained against the skull.

Cliff shook his head. "Not again. I can't lose another batch of test subjects."

"We are making progress, Doctor Beck. This time the brain development slowed at the end. It's possible that it might stop before …" Tim smiled thinly. He was twice Cliff's age and the most optimistic person that Cliff knew. He could see the silver lining in a hurricane, but even he could not finish the thought.

"We are missing something critical. We need to stop the brain development before it overwhelms the patient," Cliff glanced through the glass wall that separated the autopsy room from the rest of the laboratory. He could see the remaining five test subjects, each sitting perfectly straight, staring mournfully at the glass as if their gaze was drawn to Cliff and the autopsy table. Cliff shook off the icy chill that ran down his spine. The other five test subjects had no idea that Zeus had died. It was not uncommon for one of the test subjects to be separated from the others.

To them, the glass wall was simply a mirror. They had no idea that a laboratory was beyond it.

Cliff nodded toward the remaining patients. "It's odd that they haven't eaten their breakfast. It is already past noon. They must be hungry."

Tim's face drained a little of its color, turning two shades whiter than usual. "It's not natural for them to stare at the mirror like that. It's almost like they know about Zeus and what we're doing back here."

Cliff pressed a button on the keypad next to him, and the one-way glass window turned gray, blocking the other test subjects from his view. Cliff turned toward Tim. "It's just our imagination. Hand me the circular saw, and let's hope that we can learn enough from Zeus to save his friends."

Tim stoically handed Cliff the shiny autopsy tool, but before Cliff started, the lab door swung open. Nurse Callaghan darted into the room. The normally composed, rather pretty nurse looked ashen, her jaw clenched tight.

"What's wrong, Brenda?"

"I came as soon as I heard. I'm sorry about Zeus, but there's something else you should know."

Cliff stared patiently at Brenda, waiting for her to continue, noting the small tablet in her hands, and realizing with dread what she would tell him before she spoke.

Brenda sounded shaky, her voice trembling. "Wickersham has authorized that EBF-202 be administered to a new patient. He doesn't know about Zeus, but the injection is scheduled for later today."

Brenda handed Cliff a thin tablet with the new patient's information on it. Cliff's eyes narrowed as he looked at the chart. "This is a young patient. How can he do this? This is my trial! We're not ready!" Cliff's voice rose angrily. He clutched the tablet so tightly that he cracked the screen. "I'm going to ..." Cliff didn't finish the thought. The violent images that passed through his mind came too quickly and were too graphic to put into words. Instead, he tossed the broken tablet on the table and raced from the lab.

Cliff hurried toward the elevator. His white lab coat flapped open in the breeze, revealing a vintage Apple t-shirt, worn blue jeans, and flip-flops. Cliff's usually affable face was twisted into an angry grimace as he roughly punched the elevator button and waited impatiently for the elevator to arrive. The bell rang. The door swung open, and Cliff darted inside the empty elevator.

Someone asked him to hold the door, and instinctively he thrust out his hand, preventing the doors from closing.

A young female lab assistant entered the elevator. Her long, pin-straight blonde hair was pulled back in a ponytail and bounced as she walked. Cliff noticed her golden-brown tan and her crystal-blue eyes that sparkled behind long eyelashes. She smelled like jasmine and vanilla. *She must be new*, Cliff thought. Perfume was frowned upon in the labs, and no one retained a tan after working the long hours that the lab required. "Thanks for holding the elevator for me." She smiled sweetly.

"No problem." Cliff tapped the button for the top floor, and raised his eyebrows, looking quizzically at the lab assistant.

"That's good for me," she said, answering his unspoken question. The elevator stopped on the second floor to let in three additional passengers, and the lab assistant slid closer to Cliff.

"My name is Rebecca," she told him and held out her hand. Cliff gave her a firm squeeze, but her hand lingered on his.

"I'm Cliff Beck." Cliff was so angry and preoccupied that he almost forgot to notice that Rebecca was a knockout. Almost, but some things came as naturally to Cliff as walking and talking. The elevator stopped at the main floor, letting out everyone but Cliff and Rebecca.

Rebecca stayed close to his side. A seductive smile spread across her lips. "I've heard your name mentioned before, Doctor."

Cliff smiled despite his surly mood. "Only good things, I hope."

"Mostly," she answered playfully.

The elevator doors opened when they reached the top floor. Cliff swiftly exited the elevator, anxious to be on his way, momentarily forgetting about the new lab assistant with the sweet smile and perfume. The top floor hardly resembled the rest of the research and teaching hospital. Gone were the gray tile floors, fluorescent lights, plain hallways, and metal doors. They were replaced by dark-cherry paneling, antique ink drawings, white wooden doors that led to private offices, and a soft burgundy carpet with small, evenly placed golden specks of color that covered the floor.

Cliff strode angrily toward the corner office. With each step he grew more agitated, as if his anger rolled down a hill with an ever steeper slope, gathering intensity as it went. He stared hard at the nameplate on the corner office door, *Samuel Wickersham – Head of Research, PhD*, and shoved it open. He entered the empty waiting room and startled the receptionist, who was busy surfing the web for trendy vacation ideas. Regaining her composure, the receptionist grinned at Cliff. "I'm sorry, Dr. Beck, but we don't have an appointment for you."

"Not to worry, Clair, he'll want to see me." Cliff quickened his pace toward Wickersham's door, ignored a mild protest from Clair, turned the doorknob, and plunged into the corner office.

Wickersham's office was larger than Cliff's studio apartment. Floor-to-ceiling windows covered both exterior walls, offering stunning cityscape views of New York City.

Cliff marched directly to Wickersham's desk. Four-inch risers were added to the desk's base to prop it up. Wickersham's chair was similarly raised. In reality, Wickersham was short, but from Cliff's vantage point he looked well over six feet tall.

Before Cliff could start talking, Wickersham raised his left hand, forcing him to stay quiet. Wickersham's vast, oval desk had nothing on it except a flat-screen computer monitor, a new holographic video display that was turned off, an old-fashioned intercom box, and an old photograph of a smiling Wickersham with his left arm draped over the vice president's shoulders. Wickersham told everyone that would listen that they were childhood friends.

Wickersham's eyes never lifted from his keyboard. He typed obscenely slowly, adding to Cliff's agitation. Cliff seethed as he heard the snail-like progress of Wickersham's fingers across the keyboard. He unconsciously balled up both hands into fists. Wickersham's hair was dyed blond. He had a few strategically placed artificial freckles on his cheeks that made him look younger than he was, and there was no way his perfect nose was the one he was born with.

Eventually, Wickersham finished typing and looked up from his computer screen. Cliff was unable to read his emotions because Wickersham had injected a river of Botox into his face, preventing him from any facial expressions even if he wished to show one.

"Doctor Beck, I didn't know that we had a meeting scheduled? I imagine that you have something important to tell me. Perhaps you have a breakthrough to report? Please take a seat, Doctor." Wickersham gestured toward one of the two leather winged-back chairs that faced the desk, but Cliff remained standing.

"We can't try EBF-202 on patients yet. It's just not ready."

"I disagree. The drug has shown remarkable potential." Wickersham crossed his manicured hands on the desk in front of him. He sat perfectly straight, tried his best to smile, and sighed slightly.

"The first version of the drug ended up killing all of the test subjects." Cliff leaned onto the desk, wondering if he could hurdle it and reach Wickersham's throat in one leap.

"That was the first version. The second version hasn't produced any fatalities. I visited with all six of our canine test subjects last night. They all look healthy," Wickersham explained, calmly.

"Zeus died this morning!" Cliff stared hard at Wickersham, hoping that Zeus's death would have an impact on him, but if it did, the head of research showed no signs of it. Cliff continued angrily, "We only started this trial two months ago. Their brains are still developing. The pace has slowed considerably, but it hasn't stopped yet. If it continues, they will all die over the next month. Plus, their behavior has altered. It's just not safe! We don't understand all of the ramifications of the drug. We can't use it on humans."

Wickersham leaned back in his chair. "How did you know that I was planning on using a human test subject?"

Cliff's face reddened.

"I see. Nurse Callaghan must have told you. My mistake."

"That's not important. EBF-202 permits brain tissue to regenerate, but we can't control it yet. It will likely kill anyone you inject it with! We need more time with the animal control subjects." The anger in Cliff's voice ebbed and was slowly replaced with helplessness. Wickersham was the boss.

"This drug will revolutionize how we view the brain. It will not only end Alzheimer's and senility but can increase cognitive powers. The applications are endless and so are the profits. You are young still. You must see the bigger picture. With your share of the profits, most of your educational costs will be paid off." Wickersham's moss-colored eyes gleamed brightly.

Cliff's spirit sank. He knew that look in Wickersham's eyes. Wickersham sniffed money, and when he thought he could get paid, it was impossible to change his mind. Cliff's shoulders slumped, and he used the only argument he had left. "Did the patient's guardian sign the consent forms?"

Wickersham's lips tried to turn up into a smirk, but gave up under the strain well before anyone could have recognized the reaction. "You've seen the young man's chart. He's not going to recover from his head wound if we do nothing. At least we give him a chance to benefit all humankind. Besides, he is the perfect test subject—young, strong, and suffering from a severe head trauma."

"He still has a fighting chance to come out of the coma using traditional treatments. His mother should be told of the choices and the risks."

Wickersham stood, his head barely clearing the high back of his chair. "He doesn't have premium insurance. Under the law, I can make this decision."

The knuckles on Cliff's hands turned white as he clutched the edge of the desk. "But the Sheppard Group is paying all of his bills. They have the required riders in their insurance."

Wickersham walked toward the side of his desk. He wore a crisp navy-blue suit, white dress shirt, and solid light-blue tie. "Yes, but the tennis instructor is not covered by that insurance. They are paying for his costs out of pocket." Wickersham waved his arms in the air. "This is for the best, Cliff. Don't worry about the ethics. You should stick to what you are good at—neurobiology and making friends among the female staff members."

"Just give me another two months with the dogs. We'll be in a better place," pleaded Cliff.

Wickersham stood beside Cliff, his head just slightly above Cliff's shoulder even though Wickhersham wore ridiculous platform shoes. "You'll be fully involved in his case study. Just imagine how much we'll learn! Think of all of the people he will be helping."

The intercom buzzed. Wickersham was probably the only person alive that still used one of those things. "Your daughter is here for your meeting, Doctor Wickersham."

"That's great. I've just finished with Doctor Beck. Good day, Doctor."

"His name is Jack."

"Whose name?"

"The tennis instructor. Your *case study*." Cliff had a fleeting fantasy about smashing his fists into Wickersham's surgically altered nose, but spun around instead, and trudged out of Wickersham's office.

Cliff swung open the door and bumped into Rebecca, the new lab assistant.